Sincerely
2/2/2019

Frank Beck
02 - 2019

The Land of Noir

Book I:

The Calling

Created by

Shawn Arthur Vento

Written by

Frederick Lee Bobola

Art & Illustrations by

Shawn & Steven Vento

The Land of Noir

Book I:

The Calling

This book is dedicated to Mike and Rachelle Joplin. Thank you for inspiring me to always chase my shadow.

Shawn

To Angie, my first fan. The day we met changed my life forever. Thank you.

Freddy

A Special Thanks To: Angie "Tao" Sanford, Miguel Chavez, Brian Barr, Jon Seo, Eric Mizufuka, Brian Emmons, and Mike Bobola

III

Prologue

333 years ago

"You must always follow the prophecy, for if not, the portal shall be unsealed, and darkness shall rise again," bellowed a deep voice that cut through the hurricane like winds. He held up his two feathered arms to cover his eyes as the portal continued to vacuum the air in as it prepared to seal. Massive trees snapped, crashing into rivers, striking fear into the feathered faces that gathered to bid their heroes farewell.

"Here! Take this Femmerel and protect it always. Babarosa thanks you for all you have done and wishes you the best," Babarosa yelled as she thrust the Mirror of Libra through the windstorm, inches from Femmerel's fingers. The monstrous zephyr increased, and the hundreds of birds gathered by the portal all went scattering through Vadu Forest. The wind ripped the mirror from Babarosa's outstretched hands, sending the Mirror of Libra flying far out of site. Femmerel calmly reached an arm out and slapped her palm against an invisible wall. Only two figures remained in the tempest as they watched in awe while Femmerel summoned the mirror back to her, as if the deadly winds were not there. She held it deftly in her gentle hands. The glowing blue runes on the frame of the mirror matched her eyes as she held her final gaze on The Land of Noir. Behind Femmerel, into the portal, Wizards and Sorcerers with robes and long gnarled staffs awaited her.

"We Sorcelle have always upheld our duties. It will always remain as so," Femmerel spoke defiantly as she spiraled into the portal.

Chapter 1

Dark Disturbances

The sight of the closed coffin suffocated Elizabeth's lungs and paralyzed her mind. It was a beautiful, frigid, spring day, the sun shining brightly but the cools of winter still danced in the wind, which—along with the floral scent of hundreds of roses piled on the white coffin—failed to appeal to Elizabeth's numbed senses. Everything had been a whirlwind the last few days.

"…And guide this man's soul into the next life, where he will live on forever, and always here in our hearts. Amen," spoke the man in all black with a white collar solemnly, his head bowed.

"Amen," mumbled the large crowd cryptically, devoid of life. Elizabeth's head hung down as she blinked through tears. Only the mechanical sound of the platform lowering made her notice that the coffin was going into the ground. Tears splashed loudly against the closed lid, the droplets

1

ELIZABETH

trickling down the side of the coffin, disappearing forever, just like her father was about to.

Her heart was broken into tiny pieces as she watched her father's corpse finally stop six feet underground. The next few moments were a blur. She felt a hand on a shoulder, words of condolences, but they all fell on deaf, mute senses; she was as stoic as a stone statue. Her face never wavering, just a blank emotionless void that was the result of the spontaneous overflow of emotions.

A vaguely familiar voice slowly cracked away at the armor and when she realized it was her mother Susan's, Elizabeth finally noticed everyone had left. She was the only one left standing at the grave site. The huge cemetery was empty. Just like her soul. She looked around and saw the lush green hills and the tall trees that scarcely populated the graveyard. The irony depressed her.

She tried to enjoy their beauty but the harder she tried to force herself to feel better, the deeper her despair became. She looked down at her father's final resting place one last time. The last time she would ever see him. The thought of turning away was too much to bear.

"Elizabeth. Let's go honey," interrupted her mother's soft voice before she could ponder further.

Elizabeth did not want to go. She wanted to stay and sit on the ground. Her mind could not accept that her father was gone.

He had left them so quickly, so unexpectedly. Life had always been grand. Her parents loved each other dearly and her father, Robert, took great care of them. He always adored her mother with fairytale like love. Elizabeth longed to feel his strong embrace around her. She just couldn't accept reality. She just could not say goodbye...

The next thing she knew the ground was getting closer and she saw her fingers reaching towards the coffin. Further she slid down into the grave, desperate to never let go of her father. Elizabeth screamed when she felt arms wrap around her waist and pull her back.

Elizabeth coughed from the dust invading her lungs. Her tall height only made it harder to move around the attic. It was the last room to pack in their mansion. It would be the same as the other rooms had been: mainly deciding what few things to take and what they had to sell to cover their debts.

Ever since her father's funeral a few months ago, their world had crumbled into rubble. Elizabeth had offered to help her mom look for a new place to live but Susan had refused. Elizabeth knew the search wasn't going well from the way her mother's face would crinkle up with stress. She had hoped Susan would find something soon. They had to be out in less than a week.

Elizabeth held her breath as she fumbled through a huge box full of old black and white photos. After brushing off cobwebs and an inch of dust, the pictures revealed faces of women. Some looked alike, others not so much. The last one on the bottom was a hand-colored portrait that looked just like her. Piercing blue eyes shined brightly at Elizabeth as if the painting were alive. Icy chills froze her blood and stilled her breath. Elizabeth quickly stuffed all the photos back in, burying the colored portrait. She turned to escape but slammed her foot painfully into something, which sounded an audible clank. A dark green container she failed to notice in the poor attic lighting was the culprit. Sadness filled Elizabeth's heart when she opened the little footlocker. It was her father's military fatigues and gear. Quickly she closed the lid and headed for the stairs to get some fresh air.

"Pssst," whispered the wind. Elizabeth's heart froze as she held her breath, eyes darting around for the source. Ever so slowly she crept backwards towards the stairs, her lungs nearly bursting, but she dared not risk a breath. The second she felt her toes touch the stairs, she turned to bolt

but a voice stopped her dead in her tracks. "Elizabeth," hissed a sinister voice. Fear paralyzed her mind, but her legs moved against her own will. She screamed at her mind to stop but some strong force pulled her towards her father's green footlocker.

Elizabeth heard the latches snap and the creak of the lid but did not remember opening it. Her hands worked on their own as she felt around the bottom of a container and discovered a secret compartment. A smooth metallic surface chilled her fingertips. Her body finally returned to her control as she held up a gold chain with a huge "N" hanging from it. Dozens of dark voices began whispering inaudible gibberish, but their words forced a need for her to don the necklace.

Elizabeth felt the comfort of her father's warm presence as soon as the chain rested upon her neck and the voices vanished. Suddenly, the back of her neck tingled, and she felt an overwhelming feeling of pressure weighing her down.

Eyes watched her from behind. No matter how fast she would turn around to look, Elizabeth could never see her attacker. Invisible icy fingers wrapped around her throat. Terror replaced the air in her lungs as she trembled and sweated, nauseous and dizzy from the shortness of breath. Elizabeth felt herself blacking in and out, fading away as if she was detaching from her body.

Elizabeth choked in surprise from the sudden rush of air. It was the dusty, moldy, stale air of the attic but it was the sweetest spring tasting air she had ever inhaled. The dark presence had disappeared, but Elizabeth still felt eyes watching the back of her head as she took her first step. When her foot landed energy erupted from the necklace and Elizabeth felt the air ripple with a supernatural force. The house rumbled like an earthquake, and the last thing she heard before blacking out was something falling and crashing downstairs.

Lumiere: Lake Market

A hunched gnarled figure felt a great disturbance reverberate through the universe. "Not good," concerned a raspy voice, "Not good at all." She heard a sound, like that of a heavy rusted door being forced open. "No. No this cannot be. This is impossible," she spoke as she fumbled through her stack of items. Disbelief and numbing terror attacked her as she saw the fire dance, the earth rumble, the water flow and the wind sing. But what struck fear into her old bones the most was the ever so slight opening of the eye. She knew the end of time was near at hand, The Calling had commenced.

Noir: Swamps of Sorrow

Dead trees sprouted out of the stagnant murky water like spears. Their sharp tips snapped off and dead long ago. Just like the heart of the Toad Queen. The bright moonlight illuminated the graveyard of what once was a beautiful forest. The Mudsepy River had overflowed centuries ago, turning it into the fetid swamp it now was. Moss hung from the dead tree branches like curtains, draping down over the gloomy moonlight like phantoms. The scent of rotten eggs filled the Toad Queen's nostrils as she bathed in her lair's putrid smell. Inside her protected alcove of dead trees on a swampy, grass sprouted bank, stood her statues of swamp creatures perched atop the sharp points of the trees, like gargoyles on a cathedral. Her webbed feet flopped as she walked along the bank, inspecting each statue, some with wings like giant insects, and others like huge alligators and snapping turtles. And last was her favorite, Indra, a massive snake frozen in still animation, tongue darted out, venom dripping from her fangs. She petted its wooden head lovingly.

"Soon my pretties, very soon thou shalt taste what thou desire the most," croaked the Toad Queen as she made her way past her throne of bird bones, her favorite resting spot to think upon her plans of conquest. The bones were connected in intricate geometric patterns and spiraled into a huge bird skull that  crested over the throne. Her arm rests ended in sharp talons, just like her magical wombat-mounts she had created for her army of Googins. If those stupid Googins were wrong and the portal to Lumiere was not breached as they told her, she would summon Indra to eat them all.

The Toad Queen reached her destination and entered her treasure room. She nearly tripped over her dragon's hoard of gems, jewels and gold stacked messily on the swampy floor of her lair as she tried to make her way to the mirror hanging on the far wall. Dazzling green emeralds, shiny white pearls, and diamonds shined brightly in the moonlight that illuminated her throne room. Paranoia flooded through the Queen's cold blood as she quickly counted every last gem, ensuring none were out of place. Assured that none were missing, she strolled over to her mirror, sending treasure flying everywhere with each step, crashing like unharmonious instruments. Intricate runes were carved into the rotted wood that made up the frame. The glass itself was square which she felt gave her the best view of her figure. The Toad Queen stared into the reflection narcissistically and admired the cold crown that sat upon her head. In the middle was a small ruby, her most prized possession that gave her the power of sorcery. She also felt it went well with her sparkling red lips and the ball of rubies that were strung like beads around her neck. She reapplied heavy coats of blue eye shadow to her green eyelids and made sure her eyelashes were popping out as she blinked like a princess. Her tight red dress with white stripes showed off her dashing figure marvelously.

The Toad Queen was content with her beauty but sighed angrily when she felt the blackness of her heart. What good was it being beautiful without someone to share her life with? She thought of the empty throne made of stone next to hers. For too long it had sat empty. For too long she had taken orders. She longed for the day when she would rule the Land of Noir and reclaim her love that was stolen from her.

The scamper of feet aroused her from her daydream as two Googins mounted on oversized, mutated wombats scuttled into her view.

"My Queen," spoke the grey one with the sweep of its helmet, his huge ugly pointed ears looking even bigger.

"Why dost thou disturb me?" she demanded angrily.

"Your plans are ready for action. It was just as you said it would be. The way to the other side is open," he spoke, giant white eyes with tiny black pupils never leaving the ground.

A wicked smile curved up the Toad Queen's face. "Excellent, soon I will have the power to rule this land."

"Elizabeth!" Susan yelled, as she hovered over her daughter, "Oh good you're awake. You had me so worried."

"I'm fine, mom," Elizabeth gritted through her teeth as she rubbed her new necklace. The attic room was still a blur, but the annoyance caused by her mother's usual over-worrying revived Elizabeth's senses.

"What happened?" Susan asked hysterically.

"I found this necklace in dad's old footlocker and then I don't really know what happened. I had this really weird dream about a Toad Queen in some swamp talking to some little, grey reptile monster."

Susan seemed to not hear her and just stared at the necklace. Her mother's eyes looked lost in another world. "I never thought I would see this again. It belonged to your grandmother. Your father always was waiting to give that to you one day. He always said he was waiting for the right time. And now…" Susan sobbed, as Elizabeth did her best to not cry with her as she held her mother close.

Chapter 2

Be Careful What You Wish For

The bleakness of the fading, cracked, beige paint on the wall reminded her of the bathroom stalls in an old, dirty public restroom. Elizabeth would have never believed a wave of nausea could be induced by sight until she experienced it herself. She looked around her tiny room. It felt cramped and her tall height didn't help alleviate her growing sense of claustrophobia. Holes in the drywall had been covered by sheets of plastic that failed to hide the rat droppings. The cinder brick ceiling had half the blocks painted over with the ugliest mud color she had ever seen. The jagged cement ground was covered randomly with patches of carpet. To call the ripped red carpet filthy would be a compliment. Elizabeth had to be careful where she stepped, the rough uneven concrete ground was a minefield for stubbed toes. All the cement made the room freezing despite the heater being on, but she supposed since the heater was from the 1950s that blew a whistle out the pipes like an ancient black and white

ELIZABETH'S ROOM

cartoon, that she shouldn't be surprised. There were no windows, save the tiny one in her disgusting bathroom. Only after a monumental struggle did it screech open. The thick wooden frame of the window, that she supposed was once white, matched the filth of the rest of the apartment. The entire sink was exposed, pipes and all and no amount of scrubbing would make the grimy scum come off the ceramic or the tiles in her shower that was not even large enough for a small child, much less a 14-year-old girl.

Her entire life now fit in the half dozen or so boxes strewn haphazardly across the stained carpet floors that had more rips than the design patterns that once shined. Aside from her bed nothing else fit, not even a desk to do her homework. She tip-toed between the boxes towards the bathroom, and the coldness of the ground shocked not just her body but her mind as well. A cold, frigid reminder of her new life.

They had traveled and lived nicely but her father was a humble man and always preached to her the importance of hard work and never giving up. Robert had grown up poor, worked his way up and had amassed an empire of wealth and invested largely. Elizabeth had a great family life growing up and her father was an amazing man. She adored the way he always treated her mother with so much affection and love.

Today, her mother Susan was starting her first day at the sweatshop. Growing up, she was always so worried about Elizabeth and constantly nagging her. Despite having a chauffeur, Susan insisted on taking her to soccer where she had to stay the entire practice—just like she did at ballet— scrutinizing every movement Elizabeth made. She knew her mother did it because she loved her, but it felt like Elizabeth never had an inch to breathe.

Ever.

And now with her mother starting a second job, Susan would be around even less. Elizabeth supposed she would finally have the freedom she craved as a teenager but at the cost of her father's life…

They had managed to stay in the estate for a few months, but since mother never had a hand in running it, she did not realize how quickly the savings would go without cash flow coming in. And according to her father's business partner, Henri, a couple investments had gone bad and selling the estate barely covered the losses. However, Elizabeth had never trusted Henri one bit. There was always a glint in his eye that made her feel uneasy around him. Henri seemed to only look out for himself and Elizabeth did not understand why her father even worked with him. In the end, it was a wash and they set out from scratch to start a new life in the Iberville Projects in New Orleans. Elizabeth spent the first part of her day killing all the roaches she saw and plugging up mouse holes in the kitchen, but quickly realized how pointless of an effort that was. But this was the best they could do… all her mother could afford.

It pained Elizabeth to see her mother suffering so much. She was out working for what Elizabeth believed was an illegally low amount of money. She had meant to research it sooner, but her phone did not even have a data plan anymore, so that would have to wait until tomorrow, her first day of school where she could finally get on some Wi-Fi.

After rinsing off with the brown water from her sink, Elizabeth unpacked a picture of her father and mother when they were newlywed. She looked up at the ceiling when she saw water drop onto the frame, but then she realized the rain was her own tears.

Elizabeth rubbed her big, round, almond eyes with her sleeve and sniffled. *Why did you have to go daddy? I miss you so dearly…*

When she opened them, the bleakness of the room only dimmed her mood further. A deep sigh came out as she fell onto her bed face first, her long brown hair cascading gently on the smooth bed comforter. Elizabeth felt so uncomfortable for no apparent reason and rolled over onto her back. She stared directly in front of her into the tiny bathroom attached to her room.

Even the bathroom was barren, not even a mirror. But she imagined that would change today—hopefully when they went looking for furniture. One benefit to her mother's shady employment was that she got paid in cash every day. It would take a few weeks but eventually, they would have the bare necessities needed to have a sustainable life. Elizabeth just stared into the bareness where an imprint of a mirror used to hang on her dirty bathroom wall that was falling apart.

Just like her life.

She could not stand reality another second. Elizabeth closed her eyes and escaped to memories of better days when she still felt alive.

The closing of the front door bolted her up. Elizabeth had not realized she even fell asleep. Her vision was still on the bare wall in her bathroom. For a reason she couldn't explain, something inside of her was telling her to get a mirror today. Elizabeth and Susan were supposed to do some shopping at the lake market, although she knew she could use other things before a mirror.

As she ran down the stairs in response to her mother's calling, Elizabeth decided that she would only get a mirror if the essentials that were a higher priority were not available. She felt terrible for wanting something so vain when she knew her mother could use a chair and table for them to eat at.

That is if her mother would ever be home to sit down and have a meal for once, she thought harshly.

This was the first day her mother was able to get off before sunset since they moved into this hell hole last week.

"If we hurry we can be back by dinner time. Hopefully we can at least find some chairs for us to sit on while we eat," her mother said, trying to hide the exhaustion in her spirits. But Elizabeth was smarter than most 14-year-olds and knew her mother was already on the verge of a breakdown. She didn't know how Susan was going to last. Elizabeth knew it was on her to somehow get a job after school. Her mother just wasn't strong enough to support them. Her father had treated her so well and now they were paying for it.

"If not, it's okay," replied Elizabeth, "I like our bed picnics," she lied with a forced laugh. Thankfully, her mother seemed not to notice the forgery.

When they finally arrived at the lake market on the outskirts of town, the sun was already nearly set, and some booths were shutting down for the day. The trolley system had been so confusing. It felt like they rode the streetcar for hours even though it was closer to two. All because her helpless mother had made them take the wrong one.

Elizabeth tried to tell her so, but her mother insisted. Elizabeth did her best to not get mad. She never was an angry person, but since her dad died, it had been hard not to snap. And when rain decided to suddenly pour out of nowhere the second they stepped out into the open air, her wet stomps revealed how she truly felt.

They were quickly soaked to the bone as they tried to navigate the dark lanes of the large swap meet. Surrounding a lake were rows and rows of makeshift booths with canopies on top that went as far as the eye could see. The dirt field that housed the lake market was soft and some places muddy, making the walk even more irritating. Unfortunately, most booths were now empty. Elizabeth looked over and saw her mother shivering from the cold, doing her best to stay strong but Elizabeth thought she was doing a poor job. She wished sometimes her mother would just admit how she felt. Their lives sucked now. It was the truth. Instead, Susan put up this cheerful optimism which frustrated Elizabeth even more.

The sun was disappearing over the tall, crumbling brick buildings in the distance and they had found nothing. The wind howled fiercely, whipping harshly against her skin, stinging her eyes and chapping her lips. Elizabeth felt terrible for her mother who she knew had to go to work her shift at Monty's Tavern in a few hours. "Mom, let's just go home, this is a waste of time. We got here too late because we took the wrong trolley." Her mother didn't notice the smugness of her last comment. Susan just answered with that fake cheerfulness that only made it worse.

"Just a little bit more Lizzy, it can't possibly get any worse," Susan pleaded with a laugh to her cross armed daughter.

"Fine," Elizabeth sassed as she power walked on ahead, leaving her mother behind.

Elizabeth rounded a corner of booths that led to another four-way intersection. Elizabeth was lost in her bitter thoughts as she felt her mother's desperate grip on her forearm pull her away from the path as an out of control speeding truck splashed through a huge puddle in the middle of the dirt road, right where Elizabeth would have been. A tidal wave of splattered mud and things that tasted worse soaked them. That was the final straw. They didn't say a word to each other; none were needed. They both turned around in unison and began the cold bitter walk empty handed.

In silence they gloomily marched in defeat back towards the trolley stop. Elizabeth felt lost, but her mother seemed sure of their path, which worried her considering what happened on their way to the lake market. It was dark now and the market had completely shut down, poorly lit by the street lights in the distance. Suspicious figures stared at them from the shadows and Elizabeth wished they could get out of this suddenly dangerous, scary place. It had seemed like a normal part of town, but as soon as the darkness fell, fear flooded through Elizabeth's veins. Her mother seemed to share her urgency and their feet moved quicker before the shadows could close in. Just as they were nearly clear of the dirt roads of the lake market, a lumpy, awkward figure in the distance became larger. It moved clumsily, bobbing back and forth, like a donkey that was carrying too much on its back.

Elizabeth at first saw a pack mule in the misty haze of the poorly lit street. Weak blinking street lights tried to light the dark. As they got closer, she saw the pack mule was actually an older lady wearing a ragged and faded brown pea coat with patches sewn into the elbows that had seen better days. She looked like she was a long way from home. Her hair was short and tied in a polka dotted bandana as she leered over at Elizabeth with one eye open, her eyebrow arched up suspiciously to her hairline. Oversized golden dangling hoops hung from her ears and matching bracelets shook as she somehow waddled with laborious steps, the huge enormous load of items somehow balanced on her back. It looked as if every step would send the entire stack tumbling down in a crashing heap. But what creeped Elizabeth out the most was her long-gnarled fingers. They seemed to have no fingertips; they just ended in skinny tree branches. She looked like she had not eaten in days, nor bathed in weeks.

THE WANDERING GYPSY

The wandering gypsy hunched over from the crushing weight of her cargo. The base of the pile was a dresser with the back of a chair keeping the drawers shut that seated a picture frame on it, while a long pole with a thin pirate flag waved above her head. Behind the dresser was a magician's hat with stars on it.. Wrapped around the entire circus of items was a wooden buckler shield with two large cooking pots. Somehow there was another flagpole jammed through the center of it all with a burning candle on the top, waving a flag with a coat of arms brandishing thorns growing out of the shield with a sword stabbed through a crown. Elizabeth thought her to be a traveling lake market booth.

What caught Elizabeth's eyes the most were the most intricate symbols she had ever seen, carved into the wooden frame of a mirror buried in the pile of odd goods. The carvings looked elemental. It was hard to tell from her position, but Elizabeth swore she saw waves of water, and earthy mountains on another. She couldn't see the rest of the mirror because it was buried in the heap of junk. The carvings were beyond foreign to her mind, but Elizabeth swore she felt like she could read them…somehow understand them. She was drawn to them. She felt a power emanating from her chest as she felt the heavy golden letter "N" of her father's necklace suddenly in her fingers. Her next movements were a blur and trancelike: the world melted away, the rain, the cold, the despair and the fear of getting mugged in the darkness of their rough neighborhood dissipated. She nearly was upon the old lady before her consciousness regained control.

"How much for the mirror?" Elizabeth shot out quicker and ruder than she intended. She suddenly felt embarrassed.

"I 'ave no mirror to sell. Mirror is no for sale," she snarled at Elizabeth in a heavy and raspy French accent that made Elizabeth second guess her decision to approach the lady who smelled like a dusty old book that had not been opened in years.

Elizabeth saw her mother inspecting the disarray of items the woman had; the look she gave Elizabeth showed she had no interest in what the lady carried.

"Lizzy, we can get a mirror elsewhere, let's hurry along to make the trolley," suggested her mother.

"Fine," huffed Elizabeth. Why did she feel so dejected? It was just a dumb mirror. It made no sense, but it must have showed on her face as she saw her mother catch up to the lady. She could hear the words that were exchanged as she walked over to the haggling pair.

"Are you not a vendor here?" questioned Susan.

"Foolish lady. I see where daughter gets it from. I no 'ave mirror." Hissed the old lady venomously, making Susan take a step back.

Elizabeth knew her mother would back down; she was no fighter.

"Then what's that thing on the bottom of your... your... pile?" Susan questioned to Elizabeth's shocking surprise.

"You need chair? Yes, you buy chair. Or dresser with lamp. I give good price," the lake market lady reasoned with her raspy voice and French accent.

"How much for the mirror?" asked Susan timidly.

"You need pots, yes? Pots to cook for daughter, yes?" tried the gypsy.

Their conversation faded from Elizabeth's ears as she was just once again staring at the symbols carved into the mirror. They looked like magical runes and Elizabeth could somehow feel them calling to her. The heavy imprint of her necklace suddenly felt warm and burned her chest. Tracing her fingers along the large letter "N" that hung from the thick chain around Elizabeth's neck, she wanted to touch the mirror so desperately. It was the weirdest feeling ever and she could not explain it. The runes began getting further and further and by the time Elizabeth snapped out of her trance, the lake market gypsy was fading away into the rainy night. Elizabeth felt like she was going against her own will when she started running after her.

"Wait!" yelled Elizabeth.

"Leave me be!" the gypsy spoke in a menacing tone. Elizabeth backed up a step but just could not let it go for some reason.

"40 dollars," interjected her mother.

Elizabeth froze. There's no way they could afford to spend that on a mirror. They needed that money to eat and pay rent. That was what her mother made in an entire eight-hour shift at work. Was her mom crazy? Or perhaps Elizabeth was the crazy one… she felt a fool for acting like she did.

"Mom…it's okay, let's go home."

"No," her mother stifled with a tear, "I haven't been able to give you anything in your life. Your father always did. I just wanted to be loved the way you loved him. I worked for this money and I want to use it to make you happy Lizzy."

"Mom… of course I love you, don't say that. We need that money to eat, and for bills…" Elizabeth said with her head down, completely ashamed.

"45 dollars!" was Susan's next bid as she chased after the lady waddling away with her mountain of goods.

Her mother's last exchange seemed to finally change the lake market lady's mind. The goods on her back began to teeter and Elizabeth felt herself step back, waiting for everything to come crashing down. Somehow the mirror slid out from the bottom and like magic, nothing fell. The gypsy just stood there, staring into the mirror until she started talking to herself.

"Let me be rid of this thing!" she whispered harshly to herself, the reflection replied back in what sounded like French that Elizabeth did not understand. Back and forth the crazy lady went and Elizabeth thought she was going crazy too. How was the lady's reflection in the mirror talking back in French? Before she could ponder about it further, the lake market gypsy began reaching for a pocket and her pile nearly came tumbling down as she pulled a coin purse out of her coat. Elizabeth saw its emptiness and was shocked the gypsy would not want to sell the mirror. She took out a small piece of paper from the coin purse and held it in two fingers with each hand and seemed to be reading.

It looked like a fortune cookie slip. She saw the lake market gypsy look up and give her mother a smile. "45 dollars it is. But, one condition…" she bargained while waving a long, gnarled finger at them, "I sold you no mirror. You never got this from me. Do you understand!?" she shouted angrily. This lady was beyond looney, thought Elizabeth.

What am I doing? Why am I dealing with this lady? Elizabeth held her huge prize. Her fingers traced along the different elemental runes, and she felt a strange sensation tingle through her entire body from head to toe. They heard the old lady cackle with laughter as she hobbled off, a pack mule in the distance once again. Susan reached down and picked up the tiny piece of paper the gypsy had dropped and handed it to Elizabeth. She looked down and it read, "Someone will finally alleviate your burdens".

Elizabeth furtively peeked out from her hiding spot. There was a horde of the little reptiles, mostly brown but one green, riding on a giant wombat looking mount. They surrounded a snapping turtle that was bigger than any turtle she had ever seen, but it was crying like a baby calling for her mother. A heavy coarsely roped net entangled her and a reptilian cheer screeched the air. Elizabeth felt bad for the turtle, but what could she do? And why was she here? Suddenly, the Googin herd silenced their cheers and looked

her way. Elizabeth held her breath as felt her neck tingle and goosebumps spread from her arms up to her shoulders.

Elizabeth turned to escape but her back was to a mountain wall. When she turned back around, somehow the Googins were already upon her. Scaly hands reached for her as she screamed in horror. Their fingers felt like rough sandpaper as they clamped over her mouth and face, while fetid breath and scratchy voices invaded her senses.

"Lizzy! Lizzy!" Susan yelled. Elizabeth opened her eyes, back in her bed. "You were screaming bloody murder, are you alright?

Elizabeth felt her necklace tingle and fill her body with a foreign sensation. "Just another bad dream…"

Chapter 3:

First Day In Paradise

The bright morning sun's blinding glare finally subsided as Elizabeth walked up the last of the steps to her new life. It was a bleak and dreary run-down building that looked like a haunted house in a horror movie. She knew her new school would not have the Roman architecture of her old private school, but this was abysmal. A rusted chain link fence imprisoned the building that was all rotting brown brick, with white framed windows that looked like they had never been opened. The windows ran in threes, horizontally, three stories high. Above each set of windows, the roof formed into sharp triangles like a gothic castle from medieval times.

The hefty metal doors strained Elizabeth's arms and creaked loudly as she pushed them open. Elizabeth shuddered slightly from apprehensive thoughts of starting at her new school. So far nothing had gone right. On their miserable journey home last night, Susan had gotten sick from the cold and rain, yet somehow, Susan survived her shift at Monty's tavern that night. Elizabeth saw her this morning leaving for her other job at the sweatshop and she looked awful.

They had just started their new life and her mother was already broken. She looked down at her phone and her face crinkled in surprised confusion. There were no Wi-Fi networks available, maybe she had to go deeper into her new dungeon school to get a signal. As soon as she did, she would start looking for a part time job after school. Her mother was clearly out of her wits. Why did she spend all the money they had to survive off of for the rest of the week on that stupid mirror Elizabeth had wanted so badly for some reason? The pull that it had on her yesterday was something out of a movie… it was as if it was calling out to her. She quickly dismissed those thoughts as she knew that was impossible. But for some unexplainable reason when she brought it upstairs last night, it made her room feel a little more complete. Elizabeth was excited to fully unpack her room and hang the mirror when she got home today.

The white hallway walls with a blue stripe in the middle peeled with rot. The ceiling panels were missing and at one point, she could see right up to the ceiling of the third floor and noticed water-logged rafters that looked like they would collapse if a butterfly landed on them. The tiles were smashed out in places, and Elizabeth dodged ankle sprains as she followed the signs to the enrollment office. Kids of all different ethnicities and sizes packed the wide hallway, making it feel more crammed than it really was. Some floated like lost souls, depressed looks on their faces as they tried to avoid the attention of the other bigger packs of animals who huddled closely with raunchy laughter and lewd stares directed at those perceived weaker than them. Elizabeth had learned due to the closing of other schools in the neighborhood, Lumiere High had been converted to take on seventh and eighth grade students as well. She took small comfort that in being a freshman, she was not the youngest prey of the packs of upperclassmen. She hoped her height would pass her off as older than she really was.

Elizabeth noticed to her right a rotting wooden door that read "Principal Justice" on the small window in the middle of it. Elizabeth looked through the window and she saw a tall Asian looking kid dressed in all black with a "too cool for school" vibe being scolded by what appeared to be a teacher, and a man in a suit who she assumed was Principal Justice. When the boy turned and looked her in the eye, he seemed to be enjoying being berated as he smirked at Elizabeth. He had piercings all over his face: ears, nose, lips, but his smile was warm and pleasant with a perfect set of white pearls. She quickly turned her gaze away and hurried her pace but turned when the door opened in a banging rush.

"You must be Elizabeth," exhaled the tall man in the suit, huffing out of breath. "Welcome," he greeted with a forced smile. "I can't wait to get you orientated, please come back and see me later. I apologize for this young ruffian, I promise you most the kids here at Lumiere High are good ones just like you," lied Principal Justice unconvincingly. The kid in all black poked his head out of the door and around Justice's arm, flashed her that perfect smile and blew her a kiss.

"Steven!" berated Principal Justice, and Elizabeth took off.

Elizabeth wanted nothing to do with that boy Steven; she was trying to avoid trouble and he looked like he was good at finding it. But she could not get his perfect pearly white smile out of her head that gave her the feeling that she knew him somehow. But that was impossible. Right? How could she possibly know him?

The hall ended, and the sign above the door read "Admissions". Elizabeth felt the lump in her stomach rise to her throat. There was no line as she was enrolling mid semester. Elizabeth saw a hardened Jamaican woman behind the tall counter at the desk closest to her, furiously pounding away at the keyboard on her desk. It made her feel intimidated. The rest of the cubicles were the same, administrators with their eyes glued to computer screens. At least there was blue carpet in this room and the walls were intact. Some of the workers even had flowers and picture frames on their desks.

Elizabeth felt her head get lighter and her thoughts scatter as she walked closer. The fluorescent lights in the ceiling only seemed to get brighter and the pounding of the buttons was the only noise in the room. She looked at the rest of the office administrators behind the counter and none seemed to notice. They were all focused on their screens or stacks of papers on their desks at their cubicles, completely absorbed in their work and oblivious to everything. Elizabeth had no choice; she supposed the angry administrator pounding away would be her judge and executioner. Even the woman's braids were tied too tightly; Elizabeth could feel her intensity from ten feet away. It was only another step or two before she would be in the predatory gaze of the admission's lady who seemed to hate her job and most likely her life.

Elizabeth looked deep within for courage but could find none. She lingered in the same spot for what felt like minutes, but she knew was only seconds. Deep breaths with her eyes closed helped her focus momentarily but when she felt the comforting touch of the letter "N" on her necklace, the memories of the last few months played through her head. Her Catholic, private school had always seemed so boring and she always wanted more adventure. But just five minutes at this place and the energy and vibes were already defeating. Elizabeth felt this place was about as alive as a corpse. There was no pulse, nobody was home.

Elizabeth looked down again at her phone for the tenth time since she got in the school and still no Wi-Fi signals were available. She could not believe that there was no wireless internet here. What kind of place was this? Elizabeth would have to find a computer and hoped it would be wired to a network, so she could job hunt. She had to do it; her mother wasn't capable on her own. Tears started welling up. Was it her fault her dad died? All those times she prayed for her own space and more adventure?

For the first time in her life, Elizabeth wished she was older, capable of accomplishing more.

She had been living in her safe, comfortable bubble her entire life. Ever since that had been popped a few months ago by her father's funeral, her mind had begun changing, she saw the world differently and Elizabeth suddenly felt the strange desire to do things she had never imagined doing before.

Yesterday was still strange to her. She had never been an impulsive person, never wanting of much, especially material items.

Yet, she had to have that mirror.

Why?

It bothered her. Maybe it was just the move and the new city, and but Elizabeth couldn't help but feel a little strange. Back when she saw Steven in the principal's office, Elizabeth got the same weird tingling feeling on the back of her neck as she did when she saw the mirror at the lake market yesterday.

Never before had Elizabeth experienced this sort of sixth sense sensation.

But that's just crazy, Elizabeth thought to herself. Before she could finish yelling at herself, a booming voice aroused her from the daydream.

"Oh, I am so sorry!" shouted a sweet pleasant voice with a heavy Creole accent. Elizabeth had been so absorbed in her thoughts she forgot where she was. She looked up from her daze to see the admission's lady, smiling warmly with a large set of white teeth under bright, red lips and warm, motherly eyes.

"Sorry to keep you waiting dear!" she continued as Elizabeth stood there paralyzed.

"Oh My! You must be Elizabeth Montgomery! Come here!" she motioned over excitedly and waved her arm more quickly than Elizabeth thought a woman of her size could. She reached over the counter and crushed Elizabeth with a hug, pulling her face into her white blouse.

"Oh sweetie, if you need anything, and I mean anything at all, you just let us know." She broke the embrace and kept her heavy hands on Elizabeth's shoulders. Her fingers felt warm and safe and she looked into Elizabeth's eyes. "I am so, so sorry about your father young lady. I know this place is going to be a bit of a change, so you just let us know what we can do for you, okay?" Elizabeth fought back unexpected tears. She was overwhelmed by her emotions. The rollercoaster she had just ridden in twenty seconds put her through terrifying fear, an epiphany of self-awareness, to being consoled by the very thing she was fearing.

"Thank you," she managed to choke out.

"Aww. Well here is your schedule. Your first class is just down the hall and on the right, room 13, just head past the lockers and you can't miss it! Oh, how I remember my days in grade school! I'm so excited for you! Come back and let me know how it goes!" she shouted with a huge smile as she gazed up and down upon Elizabeth. "Make sure you eat up! You're such a pretty, petite sweetie!"

"Yes. Sure, I will, thank you again so much," Elizabeth replied as she curtsied gracefully. She realized she would have to get used to not doing that in her new life.

The bell screamed right above her ear and made Elizabeth cringe as she futilely rose her hand to her ear while exiting the admissions office, back into the hall. She felt her head get light again and her ears had a slight ringing in them as the hundreds of conversations began drowning her own thoughts. Elizabeth had never seen so many kids before. If the hallway was crowded earlier, now it was like a packed concert, elbow to elbow everyone bumped and moved in orderly chaos. Conversations were going everywhere, and people seemed to not lose a step or miss a beat. Elizabeth was completely overwhelmed, and she stood there in the sea of kids until she was bumped roughly and forced to keep moving. There must be thousands at this school. She was used to having a classroom with five kids and one teacher.

A scrawny Indian boy with glasses too small for his head wearing a green checkered shirt that was two sizes too big, and some yellow cargo pants with rips at both knees caught her attention. His eyes were lost in another world, staring off at something as he obliviously bumped right into Elizabeth. He turned to her in embarrassment and Elizabeth tried to not react when she saw his face. He had the worst case of acne Elizabeth had ever seen. He opened his mouth to say something, but no words came out. The shy kid looked back one more time and disappeared into the mob.

Elizabeth followed his eyes and saw a regal looking tanned girl with perfectly straight hair cascading down her back. Her eyelashes batted lusciously when she laughed. Elizabeth recognized her orange tightly fitting dress. She used to have one just like it… before she had to sell most of her things… Moving through the crowd, she came closer to the noble looking girl who gave her a pleasant smile in passing. Elizabeth tried to return it, but she just couldn't force one in her current mood. "Bianca," resonated the deepest voice Elizabeth had ever heard.

A huge boy, bigger than any adult she had ever seen wearing a letterman jacket displaying his athletic accomplishments like badges of honor, smoothly slid his arm around Bianca. His hair was like a greaser, shinier than a diamond, and looked like he spent two hours a day combing it.

Elizabeth finally shouldered her way out of the living blob of flesh and was able to grab a breath of air. She saw her classroom door and went to open it. Something caught her eye and she looked towards the end of the hall as she turned the handle.

A chubby kid was plopped on his back uncomfortably like a turtle who couldn't get up. Three mean looking girls each had a foot on his stomach, pinning him down as he squirmed and cried while they jabbed him with their rulers like knights skewering a hog with their lances. His sobs only seemed to increase their pleasure and cruel laughter. In the middle was a blue-eyed blonde-haired girl with her very long hair perfectly flowing out from her headband and over her shoulders who looked right out of an old-fashioned hallmark card. Her pale skin was contrasted by her bright red lipstick. She was decorated with jewelry like a Christmas tree is with ornaments: necklaces, bracelets, rings and earrings glittered brightly even in the pale gloomy light of the run-down school.

To her left was a much shorter girl with long thick black hair that was parted to the side with her bangs hanging over her angry face with matching dark brown eyes, and a perfect golden-brown tan. She wore an all-black dress and gritted her teeth in concentration while painfully digging the heel of her shoe into the poor kid while she furiously poked him with her ruler. The girl on the right was even taller than Elizabeth and looked like she was a distant relative to the admissions lady. She had wavy hair that split in the back into two ponytails and was enjoying her torturing like a person would their favorite food. Her skinny jeans and skin-tight orange blouse seemed to accentuate her daunting height even more as she flawlessly twirled her ruler like a magic wand, carefully picking her strikes, opposite of the short, dark haired girl. Despite their differences in appearance, they all had one strong commonality: they had their faces iced like cakes with makeup, as if they were about to go pose for a beauty magazine.

They stopped their taunting of the overweight kid pinned on the ground when they noticed Elizabeth staring with wide eyes. The blonde girl smiled at Elizabeth, while the tall one looked disinterested as she went back to work on her torture subject but the venomous stare the short dark-haired girl gave Elizabeth, scared her quickly into the classroom. She swore she heard one of the girls growl like a Troll as the door closed behind her.

Elizabeth quickly found a seat in the rear of the classroom near the window. It made her feel as if she had some point of escape, even though she knew the window was completely sealed. Unless she was planning on smashing through the glass, she wasn't going anywhere. Elizabeth was a prisoner in this strange new land, with strange, new rules and ways. The clock on the wall told her class would begin in a few seconds. Thankfully, no one had sat down beside her yet.

Her teacher had a name plaque on her desk that read, "Ms. Thorn". She looked mean just like her name, with a permanently furrowed brow and a scowl that looked like it never took a break. She wore vibrant colors that seemed out of place, yet somehow all matched in a weird way. Dozens of bracelets clanked around her wrists every time she moved. Elizabeth pulled her English Literature textbook out and took a deep breath. She knew it was going to be a long day. Ms. Thorn began lecturing and the door opened before she could start her second sentence. It was the blonde girl that was torturing the heavy-set kid a few minutes ago. Ms. Thorn's eyes burned the tardy student like laser beams, but the girl acted as if she couldn't care less. She passed several open seats, striding boldly to the vacant seat next to Elizabeth and plopped down hard with an air of authority.

"Hi, I'm Nora." She stuck her hand out and when Elizabeth squeezed it for a shake, it felt as cold as ice. Nora smiled when Elizabeth looked up quickly and seemed to anticipate Elizabeth's reaction. "Sorry, my hands get cold easily," Nora said warmly with an embarrassed laugh. She seemed nothing like the torturer from a few minutes ago.

"Excuse me, Ms. Alcina!" exclaimed Ms. Thorn. "You walk into my class late and you immediately disrupt the class further as soon as you sit down. Quiet down or I will send you to the principal's office," she threatened as she narrowed her eyes.

Nora tossed her long hair to one side as she leaned back in her chair, arms crossed, and smiled at the teacher. "I don't think so," she replied coldly.

Ms. Thorn balked for a second. Elizabeth thought she should be mortified by Nora's rebelliousness, but she was actually impressed and kind of admired Nora. She talked like an adult, she had so much confidence and poise, things Elizabeth knew she lacked.

"What a disrespectful young lady you are. No wonder you and your friends got expelled from every school in the district. Go to Principal Justice's office and be gone from my classroom at once," Ms. Thorn spoke sternly.

Nora flashed Elizabeth a quick smile and a wink as the teacher berated her, just like Steven had earlier. Why did she keep thinking about him? On her way out of the classroom, Nora looked over her shoulder and said to Elizabeth, "See you at lunch." The regal clacks of Nora's high heels echoed loudly in the stunned silence as she exited. Elizabeth swallowed the lump in her throat when everyone turned to look at her awkwardly. Elizabeth had been in class for not even two minutes, and she had already royally embarrassed herself.

Just great, what a wonderful first day.

Chapter 4:

Uneasy Feeling

The sloshing noise Elizabeth's potatoes made when they hit her lunch tray queasily echoed through her mind and stomach. The day had crawled by and she found herself in a trance like state, not even remembering her steps from the last classroom to the lunch line. The cafeteria was much the same as the halls lined with lockers: a loud disharmonious symphony of teenage hormones expressed in foul language and obscene gestures. Her food looked disgusting, just like the crumbling cafeteria walls and floors, it matched everything else in this crummy school.

Long rows of faded-teal, plastic picnic tables with matching benches littered the lunchroom. Cliques formed in each section, blaring their choice of music with little speakers plugged into their phones. Elizabeth skittered past hoping to not draw any unwanted attention as she made for the empty tables in the back. She gently set her red tray down with her plate of chicken fried steak that looked like it was from World

War II. Elizabeth forked through the mushy mashed
potatoes, fading in and out of reality between the blaring
music, raucous laughter and audacious shouts. The only thing
that occupied her mind was getting home to hang her mirror.
Elizabeth was fascinated by the pull it had on her. She was
never impulsive and usually pretty predictable, but
mysteriously she needed to hang that mirror like a fish
needed water. It was a depressing thought, realizing how
boring her life had been if hanging a mirror was adventure for
her. Or perhaps it was her only solace in this strange new
world and new life, as she felt out of place—a dandelion in
the bed of roses. Or was it the other way around? Was she
too delicate to fit in with the rough crowd of Lumiere High?

Before she could ponder further, Elizabeth saw Nora
cat-walking with supermodel like movements in her designer
clothes across the floor with the same two devilish girls from
this morning. Their long strides in high heels clicked and
clacked in echoed unison across the tiled floor of the
lunchroom. Every group stopped and stared, some with
admiration, others with jealousy and a few with hate. Nora's
gaze never left Elizabeth's eyes as she stalked towards her like
Elizabeth was prey.

The girls invited themselves to occupy the empty
bench across from her by plopping down without a word.

RAQUEL, NORA, TANYA

Their trays slamming loudly on the table, they scooted closer, the bench screaming loudly across the rough tiled floor, causing Elizabeth to cover her ears and elect more attention from the crowd. This was the absolute last thing Elizabeth wanted, but how could she object since there was plenty of room at the vacant table? Elizabeth tried not to tremble in fear. Confusion loomed in her mind. Were they here to torture her? Or would they be nice like Nora was in class?

"Lizabeth? Right." Nora commanded with a smirk of authority as she stroked a large red ruby hanging around her neck.

"Ye—"

"We know," said the dark-haired girl to the left while smacking her gum so loudly it nearly popped Elizabeth's ear. "Where you from? What's your last name?" She shouted out quickly, as she leaned forward with expectation.

"Uh…"

"We know that as well," chimed in the tall girl while she looked down at her long-extended fingers, admiring her orange nails.

Nora continued before Elizabeth's stunned mind could respond, "We heard about your dad. That was very tragic." Nora's sincerity surprised Elizabeth. "All of us are stuck here, in this place due to misfortunate circumstances as well. This place…" Nora trailed off as she gave a panoramic look across the large room, "Is Loserville."

"Totally!" yelled the raven-haired girl on the left as she combed her long hair vainly while looking into a black compact that matched her outfit. Nora continued, "This place is beneath us. And you as well Lizabeth. We are the only ones here with a shred of decency and class," raising her voice on that last sentence as she flipped her long hair to the other shoulder. "That's why we want you to join us."

Elizabeth didn't know what to say. This was the last thing she expected. And she thought she should correct Nora's pronunciation of her name but the loud girl with the black dress jumped in before she could get a word out.

"For starters, ditch the commoner garb. I mean I know you like want to fit in this new place you're at, but no way! Not with that! You and Tanya should link up! You guys are about the same dress size, gives you more options, so jealous!"

"You're totally right Raquel," said the taller girl Tanya. "I'm too tall for both of you," she sighed overdramatically. "It's a pity you will never know what it's like to be a future supermodel like me!" Tanya teased as she put the back of her hand to her forehead and pretended to swoon, falling right into Nora who just laughed, her jewelry shop assortment of items hanging everywhere, bouncing with her body in rhythm with the chuckling.

Raquel's eyes lit up like an angry fire. "Shut up broomstick. Here Tanya," spat Raquel as she piled her food onto Tanya's tray, "You need to eat before you wither away into nothing."

"Maybe you should lay off. I mean I know you think you've got curves but ain't no boy going to want to take you out if you keep it up," sniped back Tanya.

"Easy girls, easy, we're here for Lizabeth remember?" reminded Nora with even more giggles.

Out of the corner of her eye, Elizabeth spotted the kid from earlier who bumped into her, lanky and dark skinned with his terribly mismatched outfit, shuffling over towards them. His walk was tainted with self-consciousness and his eyes were not to be seen as he walked with his head down, but he peeked up every few steps to make sure he was still on course for his destination. It made his giant nose stand out even more. Someone threw a piece of steak and it smacked right against his face, slowly sliding down. Pointed fingers and mean laughs followed, but he just kept walking with the gravy dripping down, as if it didn't bother him. However, Elizabeth could tell by the way his head hung even lower it surely did.

"Anyways…" continued the short raven-haired girl Raquel, but Elizabeth's mind wandered, and she only heard gargled rambling. She was curious as to why this kid was approaching her. Or maybe he was just going for the empty table behind her? But there were several other empty tables much closer to where he came from. Elizabeth deliberately chose her spot to be out of harm's way. It seems that did her no good. But maybe he had the same idea, especially after what just happened. She awoke from her daydream to the snapping of fingers in her face.

"Hey, hey, hey!" snapped Raquel's fingers with each word. "Are you evening listening!? I'm like trying to help you here! What kind of person does that!?" Raquel yelled, offended and looking at the others for agreement.

"Oh…sorry," replied Elizabeth meekly, slightly embarrassed.

The crashing of a lunch tray, followed by a large thud, made her jump out of her seat. She looked down and recognized the green checkered shirt and yellow pants and instinctively reached a hand out to help.

"Ewww! No. No, no Lizzy, don't touch him!" shouted Nora frantically as she waved her arms. "He has a contagious disease," Nora attempted to whisper but obviously she wanted the poor kid to hear her. "Eww, I need to get away. His cologne smells so bad it makes me sick," gagged Nora as she fanned the air and slid down the lunch bench.

Elizabeth recognized the smell. It wasn't cologne. It was bug spray. She only knew because she had spent the first day in their apartment spraying every corner, crevice, and insect in sight. She saw Nora hold her breath and cover her mouth. Despite her typical cruelty, this act was no ruse. Elizabeth almost felt bad for Nora's discomfort while looking back and forth between the sprawled-out kid and her new pack of what she supposed were friends. The fact that the boy was laying down face first and not staring at her made it an easy decision. But still, she felt the need to help him.

Raquel continued rambling on and Elizabeth felt terrible as she heard the boy pick himself and his belongings up. He obviously was poor like her, probably living down in some outdated apartment run by a slum lord. It almost made more sense that she should be eating lunch with him, not these three rich girls. When he walked away the girls started snickering and Nora finally took a breath. It hadn't dawned on her until then that one of the girls probably tripped the poor kid.

The trio huddled in close and Tanya reached across and gently grabbed Elizabeth by the shoulders and pulled her closer. Her long slender fingers felt uneasy against her skin. Something about Tanya's touch made Elizabeth shudder inside. "Wally has Pumpkin Pox, those moon craters on his face are a telltale sign. It's best not to even breathe the same air that touches his face." The other girls erupted in laughter as Elizabeth tried to pretend to enjoy their cruel joke. She knew there was no such thing as Pumpkin Pox. The boy just had really bad acne.

The second half of the day dragged on slower than a tortoise. Maybe it was because Elizabeth was so anxious to leave, the hands of time had slackened their pace. Her day was one of confusion and bi-polarity. She was glad she had made friends, yet at the same time she was not. These girls seemed to want to befriend her solely based on the fact that she came from wealth, which she assumed based on their dress and mannerisms. They were just like all the spoiled kids Elizabeth grew up with. Except they were much cruder, not proper ladies.

Hopefully seeing her mother would brighten Elizabeth's spirits. The walk home had drained her remaining energy. Disappointment filled the air as she entered the empty desolate apartment, forgetting her mother was already gone to her second job at Monty's Tavern. She saw a note on the grimy tiles of their kitchen counter. Elizabeth swiftly bounced between boxes and leapt over trash that covered the kitchen floor. Her poor mother had to start work before they could properly unpack. Susan was so busy with work, how would she find time? Elizabeth supposed it would be on her.

Merde. I forgot to look for a job on a school computer, she suddenly realized.

She grabbed the note and it read:

"Dear Elizabeth, I hope you had a great first day at school honey, I made you some delicious dinner, it's waiting for you in the oven. I'll see you in the morning.
Love, Mom."

Excitedly, she yanked open the creaky oven. The door handle half snapped off as she did. The inside of the oven was beyond disgusting, riddled with rust and crusted food of the past. The aroma wafting in the air was anything but pleasant. Her stomach churned worse than when she saw the slime of potatoes she had for lunch. She knew she shouldn't be surprised, her mother couldn't do anything, much less cook. Elizabeth missed their private chef Pierre's mouthwatering boeuf bourguignon and his personal favorite, made with a family recipe generations old, gougères. With the delight of getting an ugly sweater for Christmas, Elizabeth pulled out what she surmised was a green bean casserole after sniffing it cautiously. Her hunger quickly faded, and she shoved it back in the oven and slammed it shut, the old corroded metal clanking loudly with a piercing squeak that popped her eardrums with pain.

She sighed as she marched up the stairs. Elizabeth banished thoughts of Pierre's succulent food and convinced herself eating could wait since she was anxious to begin her unpacking anyways, especially now that she had a mirror. Elizabeth needed to unpack the few designer outfits she had left from her old life to fit in with her new friends. But why was she wanting to befriend them? She seemed more inclined to be friends with the very kids she saw them torturing today. Some strange feeling in her mind was pulling her towards the depressed acne ridden Wally and the portly boy who looked like he was from a farm in the Midwest, with clothes that seemed too small for him. It was a very strange feeling, then again, everything had felt strange since they moved, so Elizabeth dismissed those thoughts and set out on the task of unpacking and making her room feel like her own.

The mirror was stacked against the wall next to the bathroom entrance just where she had left it. As she bent her knees and walked on her toes to maneuver through the scattered disarray of boxes, the intricate runes carved along the mirror drew her in, just as they had when she first saw them at the lake market. The runes felt smooth and comforting to her fingertips as her hands stroked the mirror frame, like a mother would to her child's cheek. The familiarity of the runes gave her an uneasy feeling of Déjà Vu. Where had she seen these markings before? Elizabeth searched the file cabinets of her memory. The mirror was ancient, made hundreds of years ago, but how did she know that? She tried to recall her father's collection of antiques and attempted to find a connection in those shadows of the past.

Elizabeth's sensitive nerves felt the life of the mirror as her fingertips caressed the frame. It somehow pulsated with energy and vitality, like a tree—a tree did not speak or move but if you left your hand against it long enough, sometimes you could feel its life force. But this was a mirror, carved and crafted long, long ago. How could the wood still be alive? The more Elizabeth felt the runes the more she felt her mind slip away into a dream. The chiseling of the craftsman engraving the runes echoed in her head. At first distant and far, but each hammering brought the sound closer and closer until she could see the markings being carved into the wood.

Elizabeth looked up and she was no longer in her room. Her reflection in the mirror shined a regal looking Queen in a majestic robe and a tiara studded with diamonds and emeralds greener than the hills of Ireland and blue sapphires deeper than the depths of a vast ocean. Elizabeth turned around to see the Queen but saw no one in her private chambers of freshly polished rosewood furniture, and grand canopy bed with white sheets hanging along the sides. Dark stained mahogany nightstands on both sides of the bed with expansive candelabras resting on top burned brightly against the pale moonlight creeping through the expansive French doors that led out to her balcony. Patterns of flowers grew in the thick padded carpet that cushioned her toes and a gasp of shock emitted from Elizabeth's mouth when she looked back in the mirror.

The Queen mirrored her movements. She curtsied, then laughed gleefully as she reached to feel the now glowing runes of multiple colors in the mirror. The runes of water glistened like ocean waves with blue light and the red runes of fire burned her fingertips. At the top of the mirror was what looked like a closed eye. The instant Elizabeth touched it, cold pain shot through her veins and up her arms, into her heart like a jolt of electricity. The room swirled like a vortex, the majestic air was sucked in, and the room swirled back into her grimy bedroom. Depression settled in again like a dark heavy curtain that blocks out the rays of the sun. The runes were normal again and they felt cold and lifeless.

Delirium ran through Elizabeth's mind. She was surely losing her sanity. The traumatic thoughts of her father's coffin, her mother hanging on by a thread, the filthy squalor of her home and new school were breaking her down.

Elizabeth felt like a mental patient. Her hallucination felt so real though, who was that she saw? Was it really her?

Gripping the frame with both hands, the mirror felt much lighter than she remembered the day before when she had hoisted it up. After setting the mirror down against the bathroom wall, Elizabeth yanked a crudely bent nail hanging halfway out of the wall and grabbed a heavy book to use as a hammer. She laughed out loud at the shamble her wall was because it did have one positive. Since the drywall was punched out in several spots, finding the stud to hammer the nail into was easily done. Elizabeth hooked the back of the frame under the nail and stepped back to see if the mirror was straight. Surprisingly it was perfect. Satisfied but still shaken up by her hallucination, she started opening boxes, searching for her designer clothes to fit in with the mean girls at school. After everything was hung in the closet with no doors and folded away in the makeshift drawers of a broken bookshelf, the sun was surprisingly already disappearing into night.

One more box, then I'll call it a day.

Now that the tiny room had a little more space, Elizabeth thought it best to rearrange her bed since there was an unsteady shelf right above it. But it was too heavy to move on her own. She shrugged it off for the time being and used the bed as a ladder, filling the shelf with her collection of bears, cats and other creatures of the animal kingdom. Her father had bought her one every year for her birthday. As she laid with sad memories on her bed, Elizabeth replayed the day in her head, dozing off into her mind's playground. The painful memory of Wally as he struggled to get up after falling face first into the ground and the sobbing cries of the overweight kid kept popping into her head.

"Pssst," came a quiet yet, piercing noise. Elizabeth bolted straight up in bed, her focus right on the mirror in her bathroom. The door was closed half way and through the tiny window, moonlight crept its way in, its reflection gleaming in the mirror. She had that same feeling again, like when she saw Steven in Principal Justice's office, and the runes in the mirror for the first time. A force was tugging on her insides, gnawing on her heart to press forward.

Elizabeth slowly made her way off the bed onto the floor, reaching for her necklace for comfort. Her hesitation surprised her, what did she have to fear? Her apartment suddenly seemed so quiet for the first time. She could hear the music of the neighbor above her, along with laughter and a loud and bawdy conversation from her neighbors next door. But loudest of all was the pounding of her heart. She reached her arm through the door before entering, searching for the light switch. Only when the light bulb finished warming up and was fully lit did she step into the bathroom.

When Elizabeth looked in the mirror her skin tingled from her calves up to the small hairs of her arms. In the reflection of the mirror, her animals on the shelf were completely out of order. Elizabeth snapped her neck back so hard she was sure she strained it. Everything looked the same. Just as it was. But when she looked back in the mirror, again, it was as if she was seeing a different world. Several times she went back and forth. Was it just the mirror? No, she had checked three times. The animals were not just in reverse order, they were in a different order. But how?!

Elizabeth closed her eyes, inhaled a deep breath that filled her lungs and let it all out.

Dad…Mom…this new place…it's just getting to me. That's all it is. That's all it is…

Elizabeth looked into the mirror again. Now she was even more baffled. The animals were in the correct order now. What was happening to her?

Quickly Elizabeth flicked off the light and closed the bathroom door. She rubbed her eyes heavily, slapped the palms of her hands against her temples, fell face first onto her bed and covered her ears by smooshing her pillow against them, just wanting everything to go back to the way things were.

Dad…I miss you…please come back…

The terror of the Swamps of Sorrow stalked menacingly across the marshy earth. The gigantic alligator's scales melted seamlessly into the dark moonlit environment. Despite his heavy frame, he soundlessly broke into the waters of the Mudsepy River and glided as smoothly as glass in pursuit of prey. He spotted a solitary figure fleeing in the shadows of the swamp. His powerful strokes propelled him to his next meal as he anticipated the taste of flesh. His tongue hung out while he salivated at the rare creature he was to feast upon. The labored breaths of the being from the other world sounded winded and deep. There would be no resistance. Not that there would have been any he supposed, even if his prey were at full strength. It was always too easy. But his gluttony could never be satiated.

Less delicious victims scattered at the stealthy approach of the behemoth. They only lived by his mercy. He could come back for them at any time; today was their lucky day since the scent of a succulent, otherworldly soul had his attention. Deeper came the labored breaths of the fleeing victim. He was now side by side as she ran along the river bank, constantly looking behind looking for her pursuer, failing to realize the jaws of death were so close they salivated onto her neck.

He felt his powerful muscles contract as he prepared to strike for the kill. He made a loud splash as he exploded out of the river, but it made no difference: there was no escape.

Chapter 5:

The Awakening

Elizabeth woke up soaked in terror sweat. Her hand rested on the "N" of her necklace, right where the giant fangs of the monster in her dreams ripped into her flesh. Once sure it was just a dream, Elizabeth kicked the covers off and rolled onto the rough floor. The aroma of something sweet baking wafted through the stale air, pulling Elizabeth from the memory of her nightmare. Rays of the sun stole their way through the small window in the bathroom. Elizabeth heard her mother's voice coming from the kitchen downstairs. Apparently, she had made breakfast. Excitedly she ambled down the creaking stairs that felt like they were about to collapse. Elizabeth was still half asleep and trying to dismiss last night's strange occurrences as no big deal.

Elizabeth nibbled on the strawberry frosted breakfast pastry as she briskly paced herself to school, still unable to shake the images of the strange mirror from her head. She felt bad. She hardly acknowledged her mother this morning

64

because her thoughts were elsewhere. Elizabeth tossed and turned all night and was exhausted. She just wanted this day to already be over already, so she could go home and lay in her bed and hopefully not experience another "episode" involving her new mirror.

Déjà vu made its return in the main hall of the school. She could see Nora's back as she taunted the same heavy-set boy from yesterday. Today Nora had somehow managed to hang him from the hanger that was mounted on the inside of the locker door. How could she have picked him up herself? She must have had help from the other two wicked witches.

And right on cue, as Elizabeth's view left the pleading eyes of the plump kid hanging from a locker by his shirt, her vision averted to the other two girls pointing and laughing at the lanky awkward kid Wally they tripped yesterday at lunch. Elizabeth looked upon his high-water pants and ugly green collared shirt, and she felt sympathy, while the other two girls obviously felt the complete opposite.

Elizabeth tried to sneak past them as quickly as possible and make it to her first class. She could feel Wally's gaze follow her.

"Hey crater face! We're talking to you!" Tanya taunted inches from his face just as they turned to see Elizabeth failing to creep by. "Oh! Hey Lizzy! We were just telling Wally here how if he washes his face in battery acid it will burn his skin off and how that would be way better than looking at his ugly face," Raquel sneered and followed it up with a cruel cackle. Her heart raced as she realized the girls were waiting for her to join in with their game. But Elizabeth felt sympathy in her heart for Wally; however, she was alone in a new environment and these girls could make her life a living hell if they knew. She supposed she lucked out that they liked her and accepted her. But she was not one of them. Elizabeth was torn.

Thank Heaven, thought Elizabeth as the bell rang.

"I gotta run! I'll see you guys at lunch!" she quickly spat out and took off to class, hoping the promise of seeing them later would temporarily placate their need for her to be a part of their destructive ways. However, it didn't solve her problem, it just delayed the inevitable. How was she going to deal with her "friend" situation?

The morning classes passed mutely. Nora had not even bothered to show up to her first period class and Elizabeth was glad for it. But Ms. Thorn kept staring at her every time she lectured. Why did it feel like she was being singled out? But she didn't give it much thought because all Elizabeth could think about was the mirror and the disorder of her stuffed animal collection. It still made no sense. She played it out in her head millions of times, analyzing it from every angle possible, adding in variables of any sort that popped in her mind, but nothing could make logical sense. She finally decided she would just have to confront the mirror again tonight. Elizabeth's head shook at that thought, how could she confront an inanimate object? It was just a stupid mirror. Yet something inside her told her it was more. Why had the lake market gypsy been so adamant that she tell no one where she got it from? Was there something magical about it?

That's absurd! Stop it. Elizabeth told herself.

Before she could solve the mystery, a similar glopping noise splashed down on her lunch tray. It wasn't soggy mashed potatoes, but it definitely came from a similar process as an ice cream dollop of spaghetti and what she supposed was meat marinara sauce plopped onto the dirty plate that looked older than her; however, it made mom's green bean casserole look like royal cuisine. After filling her tray with the other inedible items in the lunch line, she headed over towards the girls. She saw Nora's arm motion her towards them, Raquel waved fanatically with both arms and Tanya just beckoned with a nail from one of her long, slender fingers like she was a queen.

Great. Its only day two and I am already running out of ideas and patience to keep pretending…

It was the same scene as yesterday, the jocks hung out with the jocks, the nerds with the rest of the herd, the punk rockers with their studded bracelets and extreme facial piercings, and what looked like a group of the roughest kids in the school, smoking inside! Elizabeth stared in disbelief as she kept walking and at the last possible moment before bumping into someone, somehow stopped. Inches away, Elizabeth looked into the eyes of the pleasant princess-looking girl, Bianca, from yesterday who smiled warmly.

"I'm so sorry, excuse me," apologized Elizabeth as she quickly changed her course to make it over to the three witches before they caused any more trouble. The last thing she wanted was for them to be mean to the nice girl because of her.

Elizabeth's path was cut short by a confident figure, dressed in all black leather that boldly strode into her path. He stopped and didn't move. He turned his head to face Elizabeth and at the same time, he flicked a coin in the air. It spun faster than she had ever seen a coin spin. Their eyes locked and Elizabeth felt a strange warmth in the darkness of this young man. It was Steven, the same boy from the Principal's Office yesterday. After a few seconds of staring at her, he flashed his surprisingly pleasant smile of perfect white teeth. His eyes never left hers and the coin smacked perfectly into his palm.

"Hello, my lady," Steven spoke in a deep voice, "It's my pleasure and honor to make your acquaintance again," he said as he bowed majestically and swept his right arm in front of him while tucking his left behind. She felt his hand on hers. Steven came up from his bow and the imprint of his lips on her backhand surprisingly spread warmth through her arm and into her heart.

"Oh, heck no!" shouted Raquel from across the lunchroom. Elizabeth could hear her heels clacking as she stormed across the floor. She saw Nora floating over much more gracefully, her grin like a large cat about to feast on unknowing prey. Tanya didn't bother getting up, amusement dancing in her eyes.

"Ewww. Lizzy," moaned Raquel as she took Elizabeth by the arm and led her away, "Like go wash your hands and dunk them in a tub of rubbing alcohol," sniped Raquel, "I mean he talks to dead people. He's a total creeper. I mean… just look at him!" Steven took no offense and just kept smiling at Elizabeth, ignoring the other girls.

"I know but he's kinda hot," commented Nora with a raised eyebrow. "Right Lizzy?" she asked with an exaggerated wink and a beautiful yet somehow evil smile.

Elizabeth did think he was hot. And she did not think him as bad as Raquel said he was… but still, what was she to do?

Elizabeth didn't have to decide. It was decided for her as Nora towed her hand in hand while Raquel continued to berate him. In the midst of her ranting, Elizabeth stole a quick glance back and Steven flashed her that smile.

"Don't," said Nora flatly, "Just don't." Elizabeth thought to voice what Nora was referring to, but in her heart, she knew exactly what she was getting at. She was in a harsh dilemma. She saw how cruel these girls were. Surely, they would turn their ways on Elizabeth if she allied herself with anyone other than them, especially their two whipping boys, the overweight one and the lanky one named Wally. They seemed to regard the gothic boy Steven in the same light.

What was Elizabeth going to do? She was feeling emotions she had never experienced in her life. But her father always said suffering and sacrifice make a person strong.

Elizabeth harshly admonished herself. She was complaining about life and the thought of what her mother was enduring suddenly made Elizabeth feel guilty and embarrassed. She determined she would not harbor any such thoughts further. Raquel finally came back and joined them. Thankfully someone pulled the fire alarm as a prank and it gave Elizabeth the excuse to slip away from the girls in the pandemonium: thousands of screaming teenagers went flying through the halls, overrunning the shouting voices of the adults who were trying to make order in the chaos.

The pounding of her feet rhythmically hitting the pavement was her only conscious memory of the run home.

Elizabeth was determined to get to the bottom of this mirror and its mystery. The sun still hung high in the autumn air. Soon the days would be short and the air chilled. The thought made Elizabeth dread her future even more.

To her disappointment, her mother left her the same note from the day before. She thought today might lead to a different discovery but quickly closed the oven on the green bean casserole. It was just another notch on the belt of things that depressed her.

After taking the mirror down, Elizabeth had spent hours inspecting it from every which angle and such, yet it showed nothing other than being an ordinary mirror aside from the carved runes. But they were as lifeless as a cemetery. Was everything from yesterday really just in her mind? It was getting late but still many more hours remained until her mother would be home. Elizabeth decided she would have to write off yesterday's experience with the mirror as a result of stress from her new life and the death of her father. The bed squeaked when the flight of Elizabeth's jump ended with her looking face up at the ceiling as she stroked her necklace. How was she going to face the day at school tomorrow? Disappointment washed over Elizabeth as she realized she had been half hoping all along that the mirror would lead to some new avenue, an escape from her new bleak existence. If it was just her suffering she could endure it, but it was for her mother that Elizabeth grieved heavily. She wished she could help out somehow. Her search for a part-time job at the one computer that worked in the entire school library had not gone well. She was too young to get legitimate work and would have to find another way to help her mother.

The dark hours passed on the clock and the night deepened. Elizabeth slept soundly until she heard a familiar noise.

"Pssst," came the quiet, high pitched sound.

Immediately, Elizabeth bolted up and naturally her vision darted towards the bathroom, her reflection in the pale moonlight of the mirror showed her exactly as she was, seated in her bed, the covers and blankets up to her waist. Her bedroom light was still on and she was too scared to turn it off. Just as Elizabeth began lying back down, the noise came again. She turned and hopped out of bed, cautiously walking towards the bathroom and when she looked at the mirror as she approached, her blood froze.

In the mirror she saw herself still sitting in bed. Goosebumps invaded her arms and her flesh tingled at the sensation. Elizabeth crept closer, but still the reflection did not move.

What the heck is happening!?

Fear began to take over as panic sank in like the paralyzing fangs of a vampire.

As she got closer to the bathroom, her trance was broken by the sound of human life. Elizabeth flicked the light on and noticed the window was slightly cracked. As soon as she shut it, the noise of the city faded away. All the cars, the horns and even the buzz from the street lights waned out, all but one. She could hear the whistling noise she had been mistaking all along for a voice.

Elizabeth looked back at the mirror and everything was the same again. Was she just imagining things? Having not eaten or slept properly in weeks, Elizabeth supposed that could be causing her delirium.

Ah my dear Watson, it was elementary all along, thought Elizabeth. Her building was so old and outdated it still had the original heating system from a century ago. She could feel the hot air as she put her hand towards the steam that was coming from the pipe of the old radiant heater. Mystery solved. There was no magic mirror or voice beckoning her with a "Pssst". It was just this stupid old pipe in her room.

Elizabeth laughed out loud at the absurdity of the conclusions she had formed in her mind. But at the same time, a part of her was sad that there would be no adventure. She would have to face her reality and deal with her life. No secret super powers were going to change that Elizabeth realized as she turned off the bathroom light.

When she laid back down in bed, she thought to test the mirror one last time. Her flesh prickled again in goosebumps.

The image was not moving. It was just her standing there, staring at the window in the bathroom.

Elizabeth jumped out of bed towards the mirror, tripping hard over her blankets but somehow managed to get back on her feet instantly. In a matter of two heartbeats she had covered the distance to the bathroom. Determined to face whatever it was, she tried to keep her fear in check and forcefully resisted the urge to flick the light switch on. Elizabeth raised her arms above her head and wiggled her fingers. She stuck her tongue out and hopped from one foot to another. The reflection copied everything as normal. She turned around as if to walk away and spun around like a ballerina while shooting her arms in the air. Elizabeth screamed when the arms in the mirror did not fall back down as she lowered hers. Instinctively she flicked on the light switch faster than anything she had ever done and closed her eyes. When she opened them, the reflection appeared normal.

That's it. I'm just way over stressed from everything, and the lack of rest and malnutrition is making me hallucinate.

Elizabeth swore she'd start doing a better job of taking care of her health. Determined to get a full night's rest and make tomorrow a good day, she marched herself back into bed and squeezed her eyes shut tight.

Before she could even begin to let her mind drift away, the sound was back. There was no mistake. The "Pssst" was coming from the mirror in the bathroom.

When she looked into the mirror, her face cringed in confusion as a breeze hit her face. The air smelled like wildflowers in the spring, and not the hot sewage stench that normally came through her bathroom window. But as she walked towards the bathroom, Elizabeth knew the window was closed. Again, the wind blew gently across her face. It seemed to be coming from the mirror, but that was impossible.

The faintest light was burning in the middle. It grew larger and started to flutter. It looked like a dancing flame. By now Elizabeth's nose was an inch from the mirror. She could make out the bright light; it was a firefly. She turned around to look for the firefly in her bathroom. Nothing was there but barren darkness. She heard a humming noise and snapped her hand around in self-defense and jumped back. The firefly was in her bathroom and no longer in the mirror! She tried her usual test of putting her arms above her head. When she dropped hers back down, the reflection held hers up. Elizabeth rubbed her eyes furiously. When she opened them, she screamed in spite of herself. Her reflection... was not her... but clearly it was. Just a little more... evil?

The reflection stared her down with intense, hate filled eyes, piercing through her very soul. Her hair was black, blacker than a moonless night. Elizabeth felt a sinister crushing feeling grip her heart and start up her throat. Air became scarcer by the breath and panic welled inside her. She desperately tried to suck air in but that only made the pressure in her chest even tighter. Desperate fingers grasped onto her necklace, her fingers feeling the letter "N" as she prayed to her father for help. Her reflection smiled wickedly back at her. Elizabeth could feel the negative energy emanating from her evil twin in the mirror. She had never felt so threatened in her life as the air completely left her lungs. Tighter she squeezed her necklace until the gold letter "N" begin to cut into her skin. Evil laughter echoed faintly in the far distance and the blurry, evil smile became even fuzzier.

Elizabeth opened her eyes and found herself lying on the perpetually-filthy floor. Her fingers fumbled for the sink and she pulled herself up slowly, her head spinning uncontrollably. She could still feel her evil twin's grip on her throat. Elizabeth placed her hand there, just to check if everything was alright. Her image was now walking away from her, shrinking in contrast to the firefly that came in and became larger. Every step the evil twin took made her smaller and smaller.

What Elizabeth saw next blew her mind. She saw mist begin to form around her evil twin and wrap her like a protective shroud as she walked away. A few more steps and the pajamas were now a long black gown than trailed regally behind her steps. Elizabeth reached her hands through the quicksilver of the magic mirror. It rippled like water in a pond. It felt deathly cold, colder than anything she had ever felt. She was sure her fingers and hand were frozen and would never regain circulation. Elizabeth waited in frightened anticipation for pain to follow, but the mirror quickly soothed her soul with a warm feeling. She felt the same euphoria spread all over her as she plunged her face into the quicksilver. Elizabeth could hear her favorite song in the background and it felt like the loving embrace of angels stroked her face.

Elizabeth looked through the window into the other world. The world where her evil reflection tried to harm her. A dark enchanted looking forest lit in moonlight beckoned Elizabeth. She had to investigate, what other choice was there? Was this what the gypsy at the lake market tried to forewarn her and her mother about? It was a beautiful land, something out of a fairy tale in her childhood dreams. The symmetry of the forest in front of her was impeccable and over the tops of the trees were lushly vegetated hills backed by majestic snowcapped mountains whose peaks faded into the clouds. Even though it was night time, the moonlight shined so brightly Elizabeth could make out the most intricate details.

Elizabeth was getting the same feeling: the impulse she got to purchase the mirror, the feeling in her gut when Steven smiled at her. She clutched at her throat, remembering the grip her reflection had on her.

Elizabeth's blood went ice cold and her heart threatened to burst through her sternum as she pulled her face out of the mirror's quicksilver surface. As Elizabeth grasped her throat in panic and relived the suffocating feeling, an image of when she and Nora met, and shook hands flashed in her mind. Nora's hands were cold. Dead cold. Just like the grip from her evil twin. But Elizabeth couldn't shake the feeling it was more than just body temperature that made Nora's hands feel like ice. The feel of her necklace felt warm and calmed her nerves. Her hand had subconsciously slid down to it.

Just when certain pieces of the puzzle were connecting, they all fell apart. None of it made any sense. She had to know the truth. One more time, Elizabeth poked her finger into the magic mirror's glass surface. It rippled like a pond and stung her finger with sheer cold. When she pulled back from the uncomfortable sensation the ripples continued, distorting her image like she dropped a rock into a pond. Looking down at her finger and sucking on it to be sure it was still attached, she dismissed the numbness and shoved her palm through the quicksilver. The mirror rippled deeply now, as if someone had dived into the pond. The first waves of the ripple bounced frantically, waiting for the peaceful stillness to return. In the folds of the waves Elizabeth squinted and got so close her eyebrows were touching the quicksilver and she saw the forest again.

Her necklace tingled with urgency, the one thing she had left to remind her of her father. With how hectic her new life had been, Elizabeth realized all the times she thought of her father were negative and dark. She hadn't taken the time to remember the good memories. But it all hit her now at once. Looking through the mirror into the enchanted forest reminded of her of all the times he took her camping and backpacking through the wilderness. Further she stared into the mystifying image in her mirror, trying to decipher the image's origin and just exactly what the heck was going on.

It was nighttime in the magic forest, yet somehow the moonlight and starlight were so bright it was illuminated like it was day. Elizabeth could make out the details of the huge, broad oak trees, their infinite leaves sprouting from branches that ranged in height from just above the ground, all the way up into the night sky higher than she could see. The grass that covered the forest earth seemed to be the perfect setting for a picnic, the blades waving to Elizabeth in the wind, telling her to come join them. In the distance she thought she could see a river flowing, but with how dense the forest was, intertwined by vines that seemed to be looking at her, it was hard to tell. The details in the image seemed so… just so alive Elizabeth thought with a strong desire to explore.

This couldn't be real. Yet it was.

Before she even realized, Elizabeth's foot was on the sink as she began her climb through the magic mirror to the enchanted world on the other side. Her mind screamed no, the image of the lake market gypsy and her mother telling her to stop, but as her first leg went through the quicksilver she was immediately comforted by the mystical touch of the magic mirror. It felt warm, like the embrace of her father's touch. Elizabeth could hear joyful laughter in her ears as she inched further through the magic portal. Euphoria swarmed throughout her legs and up to her heart, making her smile for the first time since her father died. When she put her face through the mirror, Elizabeth's skin singed with delight and the burning sensation scared her. She panicked and fought it; however, unlike the time before, Elizabeth was not able to pull her face out. The air in her lungs was running out and she was trapped. But a soft voice spoke in her mind.

"Breathe. Breathe me Elizabeth," came the magic voice. Her lungs threatened to burst and break as Elizabeth held her breath. She had been fooled. Lured in by the deception of comfort, only to find she could not take in the air of the magical world.

"Trust Elizabeth. You must breathe me," came the voice again. Elizabeth fought and fought but could not pull her face out from the mirror. She leaned back as hard as she could, but when that failed she sprung forward, like a rubber band after being pulled back. Doom swallowed her.

But once her necklace hit the quicksilver, her mind was transported to another time. She felt the magic of her necklace speak with the magic of the mirror. There was no other way to explain it. She again felt her father's presence.

"Breathe Elizabeth, you'll be okay," came her father's voice! This was impossible. How could it be? But she knew for certain it was him…

Elizabeth inhaled a deep breath of the quicksilver, expecting fluid to fill her lungs. Instead her soul elevated. She felt like she was flying up to heaven and all the hurt and pain in her life faded away. She closed her eyes and laughed with joy. Her soul joined with the magic of the mirror, and they were one. She felt like she was free falling to the ground, but she actually was going up. There was no sadness, no worry, only joy and happiness. The next thing she knew, Elizabeth felt the padded grass of the forest floor littered with green leaves. It was dark, but bright star and moonlight somehow penetrated the dense thickets of trees and she saw a nocturnal world that made her jaw drop.

Chapter 6:

A Magical Land

Everything just felt alive. The concrete jungles of Elizabeth's world felt lifeless with no heart. She could feel the pulse of this land through the soles of her feet and into her heart. Elizabeth arched her head up until it touched her neck. The stars shined so brightly they leaked through the rooftop leaves of the tall oak trees like rays of sun. It was dark like nighttime, but she could still make everything out from the gnarled roots that were thicker than her body, erupting out of the ground, to the smaller purple bushes that grew where the mighty oaks did not dominate. The sound of a river flowed in the distance and she could see fish flapping their bat like wings, jumping in and out of the water trying to eat the fireflies floating about that she had seen in her bathroom. Crude, snake looking vines that grew everywhere between the tall trees and smaller vegetation took swipes at the flying fish, like large wooden snakes snapping at their prey. Some of the thin, thorny vines turned to face her as Elizabeth walked

DECHIRER AND MACHER

towards the river to get a closer look at the magic fish. They had no eyes, but she felt them watching with aggression and animosity. Elizabeth backed up, fearing they would sink their fangs into her. As she took a step back, questioning her decision to enter this strange world, a rustling sound right behind her spurned her attention and her heart began to beat fiercely. Elizabeth snapped her head around but saw nothing but dark emptiness. Despite the eerie beauty of this place, the darkness was quite frightening. The sound of something sniffing made her look up. Elizabeth screamed and jumped back when she saw a skunk, inches from her eyes. Leaning down from a low hanging branch, it sniffed the air once more. Elizabeth laughed; she never thought a skunk could be cute, but it looked adorable.

"Hello, Mr. Skunk," she said warmly with a smile.

"So that's what that awful smell is…" spoke the skunk smugly and darted off into the oak tree.

Elizabeth sniffed herself in bewilderment and was still in shock from the talking animal as she cautiously looked about with her mouth wide open, anxiously awaiting the next surprise. Was this a mistake coming here? She was lulled in by the appearance of her father's voice. She was dying to explore this place and solve that mystery. How could he have spoken to her? Or was she just imagining things, going crazy from all that had happened recently?

Hidden eyes silently emerged from the waters of the Mudsepy River. They watched the mysterious creature from the other side as she screamed in surprise from the skunk. An easy kill she would be, just feet from the bank—he would be upon her before she even knew it. Agony laced through his veins and he felt the power of his master's discipline. Once the familiar presence and pain faded, the eyes splashed back into the river and swam away.

Elizabeth turned back to the river, certain she had heard something large stir in the water right behind her.

She heard a buzzing noise and when she looked a tiny dragon the size of her palm, right out of a fairy tale, made of fluorescent rainbow colors flew within an inch of her face. The powerful, scaly dragon wings flapped gently as they studied each other. It winked at Elizabeth before flying off at lightning speed like a dragonfly.

It was time to go before something really bad
happened. She felt her necklace pulsate with life against her
chest and Elizabeth had a premonition of trouble. She turned
to face the tree she had crawled out of. A circular window,
looking much like a mirror was in the tree she had fallen out
of. Through the glass she could see her bathroom and
bedroom. It was time to end this dream of whatever the heck
was happening to her because this couldn't be real! A series
of quick hard slaps and several pinches later, Elizabeth was

convinced she had entered a world of magic and not a dream. Dream or no dream, the fear in her stomach told her it was time to go home. She took one step towards the mirror.

The bushes rustled loudly, and Elizabeth froze mid step.

From one of the purple bushes behind her, a solitary eye blinked. Breathing deeply and trying to fight the panic swelling up inside her, Elizabeth turned her back to the portal and kept her vision on the eye in the bush as she began to back away towards the tree. Twigs snapped somewhere behind her, and she let out a slight whimper and when she wheeled around, a set of three eyes blinked in unison at her. When she looked back at the single eye, there were now four eyes. Panic began to sink in and Elizabeth only took one step before realizing the way back to the tree was blocked. Six little reptile looking creatures stood on two legs with crude wooden armor and eyeballed her hungrily with a glint of evil in their eyes.

Circular helmets with a spear point at the top rested upon a laurel of moss. Their elven like ears stuck out as far as their wingspan. In one hand they held wooden spears. The other hand-held wooden bucklers, small shields that were built from uneven pieces of lumber with a white circle in the middle. Long black hair flowed down past their shoulders. Poorly built wooden armor protected their torsos and ended like a skirt down by their knees. Each had a short sword tied by a belt around their waste. They could not be more than two feet tall and stared with open mouths of jagged teeth with huge gaps between each tooth. They were a multitude of earthly colors like brown and orange.

Behind them a green one rode a wicked looking rodent that reminded Elizabeth of a giant wombat. This little creature appeared to have intelligence in his eyes. The rider's mouth was closed but tiny little shark teeth still poked through with an overbite. His helmet fit securely and had two horns made of bone on each side. His spear hung from his back as he commanded the giant wombat with a harness, making his way towards Elizabeth. The giant wombat snarled at her, revealing two giant buck teeth. As it lurched forward, wicked looking claws—nearly six inches long—pierced sharply into the forest ground. Elizabeth envisioned herself being torn to pieces by those ferocious talons. Its beady eyes penetrated through Elizabeth as she felt her heart hammering in her chest.

The little green monster thankfully yanked on the reins as he was only a foot from Elizabeth. Its breath smelled like the dumpster at her slummy apartment. The mounted

GOOGIN

creature said something to Elizabeth in a language of clicks and high-pitched screams. Elizabeth stared blankly, trying to decide what to do next. The little creature tried again in what sounded like a different language, but it still sounded like gibberish to Elizabeth. It tried for a third time.

"Where from, pretty lady?" hissed the scratchy little voice.

"Where am I?" was her confused response.

"That's not what I asked!" barked the little green gremlin sharply. It dug its heels into its mount and the giant wombat took an aggressive step towards her while snarling, backing Elizabeth up a step as she cringed in terror. "Where from?" it gritted through its crooked but very sharp pointed teeth.

"You don't have to be so rude." Elizabeth retorted. She immediately regretted her snarky answer.

Cries in their guttural language erupted as the reptilian creatures circled around Elizabeth, prodding her with their spear tips while excitedly chattering. Elizabeth's neck whipped around in all directions, trying to account for her enemies and how she was going to escape. One of the foot soldiers came within inches of Elizabeth. She tensed up, not sure what she would do but she could feel her adrenaline kick in as the panic turned into fear filled power. The little creature closest to her licked its lips and began jumping up and down repeatedly while shouting, "Eat! Eat!"

A hard smack to the back of its head with a spear butt from the mounted leader was the answer.

"No! Pretty lady prize for our Queen," it snarled. "When Queen is done with pretty lady, we eat her after she is nice and rotten. Googins no eat fresh meat," it hissed, showing all its hideous teeth.

Those last words put her into action as Elizabeth bolted for the tree and her passageway home. To her surprise, she easily kicked over the Googin in her path. Hysterical high-pitched reptilian screams flooded the night air and Elizabeth had never been so afraid in her entire life. As she turned around to see her pursuers, she was thankful to see the little creatures knocking one another over in a frenzied attempt to get to her. Elizabeth could taste freedom as she turned back around and stared into the window in the tree. With each step, more details of her bathroom and bedroom began to form and she smiled, knowing she would make it.

Elizabeth reached out for the mirror, it was just inches from her fingertips when she felt her feet leave the ground and suddenly the forest floor was a lot closer. The quicksilver of the magic portal teased the edge of Elizabeth's fingers and freedom mocked her as she saw one of the gigantic, gnarled tree roots zooming in rapidly. It was the last thing Elizabeth remembered before smacking her head. Her world turned black.

Chapter 7:

Stolen In The Night

A sharp pain to the back of Elizabeth's head woke her up from the nightmare. She tried to open her eyes, but they felt like they were sealed shut. She felt like was lying in bed but strangely the room reeked of sulfur and rotten eggs, making her gag periodically.

Smack. After another rough bump to the back of her head, Elizabeth tried to kick the blankets off, but they felt as if they were strapped down to the bed. The more she kicked the more she felt like the blankets were made out of coarse string that was digging painfully into her legs through her pants. She felt like she was fighting waves on the roughest boat ride of her life. Another huge wave and another hard smack on her head made her try to remember once again how she got here. Why was she on a boat?

Elizabeth stopped her struggle to listen and could hear the chatter of tiny voices in a foreign language. Her eyes finally opened but all she saw was a world of misty haze.

Another heavy blow to the head and the sounds of the world began to dissolve.

A violent hack of Elizabeth's lungs woke her up. The tiny voices were louder now and when she tried to kick her legs to get comfortable, she saw they were tangled in the net she was being dragged in. Her head smashed roughly against another rock in the soft ground. As she groggily blinked her eyes into consciousness, she realized she was never on a boat. Moonlight revealed she was in a swamp. Elizabeth could see the little Googins dragging the net with the leader on the giant wombat in the lead. The nightmare of what happened flooded back into her mind. Quickly she closed her eyes and feigned unconsciousness. She could not make out their words but obviously they had ill intent for her. This was all just a bad dream. Soon she would wake up. There was no magic mirror that led her into another world. There were no voices of sweet comfort. Elizabeth just wanted to go home. But how was she going to escape? She tried to prop her head up a little so it would stop smashing against the rocks.

A much deeper amphibian like voice awoke her. Somehow, she had fallen back asleep.

"Bring this wretched creature back t'where she hails from. Why woulds't thou bring her here?" croaked an angry female voice questioningly. Elizabeth stole a slight peek and

CHAGRIN CHATEAU

nearly gave herself away with a scream. A giant toad with a face full of make-up, bright red lipstick and a huge golden crown with jeweled tips was staring down menacingly at the Googins who had captured her. Gold emanated brightly from all over the giant toad: her earrings, her bracelets, along with her beaded ruby necklace and a huge ruby ring. Her face was a fat toad's, huge and oversized and disproportionate to her body that was slender and figured, like a human's. If it was not for her grotesque frog face, and excessive amounts of makeup, Elizabeth thought she would be rather beautiful.

The mucky bog that surrounded her on both sides farted gas. That was exactly what she thought this place smelled like. Further up the narrow road was a castle made of stone with three huge towers and three smaller ones. Bridges connected the towers and windows were symmetrically carved along the front walls. The longer she looked at it, Elizabeth realized that giant trees growing out of the bog were the foundation of the castle. It shrouded the entire structure like a protective cloak with its skeletal arms draped with moss. The bog she heard farting seemed to be a giant moat surrounding the place.

"Pretty lady is gift for my pretty Queen. She is from the other side," spoke the mounted Googin.

"Can we eat it? Can we eat it?" blurted the same Googin that wanted to eat her earlier.

"Shut up!" yelled the Toad Queen as she violently backhanded the unruly Googin powerfully, sending him flying where he whimpered quietly out of sight. Elizabeth squeezed her eyes shut in fear. She felt the huge toad's slithery presence linger over her as twigs cracked from the weight of her steps. The smell of rotten eggs tripled. It took every ounce of willpower to not scream out. This gigantic disgusting toad was inches from her face. The scent of insects, and whatever other horrible things the toad had been eating nearly made her gag. It was the worst odor she had ever sniffed. And lately with her life in the projects, she had encountered some very nasty aromas.

Elizabeth shuddered at the slithery disgusting touch of the toad. It felt like cold slime wiped across her cheek.

"I will add thee to my collection," croaked the Toad Queen, her bulbous neck inflating as she spoke, "Captain Draccus!" she yelled.

A mounted grey Googin dug his heels into his mount and came forward.

"Prepare the ritual," ordered the large toad.

"Yes, my Queen," replied the Captain subserviently.

Ritual? What was going to happen? dreaded Elizabeth. Suddenly she heard a loud humming noise pulsating rhythmically.

"My Queen!" yelled a Googin with fear, "Mistress is calling!"

"I know you idiot! Dost thou not think I can see that?!" raged the Queen as she struck him violently. Elizabeth popped open one eye and saw the giant toad making her way down the road towards her castle. As she climbed the first steps, she veered to the right and entered an open room nestled into the massive trunk of a tree. Elizabeth heard the heavy toad crash through loads of gems, jewels and gold. On the far wall Elizabeth saw a square mirror studded in rubies. Her breath was caught in her throat when she saw the exact same runes as her mirror back home carved into the deadwood frame of the toad's mirror! She saw the quicksilver ripple, but the frog's fat head blocked her view.

A voice darker than her worst nightmare resonated deeply from the mirror.

"Dispose of that creature at once. Do not keep her alive," husked the dark voice, sending chills all the way up Elizabeth's spine—making her shudder in fear. By instinct she reached for her necklace with the letter "N" and clutched it through her shirt.

"But but—" stammered the Toad Queen.

"But nothing," cut the dark voice, "You have your orders. I expect you to follow them. Do you have a problem with that?" challenged the dark voice.

"Nnno, no not at all your eminence," stuttered the defeated Toad Queen.

"Then continue to carry on your mission. Soon I will rule Noir once again. Be thankful I will even allow you to live after that, you pathetic being." Elizabeth heard the pulsating rhythmic humming noise again and the dark presence was gone faster than it came.

The Toad Queen embarrassed, looked around with fire in her eyes. The Googins all backed up several steps, none wanting to feel her wrath. She shuffled over quickly than Elizabeth thought her capable of, kicking a large golden goblet on her way out of the treasure room. With each step the goblet clacked on, the Googins all hunched with fear in unison.

"Take this wretched creature from my lair and dispose of her!" The Queen ordered harshly as she completed the descent of the stairs.

Elizabeth's grip tightened harder on her necklace as the giant toad slithered over to her.

"Oh, what's this?"

Elizabeth quivered at the slimy touch of the Toad Queen against her bare neck. *No!!!* screamed Elizabeth in her mind. Her father's necklace. The only thing she had left of him. Anything, oh anything, but the necklace she could part with! This was the only thing that she could not bear to lose.

Elizabeth was not a materialistic person. But the sentimental value of the necklace was worth her life.

She tried to fight back but her efforts were weakened from her rocky journey and the giant toad easily held her down. Elizabeth felt the shape of the letter "N" slip through her fingers as the chain snapped off her neck. She felt the last piece of her father being torn from her grip.

"You won't be needing this anymore. A fine trophy to add to my collection," croaked the Queen. Elizabeth supposed she was right. After all she was about to be killed. What good was the necklace to her? But still…she wanted it back. If Elizabeth were to die, she would want her father's presence near her.

"Dispose of this thing. Get her away from my sight. Hopefully she grows some Pumpkin Pox while she rots in the swamp," croaked the Toad Queen with an evil laugh. "On second thought, sacrifice her to the Swamp Yeti! She will make a tasty snack for him."

"But my Queen," begged they grey mounted Googin, "Last time we did that he ate two of my Googins!"

"Doth thou dare question me!?" she screeched at the top of her lungs, all the Googins shrank back into the shadows of the swamp cowering in fear, awaiting her to lash out.

"No, my Queen…it's just that we think it best if we finally capture and kill the Swamp Yeti. He is a hindrance to our army and ultimately an enemy of yours."

"Pshhh. If thou little weaklings dare think you can, then do so." The Toad Queen wobbled back towards Elizabeth who still lay there in stunned defeat at losing her necklace, "I desire this creature to suffer greatly for the embarrassment she hath caused me and what better way than her being eaten alive by that hideous swamp monster?"

"We will use her as bait then capture him and bring him back to you. Perhaps you could turn him into a statue."

Elizabeth saw the Toad Queen's eyes light up with the idea. "Yes. Yes! Very good Captain Draccus! I now remember why I put you in charge of my army. Very good my pet," she spoke kindly with a devilish grin as she patted him gently on the helmet. This relaxed the tension in the room and the other Googins smiled their crooked shark toothed grins as they took their first breath since the dark visitor had spoken through the mirror.

Elizabeth reached for her necklace during the momentary distraction and snatched it from the Toad Queen's hand. As she planted her other arm on the moist swampy ground to standup, the Toad Queen smiled at her mockingly and waved her webbed hand. She felt the sizzle of energy similar to the quicksilver touch of the mirror and

Elizabeth's eyes became so heavy she could not open them no matter how hard she tried.

Chapter 8:

Empty Escape

very time Elizabeth heard the deep thumping noise, she saw through her net prison, the little green captors paused with hesitation. Whatever this Swamp Yeti thing was it frightened them greatly. The thumping noise continued rhythmically over and over again. They traveled right along the border of the swamp and the forest, which was divided by a river. The river was wide and mighty, but Elizabeth knew there had to be a bridge somewhere for her to cross back into the woods where the portal back to her world was. Hope lingered in her mind as she knew the way home might be close. The brightness of the moon and stars had faded, and the world grew darker by the minute, as if nightfall was coming.

Elizabeth's brain hurt, and she groggily tried to surmise the origin of the noise. The Googins resumed their method of dragging her harshly across the ground in a net and Elizabeth began to worry for her mother. She would never know what happened to her daughter. And after all her mother had been through, Elizabeth knew it would break her completely.

Elizabeth knew she had to survive. She must live. For her mother. Somehow, she must escape. Although she was afraid to fight, Elizabeth could not let her mother down, not after all the suffering Susan had been through.

Squirming and thrashing violently to attract attention, Elizabeth tried to grab the spear when the silencing poke came but she was too slow. Cursing to herself and swearing she would learn to fight if she somehow lived, Elizabeth felt despair and hopelessness increase along with the deep rhythmic thumping noise. As the noise got closer, it sounded more like drums.

The piercing cry of a falcon ripped through the silent air and sent her blood into a frenzy.

"It's the Cookapeepooh tribe!" yelled Captain Draccus.

"Fight! Fight!" the rest of the Googins shouted as they jumped up and down excitedly with stupid grins on their face as they let go of the net. Elizabeth tried to scramble out but there was no escape.

A flash in the night sky made her look up and with incredible supersonic speed, a half-bird, half-man about the

COOKAPEEPOOH TRIBE

same size as Elizabeth dove in like a falcon, swinging a battle axe downward at the Googin leader. The grey creature somehow got his shield up in time, but the blow knocked him from his mount. Elizabeth reached for her ears, it sounded like the forest was alive with hundreds of birds as the high-pitched vibrations tore into her eardrums. She saw a dozen tribal looking men with plants growing out of their turtle shell helmets wielding different weapons from spears to swords and other weapons Elizabeth had no name for. Some helmets were covered in leaves with a singular blooming rose, others had leaves tied up in a band with a daisy sprouting. All wore necklaces of string with the sharp teeth of some animal with earthly robes that hung loosely. Warpaint decorated their faces in triangular patterns. The same swirling pattern was tattooed onto the bottom of all their chins as they charged in barefoot. Piercings on the nose and ears seemed to be part of the uniform as well. The Googins responded with their reptilian war cry and met them head on, leaving Elizabeth behind in the swampy dust.

Chaos ensued as the battle erupted. Desperate for a chance to escape Elizabeth tried to find a weakness in the net but it was futile. The ruffle of feathers startled her with a scream as she turned to see a soft friendly looking bird face with thin spectacles. His beak stuck out long and pointy, sinking down at the end. The bottom of his bill was huge like a pelican's. A headband tied back his hair and held a singular feather that pointed up to the sky with a feathered talisman for an earring attached to the headband as well. He wore a loose robe and a satchel across his body. He set down what Elizabeth assumed was a magic staff—a short stick with a small hand at the end with bony fingers and sharp black claws that held a bird's egg—as he opened his satchel for something. A glint of steel appeared in his bony feathered hands and Elizabeth responded by putting her foot through the net and felt the wind leave his lungs as the bird tumbled backwards, his dinosaur-like feet kicking up in the air.

The sound of the knife hitting the soft earth sent Elizabeth frantically searching the ground for the blade. After a few fumbles in the dark, she felt the metallic object. With freedom in her hands, she tore into the thick net, but it was painfully slow. Elizabeth looked up, sure the bird would have recovered by now to finish her off, but he lay there rolling on the ground, clutching his stomach in pain. The blade was about as sharp as a plastic butter knife. Her nicks and cuts were making slow progress. Every passing second felt as if it drew closer to her death. Elizabeth's head kept darting up in fear and back down to her sawing, making almost no progress. Death cries rang out through the night. She did not know if they were from the Googins or the tribal men, but she tried to ignore them and continue her efforts. Every time she looked up she expected death to be waiting but the battle stayed away.

After what felt like an hour she finally cut through one of the bindings of the thick roped net. She was able to fit her head through, but her shoulders were stuck. Desperate, she cried out as she felt the rope rip her skin open but when she finally managed, it was stuck around her waist. She tried to hop away with the rope wrapped around her like a skirt, but it tripped her, and she fell to the ground. Thankfully the earth was mushy and soft. She stood up and screamed when the bird face was right in front of her. He had his wand pointed at her and she swung the knife in fright, nearly cutting her enemy. His eyes seemed more scared than hers as he backed up. He tried to speak but for some reason his voice failed him. The bird came closer again and Elizabeth felt the netted rope rip as she tore herself free and hopped out one leg at a time, scraping the skin off her knees and legs in the process. She didn't care. It was time to get the heck out of here. Elizabeth fled into the night, following the river along the edge of the swamp, praying for some way to cross into the forest. She thought she heard a voice calling her name. When Elizabeth looked back all she saw was the skinny bird with glasses she had kicked chasing after her. Fear made her legs pump faster than they ever had.

She spotted rocks sticking up out of the fast-flowing river. It was the thinnest point she had seen and knew she had to risk crossing the river here. Any slip would be certain death but what choice did she have? Looking back the bird was almost caught up to her as it lurched towards her, still holding its stomach from where she kicked it. Elizabeth put her toe on the first rock. It felt slippery and slimy, like the Toad Queen's touch. She put her weight on the ball of her foot and exhaled a deep breath of prayer. She swung her other leg off the dry ground and reached out for the next rock. For once in her life, Elizabeth was glad for her long lanky legs. She braved the next step onto a rock that was sharp and pointed. It nearly stabbed through her rubber shoe as she felt her weight transfer onto her foot as she tried to reach for the next one. Barely did it catch as she pushed off the sharp rock and stood there resting with both feet, gasping for air, trying to slow her heart rate as the roaring river rushed by, splashing her feet and ankles. Only two more stones to go and she would be across.

Elizabeth heard the bird behind her and when she looked back she saw him pointing his wand with the crude fingers holding the bird egg. She leapt for the next rock, landed cleanly and bounded off it instantly. For half a second victory creased Elizabeth's face with a smile but it was short lived as she slipped on the final rock and crashed headfirst into the roaring river. The mighty current swept her up and she went under. Gasping from the freezing cold water, she could see fish that looked like squirrels swimming to avoid her frantic paddles as she splashed around like a drowning child. Elizabeth sucked in a mouthful of water, filling her lungs with icy coldness as she struggled to see a way out. She felt her nails painfully scrape against the muddy bank as she reached in desperation for anything to grab onto. Down and down she went, and the world was getting hazy. She felt her lungs ready to burst. Faster and faster the current pushed her, she did not know up from down, left from right. She swam for what she thought was the surface but all she found was the bottom of the river bed. Desperately she tried the opposite way, the force of the current fighting her, throwing her around violently. Her head popped out of the water and it was the best breath of air she had ever taken.

Thinking about her mother waking up to finding her daughter missing, Elizabeth tried to hug the river bank. She caught nothing but empty air and went back down into the water.

Exhausted and spent, Elizabeth knew she was going to die. She just lied there defeated, being tossed about. Faster and faster the river carried her until she slammed into something hard. She had never been so happy to feel pain and she was finally able to get a few breaths in as she propped herself on the huge rock she had hit. Shivering from the freezing cold Elizabeth reached for a large tree root that had overgrown its territory and stuck out into the river. The river roared loudly, and the root was so slippery, but she knew this was her last shot. It began to snap and give way as she yanked herself onto dry land. Elizabeth felt the root crack and it snapped off as she plunged back into the icy depths. Miraculously her fingers found a submerged root and Elizabeth held on for dear life, her shoulder felt like it was going to rip out of its socket. Somehow, she kicked her legs around to the river bank and pushed off with her feet to climb the root.

When Elizabeth hung halfway out of the water, gasping precious breaths of air, her grip slowly started slipping as the violent current kicked her legs off the safety of the bank. Elizabeth felt her grip failing and she kicked one leg up onto the bank in desperation. With a mighty scream, she pulled hard one last time and felt her other knee brace against the riverbank. She crawled onto dry land and lied sprawled out, her chest heaving with anxiety and joy at the same time. Bugs crawled on her face but after escaping an icy death in the river, the swampy marsh of the riverbank comforted her like a baby's blanket. The cries of battle in the distance shot her immediately to her feet.

The forest trees became a blur and Elizabeth whizzed past them at neck breaking speed, her instincts telling her when to duck and when to jump. It was exhilarating; never before had Elizabeth felt like this. Was she crazy? She had nearly been killed and barely escaped with her life, but she never felt so alive. As the trees got thicker, the sounds of battle dimmed until they completely faded.

Successful she was in losing her pursuer, but now Elizabeth had gotten herself lost.

Merde.

She had to get home before her mother woke up. Elizabeth had no idea how much time had passed. Desperate for comfort, she reached for her necklace. Her heart broke at the memory of the ugly Toad Queen taking it from her.

Elizabeth closed her eyes and tried to shut the tears in. Even though it was gone, she could feel the necklace still resting against her chest. She concentrated and thought of the pain of missing her father, and the loving touch of her mother. Elizabeth could not let her mother suffer any more than she already had. Susan would be worried sick if she discovered Elizabeth missing.

Suddenly Elizabeth felt her hand pulsating with life. Starlight beamed from her hand and shot to her right. In the flash, she saw the familiar part of the river with flying fish trying to eat fireflies and snake vines trying to eat the fish.

The flash of light was gone quicker than it came, but Elizabeth never hesitated or questioned how she had summoned the light. She dashed madly towards the direction it had shown, falling down several times and every time she got up, more blood and dirt clung to her arms and legs. Her lips felt cracked and bloody, but she didn't care. She was so happy to be going home. Elizabeth ran right up to the window and dove right through it like a swimmer into a pool. The ecstasy of the quicksilver made her feel happy and safe. However, a sharp stab of regret where Elizabeth's necklace used to hang pierced her heart.

Chapter 9:

Unwelcome Guest

"Lizzy! Lizzy! Are you okay? Oh, my goodness! Look at your head!" Susan cried. Elizabeth groggily picked herself up off the bathroom floor. The room spun, and her head hurt fiercely when her mother's hands began inspecting her. She must have passed out on her journey back and crashed on the floor when she came back through.

"Did you hit your head on the sink!? Are you okay? Let's get you to the hospital," screamed her fanatic mother, as she performed her "nurse's checkup" by touching Elizabeth several times on different parts of her body. "You're all scratched up everywhere! What happened? Did you get into a fight at school?" Susan worried gravely with fear in her eyes.

"No mom… I'm fine really. I had another crazy dream; the mirror was a doorway to another world and there were these green creatures riding wombats and this giant toad with lots of jewelry and there…"

"Ha-ha, well let's go back through and get some jewelry from that little frog!" interrupted her mother with a smile, doing a complete one eighty. "We could really use it right about now…" Susan said as she walked up to the mirror. "Come on let me in," her mother teased while tapping on the glass.

"I swear, it was so real. And there was this bird with glasses with these little munchkin warriors…"

Her mother's playful face disappeared. "Maybe we really should take you to a doctor, you look really dazed and confused. I'll go down and fix you breakfast first," she said on her way out.

Elizabeth stared one last time into the mirror before shuffling into her room to get ready for the day. Thankfully she could wear her bangs down with a headband and cover the giant lump on her forehead.

Merde. Elizabeth realized she was so caught up on solving the mystery of the mirror, she had forgotten to do her homework; it had completely evaded her mind. Elizabeth tore open her backpack and unzipped it, all the way open. Grabbing her notebook, she tried to scan her notes as she headed for her closet to pick out her outfit for the day.

A textbook-falling thud came from the bathroom. Her heart jumped, and Elizabeth quickly turned, and swore she heard tiny quick footsteps along with light, darting past her peripheral vision. Before she could investigate, her mother yelled up at her, telling her how late she was. She tried to brush her teeth with one hand and comb her hair with the other, while jumping into her socks and jeans. Her mind scrambled around, darting from last night's adventure, to the girls at school, to forgetting her homework, and how she was going to explain it to her teachers, to not sleeping and eating, and her mom's stress. Too many things had been bottled-up, and her mind was racing a mile a minute, ready to explode. Elizabeth buried everything and tried to focus on taking things one step at a time. She tied the lace to her shoe and snatched her backpack up.

Her blood went cold. Like it had been lately when she detected something bad was about to happen. The backpack was zipped up. Elizabeth swore she had unzipped it.

"Lizzy! I'm not going to say it again. Get down here!"

No time to think further upon it, Elizabeth tripped going down the stairs while trying to adjust her headband and thankfully caught herself on the rail before she sustained any real damage from the fall. After grabbing her microwaved breakfast pastry, she said goodbye to her mother as she ran out the door.

"Wait! What about the doctor?" Susan yelled after her.

"I'm fine mom, I promise!" Elizabeth turned and shouted as she ran backwards out the door and down onto the jagged sidewalk, nearly tripping again.

She managed to avoid any more trouble on the way to school. Crossing through the prison gates that enclosed the campus, Elizabeth tried to slow her breathing down and make sense of what had happened yesterday. The cuts, the bruises, and her pounding head from the giant lump she had were all real.

But there was no way it could have actually happened.

Thinking it best to check herself in the mirror one last time before school, Elizabeth shouldered her way through the human blob of the hallway traffic. There was only one bathroom in the entire school that still had a mirror, all the other ways had been broken or graffiti had been tagged over them, making the mirrors useless. As she pushed through the door to the girl's bathroom, the worst thing possible was waiting for her.

"Lizabeth!" screamed Raquel in delight between brushes of her elegant hair, "I didn't think you heard me when you ran off yesterday, you big chicken. Glad you made it to the secret meeting spot." Elizabeth looked around and noticed the bathroom was empty. Tanya walked up to the door, pulling a key out of her backpack. She nimbly twirled the key in her long slender fingers and locked the door in one motion. Raquel was right, Elizabeth had not heard her say anything about meeting up here in the morning. Just her luck, again. After the girls' usual recap of how they made other people's lives miserable and laid out their battle plan for how they were going to ruin lives today, they finally noticed Elizabeth's concerning look.

"Liz, what's wrong?" asked Nora with genuine worry, "Are our plans not to your liking?" she questioned tentatively while she looked down at her hands to inspect one of her dazzling rings. Well of course they were not to Elizabeth's liking she wanted to yell, but instead, she focused on telling the girls how she had forgotten to study and was worried about the reading quiz in her first period English class. Nora's response didn't surprise her at all.

"Study? I never study! And I always get straight A's," she said with an exaggerated wink to the others. "Anyways did you see his face?" asked Nora while adding another unnecessary layer of eyeliner in front of the mirror.

"Totally!" chimed in Tanya.

"He's probably crying in the bathroom now!" squealed Raquel in delight.

"Pretty funny, right Lizzy?" asked Nora with a mischievous look and a cocked eyebrow.

When Elizabeth looked at the mirror, she froze in terror. She stared into the mirror where Nora's reflection should have been. Instead, Elizabeth saw the huge Toad Queen with a golden, jewel-tipped crown putting blue eye liner on, and not a petite, teenage girl. The large, golden letter "N" hung from Elizabeth's chain, around the Toad Queen's neck but when she looked at Nora, she was not wearing it.

Elizabeth had completely forgotten about that part of the "dream" and with dreadful anxiety, she felt her heart sink into her stomach as she felt no necklace. How could she not have noticed that she was not wearing it? Ever since she found it Elizabeth had never let it out of her sight, and most certainly never forgot where she put it. But why the heck was she seeing the Toad Queen in Nora's image? Maybe her mother was right. She should go to the doctor.

Elizabeth kept staring at the frog reflection and her necklace. She had to get home. Like now. Like five minutes ago—no, an hour ago. How could have she forgotten her prized possession that was her last link to her father? It must be somewhere at home. She had to find it.

Elizabeth's chair in her first period class felt colder than usual. Maybe it was because she was completely unprepared for the test. Her thoughts of seeing the Toad Queen from her nightmare in Nora's reflection was baffling and distracting her even further.

"Take out a pen and paper. Time for the quiz on last night's reading assignment," said Ms. Thorn. The cracking blackboard and peeling paint added to Elizabeth's feeling of impending doom. She tried to get comfortable in her desk that was barely hanging together with a few screws. Just like her mind.

Merde. I thought this day would be better, it's starting off terrible already but at least it can't get worse. I just need to get home and look for my necklace.

Elizabeth felt something slide under her left elbow, which was resting on the desk. She looked down and saw a small piece of paper folded over twice. She looked up to Nora's uncharacteristically benevolent face, inviting her to open it. When she did, she saw that the note contained the answers to the quiz!

Her eyes went wide, and Nora quickly put her finger up to her lips and mimed a silent, "Shhh" to Elizabeth as she smiled wickedly. Just like her evil twin's reflection did the night before.

This sent eerie chills down Elizabeth's body. She got that same feeling in her stomach that she had been getting lately. Why did she ever buy that stupid mirror? All it had done was lead to one bad thing, after another, like this situation.

What was she to do? Elizabeth had never cheated before. She never had to. She was studious and responsible. How would her mother feel if she got a phone call during

Elizabeth's first week in school about how poorly she was doing? It would put her mother over the edge. And how ashamed would her father be if he knew she was a cheater? But what choice did she have? Which alternative was better? Instinctively, she reached for the necklace that was not there. It was her comforter, the one thing that calmed her.

Elizabeth's heart raced as she decided what to do. Ms. Thorn began asking the first question. "In chapter two, describe the setting of where the story takes place. Be specific and use sensory imagery to support your answer."

She froze, unable to decide her course of action. The sound of her backpack unzipping quickly grabbed her attention. Further it opened, and she saw long nails come out. Soon, scaly brown hands gripped the bag and opened it fully. Out peeked a creature that reminded her of the Googin creatures. It had small, wiry hands with sharp looking talons that she mistook for nails. Its body was brown and scaled, tiny like its limbs, but its head and ears were huge, and on its face rested two giant eyes. They looked like giant cue balls from billiards with a black dot in the middle peeking out at her.

Elizabeth snatched the bag with both hands and closed it with a death grip. Her fingers ached from the effort. Quickly she surveyed the room but thankfully no one seemed to have noticed. It was for sure one of the creatures from her nightmare last night. The bag was still unzipped, and she could feel the little thing lashing about—its claws poking her through the fabric—fighting viciously to escape. She dashed out of the room, excusing herself to use the restroom while squeezing the backpack by the top until her fingertips turned white as the Googin thrashed like a shark.

She had never seen the school so empty, and with every step, she could hear the monster in hear backpack growling and fighting to break free. Elizabeth ripped passed the hall monitor who yelled out to her, but all Elizabeth could think about was keeping the monster in her backpack. However, the struggle was fierce, and she could feel it winning as she tore down the hall. Twice it nearly popped out of the bag and she fought desperately to shove it back in, smashing her palm into its scaled head, cutting her hands in the process. Her shoulder flared with pain as she rammed through the bathroom door and slammed the backpack on the ground, hoping to stun the Googin.

Immediately, the white eyes popped out of the backpack and the creature emerged faster than lightning into an aggressive stance, hissing venomously at Elizabeth, revealing its shark like teeth. Its furtive glance quickly took in its surroundings. "Kill you now!" it screeched, and Elizabeth saw it was the same Googin from the other world who wanted to eat her. The Googin lunged and Elizabeth closed her eyes and screamed, kicking wildly at the charging creature. Luck connected a solid boot with a sickening crunch that sent the creature flying onto a sink.

Rubbing its jaw gingerly, the Googin took one last sneer at Elizabeth and hissed loudly, revealing its sharp teeth to her and then it leapt onto the next sink, continuing on. Each step landed its tiny feet on a knob, turning on each faucet as the creature hopped towards the only exit and launched itself headfirst through the window, shattering the glass with reckless abandon.

Brakes screeched, tires skidded, and a violent impact thundered, followed immediately by shouting. Elizabeth stood there rigid as a corpse, eyes and ears open, not daring to breathe as she heard a woman shout about running over a giant lizard. Was she losing her mind? Was this really happening?

Last night was definitely real. How else to explain what just happened? Elizabeth dashed out of the bathroom, heading straight for home to solve all this craziness.

Chapter 10:

Prophecy

lizabeth pounded the mirror in frustration. She hit it so hard she was convinced it would break. But no ripples of quicksilver formed. She ran her fingers across the runes, but they felt ordinary and plain as vanilla, nothing magical about them. She looked back into her room. It was a wreck. After tearing through all of her items, the search turned out just as she had feared.

Her necklace was gone.

Over and over her mind played out all the places where she may have lost it. Elizabeth considered telling the school and perhaps it may have turned up there?

No, who was she kidding? She had lost it in the world beyond her mirror. Those were no dreams. They couldn't be at this point. Elizabeth had nearly died in the dark world. Yet here she was, seriously debating if she should go back. She had to. She must. Elizabeth needed her necklace back. Angrily, she concluded to get a few kitchen knives, and march back in that world to take her necklace from that ugly toad. The memory of almost drowning made her hesitate but, in the end, she could feel the nakedness of her neck where her father's last connection to her should be.

She heard the front door downstairs unlock, and she panicked. When Elizabeth looked around, she realized she had no weapons. She never considered things like this until her experience last night. Now violence seemed like it was not so far away. Gone were her days of innocence.

Elizabeth bounded downstairs to grab the butcher knife she envisioned using to make the Toad Queen frog soup with and to get her necklace back. But the door was already opening before she could get to the kitchen. Terror froze her blood as she held her breath, awaiting to see the intruder.

"Lizzy!" yelled her mother's voice in surprise as she stepped through the door with a bag full of groceries. "What are you doing home? Are you not feeling well?" asked her mother, with great concern as she felt her hand against the bump on Elizabeth's head.

"I'm so worried about you. I'm sorry, but I have to get changed and get to Monty's Tavern for my shift." Her mother's soft eyes looked so broken and old. It had only been a short while since her father died but her mother looked as if she had aged a decade. Elizabeth felt terrible. Her mother sometimes worked twenty hours a day, trying to support them. But that was her own fault for never learning father's business and always coddling Elizabeth, just like she was doing now. "Why don't you lay down and get some rest?" Susan suggested and kissed her lightly on the forehead, narrowly missing the huge bump on her head. Her mother's lips felt parched and dry, nothing like their usual moist, vibrancy that came with their old lifestyle.

"Ok sure." But Elizabeth knew no rest would come.

"Elizabeth, what's wrong? You can tell me," concerned Susan.

"Nothing. I'm fine," Elizabeth replied coldly as she marched up the stairs.

The clouds disappeared with the sunset as a muggy breeze blew through her tiny, bathroom window. She had tried everything she could think of, but nothing could induce the portal to open. It killed Elizabeth to know she had lost her father's necklace. The heartache it caused her was overwhelming. It was the one thing she had to keep her sane after her dad dying unexpectedly.

No. It was not lost. It was taken, she decided. Elizabeth made a fist but felt so weak. She never had to fight anyone in her life, how was she going to march back through a fetid swamp and take on an army of mean, little monsters

BLACKBIRD

on giant wombats, and a giant stinky toad? Somehow, she knew she must.

The flip of a table that sent coins and cards scattering ignited the fuse. A calm, leisurely night of gambling, cheating, and drinking was ending like it always did. Pirates from all wakes of life, koalas, birds, rats and monkeys sprang into action. Chairs flew and splintered on heads, bottles cracked on backs while fists, fur, feathers and fury raged in a tempest. Screams and shouts erupted as the sound of steel rang out. The sight of swords made Elizabeth shrink into the corner even further as she tried to remember how she got here. The thick scent of cigar smoke wafted through the stale, dusty air, making her gag.

An ear shattering explosion sent wood splintering into the air and Elizabeth barely ducked in time to keep her head on her shoulders. She looked to her left where the blast came from and an odd crew of pirate birds caught her eye. A maniacal looking crow held a bomb as he looked for a reason to use it. She saw a short toucan calmly sweep money off a table and into a sack, oblivious to the chaos around him. A tall, slender bird stopped sharpening his sword long enough to point out to the toucan that he had missed a few coins that spilled on the ground. A large, salty owl with a huge pirate hat on stumbled out of a hidden door in the wall. "We gotta' set sail for Vail! Dark clouds be ahead, time to beat 'em!" ordered the older and husky owl pirate.

The toucan looked annoyed as he picked up the last coin from the ground, "Vail isn't going anywhere. Besides, when things aren't right, fortune is at its highest. I smell gold in the winds," concluded the toucan with no effort to hide his arrogance. A short bird with an eye patch stumbled into the conversation, his two mugs of beer spilling everywhere. "Then let's git 'er goin'," sloshed the drunk bird as he struggled to stand upright. He leaned heavily on the massive bald chicken hawk who seemed inclined to listen to the salty old owl.

"Supplies are needed," instructed the toucan. "Aye," agreed the old owl, "Set course for Vadu Forest."

"Ohhh!" yelled the huge chicken hawk excitedly, "I likes those little guys!"

"Not a second more to waste," the old owl ordered, "Quietly now to the ship. Keep the engine off and open the sails. The wind will take us where we need be."

WALLOW

Exhaustion clung heavily to her eyelids as she awoke from a dream of being in a saloon full of bird pirates. Ever since she had obtained the necklace, she had been having the strangest dreams. A refreshingly cool, crisp, misty breeze invigorated her nostrils. Elizabeth knew it was from the mirror without having to look.

The last rays of the sun faded, and the moonlight shined down on her shambled apartment. The moonlight seemed to beckon her attention to the intricate runes of the mirror. The more Elizabeth studied them, the more convinced she was that they resembled the elements of earth, fire, water and wind. As she neared her bathroom the runes glowed brightly again and pulsated with more life than ever before, as if beckoning Elizabeth to come. On the bottom of the mirror was an empty socket, and two identical empty sockets on the left and right of the mirror. When she looked at the top of the magic mirror, instead of an empty socket there was an eye that was slightly opened. She had not noticed it the first time the mirror activated, but then again, so much had happened so quickly she may have overlooked it.

Giant meat cleaver in hand and with the intent to harm, she stepped on the sink and without hesitation, Elizabeth dived through the mirror and felt the familiar tingling of the quicksilver flood through her veins. Nothing would deter her from her course of action. Elizabeth would not stop until she got the necklace back, no matter the cost. This was the first day of her new brave self she decided.

Elizabeth swam through the ecstasy of the portal's magic, her worries forgotten, and her pains eased. She relived memories she had forgotten, and voices gave her knowledge. Philosophy, Science, and the true history of the creation of life made Elizabeth feel powerful. The world suddenly seemed like such a simple place, and she could not wait to return to make everything perfect. Time was lost, and she felt like she was in there for hours but when the journey ended, it felt like it had only lasted a few seconds. Elizabeth gently floated out of the portal and felt the air of the enchanted realm upon her face, as magic hands guided her safely to the ground. She tried to recall all the knowledge she was told but could not remember a thing...

Surprisingly, it was darker than it was last time she entered the magical world. Elizabeth broke through the portal and landed on the forest floor, padded with leaves and looked up. Inches from her face, there was the same, soft-faced bird with the thin glasses she had kicked during the battle to escape. Fear jumped her back a few steps as she reached for her knife.

"I knew you would return," he spoke confidently, with a goofy grin.

"Who are you?" she demanded while brandishing her…stock of celery…

What the heck? She searched her pockets but no knife. Somehow her mighty weapon had turned into a useless vegetable…

"You must come with me. You must see Owah," insisted the talking bird, seemingly oblivious to her confusion as she looked back and forth from the celery to his narrow face.

"I'm not going anywhere but to find my necklace," Elizabeth stated boldly as she stepped towards the bird, making him back up a step. "Where is this place?"

"Come, all will be revealed," he said again, with the goofy grin.

"Knock that stupid grin off or I will," growled Elizabeth.

"Please," begged the bird with scared wide eyes, "I am a friend, I mean no harm, I swear!" he pleaded.

"Obviously I don't trust you since you tried to kill me! And why are you taking me to this person, bird…or who knows what? Called, Owah?"

"No, not at all. I was actually going to free you before you kicked me…" he said, as he gingerly rubbed his ribs from the painful memory. "My name is Wallow," he told her as he extended his hand. She coldly refused his handshake.

Elizabeth didn't fully believe him, but it cooled her anger just a little. "So, who is Owah? How did you know where to find me?" Elizabeth interrogated suspiciously, looking around the ground for a weapon in case she needed to bash his bird-brains in.

"Come and all will be revealed," Wallow spoke with the stupid grin returning.

"No! I am not going anywhere! I was taken prisoner by those Googins, almost killed multiple times the last time I came here, and now you're just asking me to trust you blindly?"

"I will tell you just what you need to do. The rest must be revealed by Owah."

"Why?"

"Come, and all will be revealed."

"Tell me why I should trust you," Elizabeth demanded with her arms crossed.

"Because you are from the other world and descended from the men and women with robes and pointy hats. You were written in our prophecies long ago Elizabeth."

"How do you know my name?" the suspicion back in her voice.

"Because you are destined to help save this world from the dark clutches of the Queen of Mist." Wallow looked

OWAH

around in fear, as if expecting the Queen to come and strike him for saying her name.

"I don't believe you," she said crossly.

"Elizabeth, do you think it was coincidence that our war party came across you to rescue you from the Googins? Please you must trust me. We came to help you," begged the lanky bird. For some reason his face at that moment reminded her of someone back at home, in her world.

Figuring this was her only path to the impossible quest of getting her necklace back, Elizabeth agreed to go with Wallow but would do so with great caution. The first sign of danger and she would bolt out of there.

"Fine. But you have to answer some questions on our way to Owah. For starters, where am I?"

"Welcome Elizabeth, to the magical Land of Noir," Wallow said with great pride.

The entire trip, Wallow blabbed on and on about the different regions and inhabitants of Noir, but Elizabeth paid no attention. Unless he was going to say something about the Toad Queen, she wasn't interested. Instead, Elizabeth's brain went through hundreds of different scenarios, trying to envision how to convince this Owah into helping her with attacking the Toad Queen who they probably had no idea where to find. It sounded so preposterous but not as insane as fighting by herself against those monsters. But then again,

Wallow did say they knew the Googins had her… so perhaps they may know where to find the Toad Queen. However, Elizabeth wondered what it would take for them to fight so she could get her necklace back.

They walked for what felt like several hours and Wallow finally finished his tale. Elizabeth felt terrible. She never intended to, but she somehow ripped open the gateway that had been sealed for centuries to Elizabeth's world, Lumiere. The Queen of Mist had been trying to open this doorway for ages. He told Elizabeth the Queen couldn't enter Lumiere just yet, and that she would need agents in Lumiere. Their presence somehow in Elizabeth's world would make the Queen of the Mist stronger in this world. And once the Queen entered Elizabeth's world, everything she knew and loved would be no more.

Elizabeth felt responsible for what had happened if it indeed it was true. But it could be completely made-up. How could she trust this stranger, in this strange world? Besides, she was no warrior, certainly no Sorcerer. She had been pretty terrible at sports her entire life, so how could she confront an all-powerful being such as the Queen of Mist in an actual battle of life and death? The thought was absurd to Elizabeth. She had never even gotten into a fist fight, much less a battle.

But after hearing about the Great War—where men with white beards, and women with long hair, both wearing blue robes and wielding long branches of trees came from the gateway Elizabeth had come through to battle the Queen of the Mist—it seemed a war between her world and this magical one was inevitable. Wallow said they all believed the white beards sealed the passageway forever and trapped the queen in the Land of Noir, but something had changed that. Apparently, Elizabeth's world was considered paradise by some of the inhabitants of this world and the Queen still sought to gain access.

Elizabeth's feet padded across the soft forest ground. It was still dark, but her days spent backpacking through mountains and forests with her father told Elizabeth it should be daylight by now. When they finally exited the Forest of Vadu, the woods had opened-up into a grassland that left her feeling exposed. She already knew from her last encounter, Wallow did not seem very good in a fight, but he assured her the land they traveled was safe as they were near the trading town called Saint Bernard Bay that they had skirted around to get to a bridge that crossed the Mudsepy River. He said he would give her a tour another time but for now, he must take her directly to Owah as time was short.

"Wallow, why is it so dark? When does the sun come up?" Elizabeth inquired. Wallow looked her questioningly. "What do you mean? Ah!" he exclaimed with a smile of realization. "It is always dark here."

"But why?" she asked, knowing what the answer would be.

"Soon all will be revealed," was all he said, as he had for about the twentieth time since they began walking.

After a long trek through the exposed grasslands, Elizabeth began to see trees again. Hundreds of branches curved over from both sides of the path, making an archway that completely blocked out all light. Her steps slowed as she looked at Wallow who seemed to know exactly where he was going. She stubbed her toe against something hard. When she looked down Elizabeth saw they were walking on a broken brick road. Elizabeth looked back to be sure she knew where the bridge was in case she needed to escape. As she passed through the dark archway of bent branches, the forest opened into trees too tall for her to see the top of. The darkness made it harder to see more than a foot in front of her.

Wallow spoke a quick chant and planted the butt of his small magic staff into the ground, and the egg began to glow, revealing a fortress of tall, wall-logs built right into the trees. The trees here were even larger than the ones near the portal and canopied the entire sky. Not a single drop of moonlight shined through and the darkness only intensified Elizabeth's anxiety.

When Elizabeth looked in the distance beyond the fortress gate, there burned faint fires, revealing a complex

COOKAPEEPOOH VILLAGE

system of massive gnarled trees that were intertwined, making it seem as if all the trees connected. Wooden houses with straw roofs were built into the higher levels of the trees. Instead of a door, each house had a circle carved into a wall. Faint light illuminated from lanterns that hung on the end of long poles, strategically placed at each house and along the walkways. Elizabeth could hear movement in the trees but could see no one. She supposed they had at last arrived at the home of the Cookapeepooh tribe that Wallow had told her about briefly, but that did little to calm the fear that was beginning to take over her body. As they walked closer to the tree-house village, she could feel eyes on them. But when she would look up to see, she could detect nothing. Elizabeth tried to steady her breathing, but that only made her anxiety worse.

"Here we are," informed Wallow. "The entrance is made for creatures much shorter than you."

Elizabeth saw what he meant. There was a three-foot door carved out of the log wall. "Please, ladies first," offered Wallow with a deep bow, as he tapped three times on the door with his wand and it opened without a sound.

Taking one last look back at her last chance of escape, Elizabeth nodded curtly and began to squeeze her way through, hoping to not get stabbed by a huge splinter from the rough wood. Being inside the darkness made it difficult to

see. As soon as she stood, she heard the repeated whoosh of
fire coming to life and lanterns by the dozens that hung high
in the trees directly above her began lighting up all around,
revealing a huge open space. Now she could fully see the
phenomenon that was the Cookapeepooh village. There were
entrances carved into the base of the roots with magical runes
that reminded her of the ones on her mirror. Inside the
fortress, every single tree had multiple houses built into it.
Bridges connected to dozens of trees with identical houses
and lanterns, as far as her eyes could see. The massive gnarled
roots of the trees were as big as a bus. Up and up the trees
went with dozens of houses as high as her eyes could see.
The lanterns burning at the highest houses seemed miles
away. The view from the outside did no justice to the size of
these trees. Envisioning herself up at those heights instantly
made Elizabeth's stomach churn and her head spin.

　　The sound of footsteps snapped her attention to
what was directly in front of her. Hundreds of the little tribal
men and women who looked just like the people who had
fought the Googins to save her stared at her, with wide eyes
and mouths as silence hung in the air awkwardly. Screams
and panic suddenly erupted and Elizabeth could not
understand the language they were yelling in. Dozens of birds
began descending from the thick treetops and scooped up the

little human villagers from the ground. Some looked like Wallow, others looked like owls and ravens.

Once the birds cleared the civilians, Elizabeth saw armed tribal human warriors who she supposed were the defenders of the Cookapeepooh tribe come running in a tight formation. Dozens of spears prodded her harshly, pinning her back against the log wall. Elizabeth screamed out more in fear than pain every time she felt a spear tip. She threw her arms up submissively but still the shouts and pokes continued.

Elizabeth felt something feathery brush against her leg. She looked down and Wallow was crawling between her legs.

"Wait!" Wallow shouted but as he crawled further, his hands slipped, and he fell face first, his beak stuck in the soft muddy grass. The air became silent as they waited for Wallow to speak. All she heard were muffled noises in what sounded like the same language the Cookapeepooh tribe was speaking.

The spears went down a little and Elizabeth finally took a breath. Wallow spoke another series of muffled words with his beak stuck in the ground. The cries and screams doubled, and she felt a spear pierce through her arm and into muscle.

Elizabeth fell over in pain and grabbed her bleeding arm. The world slowed down and moved in slow motion.

Gone were the little war painted faces of the villagers with plants growing out of their heads. All she could see was a sky of spears, raining down like a sea of arrows. Her last thoughts were of her mother and she cringed in anticipation of a painful death.

A huge gush of wind awoken her senses and she heard the flapping of powerful wings. When the sea of spears parted, Elizabeth saw an owl with the wingspan of an Albatross. His feathers were aged with grey all the way down to his hands that poked out of his bright red robe with yellow trim around the cuffs. Tribal runes of red written on parchment paper circled his arms as he folded them. Massive, grey eyebrows at least a foot long and six inches thick sprouted from his forehead. All white hair matted his head and his moustache that hung below his mouth had chains attached that held up some unknown square device that Elizabeth had no name for. Red war paint striped down his cheeks as brown feathers of a different bird poked out behind his ears that held earrings of great green and blue beads, ending with a large teardrop ornament with the same red runes on the parchment paper. He elicited no threat towards Elizabeth and she saw the sagely wisdom in his eyes.

"I apologize, we thought you were the Queen of Mist," spoke the giant owl softly.

"No, I'm definitely not a Queen and not even from your world," replied Elizabeth with relief.

"Oh? What do you mean?" the large owl inquired.

"Shaman Owah sir! Elizabeth is from the other side! She came through the gateway!" Wallow beamed with pride, unsuccessfully wiping the mud off his beak after he finally managed to pull it out of the ground.

"What!? We had feared you would not return after your last encounter," Owah spoke with great relief. "Trust we were trying to save you young lady." Owah turned to Wallow with a smile "Thank goodness you brought her straight here! We have no time. Elizabeth, I have been waiting for you for many moons," Owah informed gravely.

Elizabeth saw Wallow cringe slightly and Owah quickly noticed as he lowered his eyebrows and his gaze pierced Wallow.

"Wallow!" yelled Owah.

"Yes sir!" he piped up meekly.

"You did bring her here AS SOON as she arrived, right?"

Silence.

"Wallow!?"

"Yes sir! I did."

"Then what's wrong?"

"I'm sorry Shaman Owah! A Googin followed her back to her world…" sniffled Wallow with tears.

"What!? Wallow!!! How could you let this happen?" Owah's mighty wings flapped and all the other birds and tribesmen jumped back a step, some flying off into the trees and birdhouses. "I try and try, I fight with the elders to keep you as my apprentice. How are you to be the tribes' Shaman one day? You continue to make terrible decisions! I gave you the simplest of tasks: to make sure nothing goes through that portal! How could you neglect your duty?"

Wallow went down to his knees and placated his forehead on the ground in humility.

"Please forgive me master, I promise I will do better!"

Elizabeth felt terrible for Wallow. When they were traveling alone, he seemed more confident and sure of himself. It hurt her to see him humiliated. After all it was her fault the Googin followed her, wasn't it? She thought to say something but before she could Owah turned to her. She tried to take a step back but only felt the wooden wall.

"As expected. If there has ever been a bigger disgrace to the Cookapeepooh tribe than Wallow then I'm a frog," spoke a displeased hoarse voice. A massive headdress of feathers shot out like the mane of a lion in the faint light. As the newcomer walked closer, Elizabeth saw the stature of a powerfully built man but with the face of a bird. He leaned

147

on a gnarled oaken staff with his bird hands showing underneath his flowing robes. From his forehead grew two wooden antlers, both with burning candles at the ends. He had the look of someone used to people doing what he commanded.

"Pathetic," he continued as he stepped closer to Wallow, "An embarrassment to your tribe and your parents."

"Chieftain Sage," came a powerful female voice from the crowd. "That is quite enough." Sage looked like he was going to say something else, but to Elizabeth's surprise he didn't. Before she could figure out who had silenced Sage, Owah continued, "I am sorry young lady," he spoke in a deep and intelligent voice. "This is grave news. But it explains what's been happening in Noir. Lately, we have been forced to live in the trees because of the Toad Queen's Googins and their wicked mounts they ride called wombats. Our people can no longer freely wander our ancestor's lands without fear of attack and death. Lately in the Land of Noir evil has been on the rise. I don't know exactly how but the Queen of Mist weakened the seal, allowing it to be broken. The gateway to your world must be sealed again. And since you are the one who opened it, you are the only one who can seal the gateway."

"What? You're kidding!" Elizabeth concluded. Owah simply stared at her and blinked at her impassively with his big owl eyes. She noticed that a candle burned brightly from his head too. She looked around and saw hundreds of tribesmen and dozens of birds staring at her, expecting her to save their world. All she wanted was to get her necklace back and go home, never to return, and now she was getting dragged into another mess. Her life at home was already a wreck. She couldn't possibly deal with anymore.

Oh, why did I ever get that mirror?

Silence ensued as everyone continued to stare, awaiting an answer from her. Elizabeth did not know how to begin explaining how powerless she was to help. She could not even get her necklace back on her own, and they were expecting her to battle some Sorcerer?

"Even if I could do something like seal the portal, I have school, and my mom is going to be looking for me," Elizabeth pleaded.

"You will not do this task alone. We will aid you in your quest Elizabeth," assured Owah.

"But I don't want to go on any quest! I don't even know what's going on!"

"There is not much time Elizabeth. Every second we don't act, is a second the Queen of Mist is closer to taking over Noir. And eventually to the Realm of Lumiere, your home. You are not just responsible for our world, but your own as well."

"This cannot be..." she lamented as she yanked on her long hair in dread.

Owah shook his head. "We must seal the gateway. I knew this day would come. I knew not if it would come in my lifetime. It is most unfortunate. I am old. Wallow is my successor, but he is not ready. However, we will send our greatest warriors to assist you. Both of our worlds depend on it."

"What must I do?" choked Elizabeth.

"The Runes of Noir must be retrieved. Once we have those, we can seal the portal," explained Owah.

"How do we seal it?"

Owah waved his large wing and motioned with his staff.

"No time for that now. We must consult the spirits to discover the locations of the Runes.

Chapter 11:

The Gathering

Smoke danced in the pale moonlight as the Cookapeepooh tribe all sat in a large circle and chanted. Tall thick trees blocked out the shine of the stars and moon from the skies of Noir. To Elizabeth's surprise the lanterns were full of the same fireflies that had flown through the mirror into her bathroom! Dozens of flies softly floated in their glass prisons, trying to escape. Their brightness revealed solemn faces, both tribesman and bird, striking Elizabeth with reverence and a need for deep respect. The meditative faces made her feel this was important and sacred to the Cookapeepooh tribe.

Elizabeth was lost among the hundreds seated cross legged, lotus style, in the huge outer circle of spectators that looked on at the inner circle. Elizabeth took them to be the higher-ranking members of the tribe. Owah the tribe's Shaman, and Sage, the elderly but powerful looking Chieftain

CHIEFTAIN SAGE

were near a large pile of special looking branches of wood that were completely white. There was a third elder inside the circle with Princess Whitecloud and Wallow. Elizabeth had been given a brief introduction, but Chieftain Sage had not much to say to her. He had regarded her somewhat coldly as if she was a nuisance, opposite to the excitement and importance Owah had greeted her with. Despite Owah's kindness, he made Elizabeth uncomfortable, pushing all this nonsense of battling a powerful Sorcerer in a land she knew nothing about. Sage's granddaughter, princess Whitecloud was the only one who had made her feel truly welcome. Elizabeth was glad for her warm heart. Whitecloud was gentle and graceful. Her features were halfway in between that of a human and a bird. Her bright smile reminded Elizabeth of someone back home, but she could not think clearly in the midst of all that was happening so quickly.

Owah stood and clapped his palms together like he was in prayer and chanted with closed eyes. The earth rumbled and the sound of wood snapping scared Elizabeth. Bright white moonlight illuminated the village as she watched the massive branches of the trees open slowly. The view into the star filled night was breathtaking. Elizabeth had never seen anything like it back in her world. Several moons hung in the air, one so close it looked like it was resting on the leaves of the ancient trees. It glowed a blueish green and she saw others of different colors.

All the elders, like Owah, had a candle mounted on their head. Chieftain Sage muttered something in their language and all leaned forward in unison, creating a huge flame from the candles , igniting the pile of white wood. The sweet scent of the smoke invigorated her nostrils and cleared her mind.

Elizabeth had been dying to apologize to Wallow for getting him in trouble, but she had not had a chance to speak to him yet. And every time Elizabeth looked over to get his attention she saw him fawning over Whitecloud, who was focusing on Owah flapping his huge wings to manipulate the smoke rising from the fire. The smoke from the white wood was blue. Elizabeth was mesmerized. It was like she was seeing magic. The blue smoke began to turn into images and she could see trees, a river running into a lake and animals like deer and rabbits darting about. The elders began chanting solemnly and deeply while Owah continued to dance in a circle and flap his wings every so often, shifting the image to some new kind of scenery. At one point, Elizabeth saw the magical smoke turn into a land of ice and she swore for a second, she saw herself dressed in robes and a cape just like in her vision when she first hung the mirror. By now everyone had their heads down and eyes closed, entranced by the chanting. Only Owah watched the images as they continued to show what Elizabeth assumed to be different parts of the world of Noir. She supposed he was searching all the lands for these runes they needed to seal the portal.

Everyone except Wallow was entranced in meditation. His gaze continued to be fixated on Whitecloud with his mouth halfway open and his eyes showing the love from his heart. Owah began making his way around the fire, slowly flapping his large wings. He began to inhale the smoke through his nostrils while affording a quick smack that went unnoticed by all, except Elizabeth, to the back of Wallow's head and snapping him out of his love trance. Wallow finally closed his eyes and joined in the chant. When Owah exhaled the smoke, he blew away the scenic images that had been playing and it was replaced by a ghostly image revealing three faces, one of an eagle, an owl and a crow. The chanting stopped, and all stared at the three faces in the smoke.

A smooth ethereal chorus of three voices rang throughout the camp:

> *"The first of which you seek*
> *Lays deep where it reeks*
> *Between two rocks*
> *Staying dry in a wet spot."*

Murmurs broke out amongst the inner circle as they tried to decipher the riddle from the spirit guides in the hazy images.

When the smoke vanished so did the fear Elizabeth held about Noir. The witnessing of that magic had done something to her. The back of her neck tingled. It was the same feeling she got when her fingers first touched the runes of the magic mirror, the same rise in her stomach and pull when she saw the mirror on the cold rainy night at the lake market. Elizabeth remembered her dream when she was in a royal palace in that exquisite gown. She turned, excited to see Wallow's response, but it looked as if he never took his eyes or focus off Whitecloud the entire time. Owah began walking towards Elizabeth and still Wallow stared at the princess with that same hopeless romantic look, taking no notice.

As the faces of the magical smoke birds began to fade, deep dark menacing laughter cackled in the air. The blue smoke turned blood-red. The image of a slim figure with long hair took form.

"Fools. Noir is mine," threatened the sinister voice.

"Be gone!" bellowed Owah as he tried to flap the red smoke away. When his wing touched the cloud, Owah's body went stiff and he collapsed to the ground, writhing in pain. The smoke stayed perfectly still, as if trapped in time.

"Owah!" bleated a scared Wallow as he ran to his master's side.

The evil laughter returned, sending chills up Elizabeth's spine. The villagers of the Cookapeepooh tribe scattered, leaving only the elder circle. When the red smoky figure turned, she stared directly into Elizabeth's eyes. Instantly she felt the cold death grip of fingers around her throat, just like in her bathroom. Slowly the air choked out of her lungs. Sucking dreadfully for breath, nothing came in but harsh small gasps. Elizabeth could feel her face turning blue as she stood up trying desperately to pry fingers away that were not there. Her chest felt like it was going to explode. Owah struggled painfully to his feet and began frantically flapping and chanting as the face in the smoke smiled wickedly.

"Wallow! Quickly help me dispel this enchantment!" Owah cried frantically.

Wallow froze with panic, eyes scared like a baby fawn. Whitecloud came running out from one of the huts with a bucket of water and hurled it onto the fire. The water crashed and hissed loudly, a huge explosion rocked the air like thunder and the inner circle went flying. Their cries sounded so far away, and Elizabeth was on her knees, her vision fading, the world becoming pitch black. It felt like she was drowning; the pressure on her chest was going to cave her sternum into her lungs. It hurt so bad. More than anything she had ever felt. Elizabeth heard more screams of the elders, both those of pain and panic. She heard her name but the suffocating agony she felt was making the world get darker and farther away.

Through closing eyes fighting to stay open, Elizabeth saw the red smoky image of the evil lady still staring at her with hate in her face, like a bitter enemy, exacting revenge with pleasure.

"Grandfather! Do something, save her!" pleaded a voice that sounded like Whitecloud's.

Father…father…

Those words played in her head. Elizabeth thought about her father. She thought of her mother and how badly she was suffering. How desperately she wanted to help her. How desperately she missed them being a family. Hundreds of memories of being with her father flooded through her in an instant. Warmth filled her heart. It began to melt the icy grip that strangled her. Power surged through her veins and the nakedness of her missing necklace suddenly felt alive.

Elizabeth gasped her first breath. It felt like heaven. Nothing had ever felt so good. Never could Elizabeth imagine something as mundane, something so taken for granted, could feel so amazing. A second gasp let in a little more air as she felt the death grip on her throat fighting to keep its domain over her. Rising to her feet she looked at the red smoky image. The hate on the image's face had manifested to disbelief. Elizabeth felt the icy fingers of invisible death try one last time to crush her windpipe. She thought about her father's coffin going into the ground, the pain she felt that day, the tired worn look on her mother's face in their new life, and Elizabeth felt an overwhelming sadness transform into anger.

Power surged through her veins and she felt the grip snap. Stomping towards the phantasm she didn't know what she would do but she was going to make this magic specter pay. The closer she got, it felt like she was looking into a mirror.

The smoky red apparition looked just like her.

Elizabeth reached out and her fingers burned at the touch of the red smoke. Pain paralyzed her mind and body. She struggled to fight it off. The last thing she heard was the dark menacing cackle of her evil twin image.

"Elizabeth. Elizabeth," came a warm female voice.

Painfully she blinked, and she saw the inside of a building. Was she back at her home with her mother?

"Thank the great birds you're alive," spoke Owah, "Princess, please watch over Elizabeth. We must confirm where we think the first Rune of Noir to be," Owah informed her as he and Chieftain Sage exited the hut.

Elizabeth felt the comforting touch of Whitecloud as she placed a cold towel on her forehead.

"That was incredible. You possess great power. To be able to dispel an enchantment that Owah could not, is no simple feat," the princess admired.

"What do you mean?" Elizabeth groggily asked, head still spinning.

"You must be a great hero where you come from. Your strength saved our tribe. Thank you."

Elizabeth laughed at the absurdity of the statement. "Me? Heavens no. I'm nobody where I come from… I have no friends… I can't even help my own mother…" she trailed off, choking back tears.

Whitecloud shook her head. "I don't believe that. Only someone with a heart of gold could have done what you did. You stood up to the Queen of Mist. She is nothing but sorrow and hate." Whitecloud flipped the towel on Elizabeth's head as she checked her temperature with a hand across her face. "I have never seen anything like what you did, it's like in the legends of the Wizards and Sorcerers from ancient times who came and saved Noir. Powers like yours can only exist from one who is a descendant from magic. You are descended from the bearded men and long-haired women with tree branches and pointy hats."

Whitecloud stared into Elizabeth's eyes with sudden wonder. Elizabeth's blood tingled before the question was even asked.

"Do you not feel connected to this world? Do you not feel Noir calling to you from your world?"

Yes. Elizabeth knew exactly what Whitecloud was getting at. It had seemed so absurd to Elizabeth and now here was someone from this magic world who knew exactly how she felt. Elizabeth wanted to deny it, she wanted to lie and go home and never come back. But she needed to know the truth. "The runes in the mirror are what called out to me when I first saw it. That's the portal from my world to yours... a mirror."

The princess nodded, "That is your magic connecting, you cannot fight who you are; it is in your blood. That is why you are here, the only visitor in hundreds of years. You are here to strengthen the seal that has been weakened. It has been spoken in the prophecies and today was proof of that."

"But I can't... I can't do what you're all asking me to do."

"Yes, you can Elizabeth. I saw what you did today. I believe in you."

PRINCESS WHITECLOUD

Chapter 12:

Cowardly Courage

irefly lanterns lit the dark hut but did little to lighten the mood of the high council. Elizabeth sat—still recovering from her encounter, trying to piece together her memory with what Whitecloud had told her—on a tiny stool around a table with the elders and a huge half falcon, half tribal looking man and ten armed tribesmen. She felt exhausted and drained and just wanted to go home and sleep. Owah stood and spoke to the room.

"The first Rune of Noir is no doubt in the possession of the Toad Queen in the Swamps of Sorrow and most likely in the dragon's hoard of treasure that buries a second throne. There are different versions on who the seat once belonged to, or perhaps it is there for a future king we know not for certain. All that we know is that the source of the Toad Queen's evil is her lonely heart. She tries to hide her inner emotions with the charades of her swamp kingdom but deep down inside she longs for something missing inside. She seeks to remedy her emptiness by hoarding precious gems and gold and harming others, like our tribe. We will send Toma, our strongest warrior and betrothed to the Chieftain's granddaughter and future Chieftain along with his personal band of warriors to confront the Toad Queen and demand she surrender the rune."

"Are you sure that will be enough?" reasoned Elizabeth, "And what if the rune isn't there?"

Wallow chimed in, "The probability of surviving this quest with ten warriors at this time of year while treading through the swamp, calculating in the attacks of the Googins, some mounted, some not, compounded by the appearance of Flying Death, the chance of success is precisely 35.67%, however if we..." Wallow's geek speech was interrupted by the thwacking of Owah's cane on the back of his head as he continued talking to Elizabeth.

"Yes. You are descended from the tall men of white beards and women with long hair and robes. Your battle with the Queen of Noir, though be it just a spiritual projection, proves it." Owah looked down at his own staff, a gnarled branch of an ancient looking tree, "Your ancestors were wielders of these large branches capable of powerful feats."

"But I'm just a regular person! I have no power..."

"Elizabeth you have more power than you realize," spoke Owah softly and wrapped a large wing around

Elizabeth's shoulder. It felt warm and comforting, like her father's arms. "Not just in Noir but in your own world too. But until you believe in yourself, you will never unlock it."

"I can't fight in a battle! I'm too scared."

"You must. Just as you did when the Queen of Mist threatened your life."

"But how? I don't know how to use magic. I don't even remember what happened back during the ceremony. I got lucky."

"Elizabeth. I cannot tell you what you need to know. Do not gather information from without. Look within and there you will find the answer to fill the emptiness. All I can tell you for certain is you have great power otherwise you could not have come through the gateway and stopped the Queen...where I failed..."

"There is no more time for delay," interrupted Chieftain Sage, "Say your goodbyes and be off." Toma bowed deeply to Chieftain Sage and yelled out an order for his men. Ten heavily armored tribesmen responded with a loud cry and lined up. They bled discipline and the hardness in their eyes scared Elizabeth. Princess Whitecloud gave Toma a huge hug and a kiss on the cheek. Elizabeth noticed the heartbreak in Wallow's eyes as he stuttered forward towards Owah and Sage. He bowed so low his forehead was on the ground.

"Honored Elders, please allow me to assist you with the preparations for this quest. It is my fault the danger has been amplified and I need to fix what I made wrong." The elders exchanged silent looks and Wallow fell to his knees. "Please! I will make up for all my past blunders! Just give me this chance."

"No," grunted Sage, "This is far too important."

"I will not get in the way! I will lay my life down if need be for my tribe to ensure they are protected and safe."

Astonished hushes went up in the crowd. Elizabeth assumed Wallow was not known for his courage based on what she had seen since they arrived at the fortress of the Cookapeepooh tribe.

"Here are the top five reasons why I should be on the committee to decide our plan. One…" Wallow continued rambling and Chieftain Sage whispered into Shaman Owah's ears.

"This may be our chance to finally be rid of this useless fool."

"It is too dangerous; he will be killed," replied Owah.

"If he is to become Shaman one day he must stand and survive trials, just as all before him have," snarled Sage.

"He is not ready," argued Owah.

"He is past of age," came Sage's quick reply, "Do not sympathize because of the loss of your student, his father. The facts are Wallow is not cut out to be your successor. This quest will prove it."

"Or perhaps this is the spiritual journey of awakening that Wallow needs to begin his path of becoming the next Shaman for the Cookapeepooh tribe," reasoned Owah.

Sage erupted in laughter. "You're funny old friend." He clapped Owah hard on the back, still laughing as he turned back towards Wallow. Owah looked as if he was about to say more to defend Wallow but simply nodded when Sage turned around with his big goofy bird grin and protruding belly.

For the first time in a long time, Owah noticed Sage had aged. Owah supposed he had as well. A reminder that dire times were at hand. If there were any other way, he would take another road. Desperate times called for desperate measures. Owah sighed deeply as he looked over at his apprentice, clueless and lost, horribly prepared to face the dangers of death.

"Wallow," commanded Chieftain Sage with his hoarse voice that always sounded like he had been yelling too much.

Oblivious, Wallow ranted on, "Reason number two and a half, a subsection of reason number two containing three elements of rhetoric to validate my argument. First— "

"Wallow!" erupted Chieftain Sage in his booming voice and the hut became as silent as a crypt.

"Uh hum yes?" came the weak reply.

"You will go with Toma on this journey," grinned Sage.

"What!? Me?" Wallow squawked in shock.

"Yes. You."

"But…"

"Anything for our home and the lives of our tribe, is this not what you spoke Wallow?" mocked Sage with a cocky grin, not even bothering to hide his obvious pleasure from being rid of Wallow.

Wallow gulped his Adam's apple down and looked about the crowd. When his eyes locked on Princess Whitecloud he instantly bolstered up and tried to huff his chest up. He firmly planted his staff into the ground and when he went to lean on it, the staff slipped on the hard grass floor and down Wallow went. Elizabeth cringed and felt terrible for him. Snickers broke out and Chieftain Sage shook his head in disgust.

The only one who didn't seem amused was Owah. He looked genuinely concerned for Wallow, as if he was watching his own child leave for the last time. Sage, on the other hand, was the opposite. Elizabeth feared for Wallow's life as well but when she turned to give him her sympathy, he was fixated again on Whitecloud with a naïve face; his attention completely absorbed as he leaned on his staff to help himself up off the grassy ground.

"Yes. Wallow will answer the call," he beamed as he stared at the princess.

Whitecloud took no notice as she gave a kiss goodbye to the huge half falcon, half tribesman called Toma. Through the slits of his half-face mask, she saw the eyes of warrior. The sharpness of his yellow falcon eyes bled toughness and glinted peacefully in the pale light. He had the face of a man, but beautiful amber red feathers covered his cheeks and stood numerous and tall. He wore the skull of a bird as a helmet and hands of a human gripped his long spear. Feathers covered his arms and over his leather armor he wore a wide necklace of miniature logs tied expertly with blades of grass. He was nearly as tall as Elizabeth and towered over all of his fellow tribesmen.

Elizabeth trembled at the thought of what lay ahead. But she should be happy. This is exactly what had been prayed for. It just seemed too good to be true that they were going right to exactly where she needed to go. Something was not right. Something was off, but she could not put her finger on it. Elizabeth could not think straight, still shaken up from her incident at the ceremony. She was having trouble thinking and reasoning. This was crazy. She was going to march into the lair of this Toad Queen? And do battle and somehow retrieve this rune and her necklace?

Before she could ponder further, Toma gave a startling shout as he and his soldiers exited the hut.

Elizabeth had that same feeling in her stomach again that bad things were going to happen. Her hand went for the necklace that was not there. Her cold bare skin did little to comfort her.

More shouts in the air rang out and Elizabeth felt eyes upon her. When she turned she saw Owah's eyes shared the same fears.

Chapter 13:

Guardian Angel

Whatever trace of joy Elizabeth had from the magic ritual earlier was gone. A few hours ago, she was safely in her house feeling sorry for herself. Now the problems of life back home seemed trivial. The silent stealthy march and the sharp gleaming tips of spears in firefly light showed the reality of the situation. Elizabeth recognized where they were when Toma stopped to study the map the Chieftain had given him. The flying fish in the river told her they were not far from the gateway to her world. She strongly considered making a run for it.

They followed Toma north up towards a mountain range. No words were spoken. Elizabeth had none to speak either. Her mind replayed all that was set upon her and the heaviness of the burdens made it hard to breathe. It seemed impossible that she could accomplish her task. The rush of a river awoke her senses from her trance of self-pity. It was hard to tell how much time had passed since there was no sunrise or sunset; her calf muscles burned with feverish fatigue from their trek. Elizabeth groaned internally as they began to ascend the mountain, the river to their right uncrossable at this juncture.

Mercifully, Toma finally stopped. Elizabeth collapsed on the ground and looked up at the sky while she greedily inhaled oxygen. Her legs were on fire and pulsated like a heart. Once the pain was tolerable, Elizabeth fell into a trance staring at the stars and multi-colored moons. She felt their warm embrace enter her breaths, and each time Elizabeth exhaled, the body hurt less. It felt like minutes had passed before she realized her surroundings. Elizabeth only saw Toma, kneeling with his head down, eyes closed, looking far off into the distance. The rest of the warriors and Wallow were nowhere to be seen. Before she realized what she was doing, Elizabeth's steps towards Toma disturbed his meditation. He turned to her and blinked his eyes a few times, as if he just woke up from a deep slumber.

"Sorry…" Elizabeth said meekly. Toma just stared at her, his face an unreadable mask.

"I was just curious about what you were looking at." Just when she was about to turn around and walk away, he finally spoke, "It is the Tomb of Warriors. Where all of the lands greatest warriors are buried. Where my father is buried. And his father as well. It is where I too will be buried."

Before she could ask another question, a few of the other warriors crept in silently. They exchanged quiet words that Elizabeth could not make out. After a few more returned they resumed their march in silence. Elizabeth kept looking for Wallow, but there were no signs of him. The downhill march did not go any easier on her legs. Thankfully she got another rest once the mountains flattened out into forest again. Toma and his warriors huddled up, discussing their next step when Wallow finally reappeared, his hands on his knees as he heaved in huge breaths of air. After a few moments, Wallow moved meekly towards the group.

"Uh um, excuse me, uh…"

"Get out of here weakling!" barked Toma.

Wallow took another cautious step.

"If we head east here at the fork it will take us to…"

"We don't need your help to figure this out," Toma interrupted.

"But you've never been this far from the village. I have and know the way…"

Toma angrily lifted Wallow by his collar. Elizabeth feared for Wallow but what could she do?

A fierce whistling noise pierced the air followed by a loud thud. Wallow cried out as he fell from Toma's grip. Elizabeth gaped in horror when she saw an arrow protruding out of Toma's chest, his eyes with no sign of life as he fell face forward, hard onto Wallow's feet. The other tribal warriors came over in disbelief that quickly turned into anger when Elizabeth heard a familiar sound.

In the firefly lantern light, she caught glimpses in the distance of what looked like the Googins who kidnapped her; their green and brown skin and raspy voices sent fear through Elizabeth. Toma's warriors let out a cry and charged into the darkness. Elizabeth froze in fear, unsure of what to do. Sounds of death came from all around and began closing in.

"Elizabeth! We must go. It's an ambush, we're surrounded!" pleaded Wallow. Numbed by the fear of the chaos, Elizabeth simply followed. Through the trees they blindly ran trying to escape their attackers. Her heart nearly burst when a squealing scream came so close she could smell the giant wombat's breath as a mounted Googin appeared.

Wallow squawked even louder as he ran for his life. Drool dripped from the fangs of the wombat as it tried to take a bite of Wallow, missing by inches. The Googin screeched and its mount responded with a cry and leapt into the air. In the light of her lantern, it made eye contact with her and she swore for half a second it was trying to reach out to her and tell her something. It looked so sad. The Googin pulled hard on the reins midair, but the wombat refused to look away from her and crashed into the ground, sending the Googin flying.

The sounds of battle rang out and notes of steel upon steel harmonized the bloody air as she ran towards Wallow who had disappeared into the darkness, no longer in the radius of her firefly light. She had no idea what she would do once she caught up to him. Elizabeth ran on, hard into the black oblivion, hearing the guttural war cry of the Googin followed by the screech of its wombat-mount.

Elizabeth ran until she only heard the heavy breaths of her exhausted lungs. She huffed in air with her hands on her knees. She had lost them all. It had happened so quickly. The raw breath of danger made her feel as defenseless as a baby lamb. Thoughts of getting her necklace back were far away in her mind. All she wanted to do was get home and never come back. Coming back here was a huge mistake. The beautiful magical world of talking animals had entranced her. The incredible powers of the shaman owl Owah and how his magic revealed their quest was so fantastic. But the Toad Queen and her little Googins made Noir a scary, dangerous place.

Out of the woods she stepped and into a field with grass nearly as tall as her. After a few strides she tripped over something but caught her balance on one hand. Before she could turn to see what caused her fall, the sound of someone whimpering stopped her.

"Wallow?" whispered Elizabeth.

"Huh?" Wallow sniffled.

"It's me Elizabeth. Let's go!" she urged.

Standing up and pulling Wallow by the hands, they took two steps before the ground unexplainably disappeared from under their feet. Elizabeth felt her bones smashing against the ground and her wound from the spear earlier reopening as they tumbled over and over down the side of a rocky cliff in the darkness. She saw her lantern crack open and the fireflies fly to freedom before her head smacked loudly on the hard ground when she finally hit the bottom. It hurt like heck, but all Elizabeth could think about was if it would leave a bump like the last one. She didn't want her mother to worry. She tried to look for Wallow, but her eyelids were too heavy.

Raspy voices nearby immediately awoke her back to reality. Something in her screamed at her to not move or make a noise.

"There's two more down there," slithered a voice.

"They're dead then, there's no way they survived that fall," came another scratchy voice.

"Good. The Queen will be happy. All dead," came the Googin voice followed by a wicked laugh.

"No," argued the voice she recognized as the leader, the solo grey Googin on a wombat-mount, "I can still smell the pretty one. We must get her!"

Elizabeth stood up and, in her haze, she stumbled. Wallow was nowhere to be found. She couldn't risk calling out for him, but she could not just leave him. Her eyes frantically searched for Wallow but no luck. And the only way she knew how to get back home was the way they had come. But she couldn't climb back up the cliff. Elizabeth would have to navigate her way through the dark in a strange land. Who knew what other dangers besides the Googins would be waiting for her?

The more time she spent in Noir, the less she liked it. She hated leaving Wallow behind, but Elizabeth realized if she found him, he would not take her back to the portal. He would want to bring her back to the Cookapeepooh Village. That wasn't happening. It was time to go and never come back. If she made it home, she swore that mirror was going in the dumpster. Elizabeth took one step and her body collapsed in a heap. Her bones hurt and were possibly broken. She wasn't sure. Elizabeth had never broken anything in her life.

Exhaustion claimed her, and she swooned out of consciousness.

The bright starlight opened her eyes. The stars seemed to shine brighter and felt like it was daytime in Noir. Mist was beginning to seep heavily into the forest.

Wait forest? I was in an open field of grass…

Before Elizabeth could think more about how she got back to the forest, the cries of the Googins sounded too close for comfort. Elizabeth painfully stood and limped heavily as she dragged herself deeper into the woods, desperate for an escape. The trees of the forest were gigantic, some looked over two hundred feet tall but from her perspective they could have been even more, she had no way of telling. The ground was soft on her feet, it felt mudded and moist with thin blades of grass growing in patches sporadically. There were no creatures in these woods, not even birds in the trees. Or perhaps they had all gone into hiding because of the Googin pursuit. The branches dipped low enough to make her duck at times and she tried to be careful, but knew she needed to keep a frantic pace up to escape.

Elizabeth tried to think but her head was swollen fiercely, and every step made the world spin. Nausea kicked her in the stomach as she strained to hold in the vomit rising up her throat, stumbling blindly through the maze of trees. It did not take long before Elizabeth was completely lost. Screams from the little scaly monsters pierced her ear drums. Terror attacked her as she envisioned them grabbing her with their crusty, reptile fingers with filthy, jagged claws.

On she went, throwing one leg in front of the other, struggling to keep going. Thoughts of her mother and not wanting her to have to live a life with a dead husband and

DOOR OF THE UNSEEN

dead daughter drove her on. But she knew she could not keep it up. Despair set in as tears ran down her face.

Elizabeth knew she was going to die. No rescue would come this time. The Cookapeepooh tribe had saved her once, and the ones she came with were killed.

She was all alone in the dark woods.

The lake market gypsy's laughter cackled in her mind. Her fingers burned at the thought of the smooth runes carved into the mirror frame.

"She is near!" hissed a googling voice in excitement.

Elizabeth thought her energy sapped, but she learned the body and spirit were very resilient as adrenaline kicked in again. Faster than before she pumped her legs like a locomotive, jumping and dodging over overgrown gnarled roots of the massive trees that seemed to reach into the sky. Her only hope was to hide, but the Googin's could smell her.

Water! She had to find a river and cross. That would throw the scent off, she prayed desperately. But how to find one? Luck was never on her side, why would it start now? The universe hated her, why else would they take her father away and make her mother suffer so? Why would it suddenly change and bring fortune now?

Climb! Maybe the Googin's couldn't climb. But then what, she would be stuck in the tree and they would just wait

it out. She wished she had a weapon. Elizabeth was no
fighter, but she was out of options.

She risked a glance back and went down hard over a
rock that was hidden in the short grass of the forest. Pain
arced through her bones and she cried in defeated frustration.

It was over. She thought about her father and all the
times he made her happy. She thought about her mother and
how she always babied her. Suddenly she wished Susan was
here to hold her and keep her safe. But that was not
happening. Elizabeth wanted to grow up and she had her
wish.

In her delirium, Elizabeth spotted a door with a
handle in the smallest tree she had seen yet in the forest. As
she got closer, she realized it was no illusion. Elizabeth could
hear the bounding footsteps of the wombat it was so close.
Yanking the door open without hesitation, she ducked in and
slammed it shut behind. She looked about for something to
barricade it with, but her mouth just opened with awe. Firefly
lanterns by the dozens hung from every wall that lit up the
giant tree. Massive scaled lines ran through the inner
hollowed trunk up to the ceiling so high it seemed to
continue on forever. It was warm and smelled pleasant, like
incense.

"Come child. Don't make a sound. You are safe
now," came a voice from a shadowy figure somewhere in the

tree. Elizabeth froze with concern. She looked back at the door where she came in and it was gone. The lining of the tree trunk was undisturbed as if no door had ever existed. But what choice did she have? The Googins meant death for sure. She would have to roll the dice with this mysterious stranger.

"Come my child. Babarosa has been expecting you."

Elizabeth moved closer to the middle of the giant room in the tiny tree and the light from the lanterns seemed to brighten and revealed a table in the center of the huge room with a crystal ball perched on a wooden mount and two chairs, one occupied by an elderly woman with huge eyes and massive eyelids painted blue. Her head was wrapped in a turban and five feathers tucked into the middle of it were held in place by a tiny bird skull. Two thick braids on each side of her head covered her ears as she stared down into her crystal ball, her ruby red lips and bright white teeth filled with excitement as she raised her arms above her head, multiple bracelets on each side slid down her forearms, some like gold jewelry, others like the leaves of the forest or the teeth of an animal. Matching necklaces hung around her neck and the runes cascading down her loose robe reminded Elizabeth of the ones Owah wore. A warm smile parted the old lady's face as her gaze penetrated Elizabeth's eyes and into her soul.

"Do not fear Elizabeth. Babarosa is here to help you," soothed the gentle voice.

"Hhhow do you know my name?" Elizabeth stammered.

"Shhh," hushed Babarosa, "Come and sit, keep your voice low or they will hear you. Do not worry child, Babarosa will keep you safe from the Googins."

"How did you know about the Googins?" Elizabeth asked with a whisper.

Babarosa let out a light chuckle and pointed down to her crystal ball. "Babarosa always knows. Babarosa knows all in the Land of Noir."

Elizabeth opened her mouth for another question, but a raised hand silenced her.

"Let those nasty Googins pass, I will show you the way home," calmed Babarosa with her grandmotherly presence. She took Elizabeth's hands in hers and they felt warm, like laundry fresh out of the dryer. Elizabeth took a breath for what felt like the first time since her near death scramble began.

"Child, you must be careful in Noir, those who seem to be your friends are not. But fear no more Babarosa will show you the way home. Babarosa knew you would be coming…Babarosa always knows who is coming to Noir." She repeated again more for herself than Elizabeth it seemed.

"Your heart is empty child. I have something for you to warm it," Babarosa spoke as she held up an oversized blue

BABAROSA

moonstone with a hint of white sitting on a ring of thorny branches, "As long as you open your heart to help others, it will always light the way. Wherever you need to go in Noir, it will show the path." Suddenly Babarosa straightened up and her eyes narrowed dangerously, scaring Elizabeth. "But you must tell no one I showed you the way. Promise me Elizabeth. Promise Babarosa you will tell no one!" she demanded forcefully with a squeeze so strong it hurt her hands.

"Of course. Yes. Yes, I promise." Elizabeth said quickly nodding her head. "Thank you. Thank you so much for saving me and helping me."

The warm pleasant smile returned, and the grip loosened. "Of course, child. You are most welcome. Babarosa only wants to help you. Unlike others in Noir who wish to use you."

"What do you mean?"

"Do not trust the Cookapeepooh tribe. They have selfish motives."

"But the Land of Noir is in danger and— "

"You must go now Elizabeth. The Googins have lost your scent but they will be back, they will not give up," interrupted Babarosa.

"Do not worry about what they have told you. You know without me telling you this is not your world. You belong back home, in Lumiere. But remember, if you do return Babarosa will always show you the way, the way that your heart most desires because Babarosa only wants what is best for Elizabeth. Go home and if for some crazy reason you decide to return, which Babarosa does not recommend, I will still help you, but you must tell no one of our meeting. If you do, you will never be able to find Babarosa again and I will never be able to help you. Go now, open your heart to what you love the most and the moonstone ring will show you the way home."

"Thank you so much. I wish I could repay your kindness," Elizabeth offered with gratitude.

Babarosa smiled warmly as she stood up from her chair and hobbled over to Elizabeth and offered her hand. She draped her bony arm around Elizabeth and her bracelets jangled near Elizabeth's face as they walked towards the door that had magically reappeared, her closeness revealing her scent of wildflowers mixed with old dusty books.

"Your gratitude is enough Elizabeth. You are a very kind girl and it is wrong for Owah and the Cookapeepooh tribe to use your kindness for their own selfish gains. Make it home safe, and Babarosa will be happy."

Elizabeth stepped out of the safety of Babarosa's home and back into the woods. When she turned the door in the tree had vanished. Her hands searched the tree trunk for any sign of a door but there was none. Questioning if that was the tree she had stepped out of, Elizabeth glanced around. She tried to look around for any clues of the way she came. There were no footprints and everything around her looked the same. Elizabeth fumbled with the ring, rotating it and observing it from all angles. She tried pushing on the moonstone, but nothing happened. Babarosa said she must think about what is dearest to her heart.

Elizabeth closed her eyes and thought about her mother back home, exhausted with no hope left. She thought about her father and his joyful laugh that she dearly missed. Tears pushed through tightly shut eyes and one splashed onto the ring. Elizabeth felt the ring pulsate with life and as she opened her eyes, it glowed a few times. On the third pulse, a burst of light shot from the moonstone and a map of Noir appeared before her! She saw different lands of mountains, deserts, swamps, and what appeared to be towns. There was a blinking dot that she assumed that was her current position. Elizabeth placed a finger in the Vadu Woods and the map reformed into a map of just the forest. Eyes darting about, she finally spotted the river with jumping fish and the giant tree with the gateway back to her world. Elizabeth tapped on the tree. The map dissipated into a small ball of light before she could even blink and shot off like a laser beam into the dark forest. The bright beam of moonlight showed the way home. Her feet were moving, and it took everything Elizabeth had to not scream in joy at the top of her lungs. As she moved through the dark forest Elizabeth remembered how close the Googins had been to catching her. It was a miracle that she would make it out alive. She continued following the beam of light and soon she could hear the rush of the river.

To Elizabeth's surprise she arrived at the tree in just a few minutes. She vowed never to return as she crawled through the ancient tree and back to Lumiere.

Chapter 14:

Wise Words

The ringing of the bell seemed even louder today as lockers were slammed closed, conversations were shouting matches and everyone began heading to first period class. Nora was in her usual mood, having Raquel and Tanya snickering their usual evil laughter at the expense of some poor kid.

"Can you believe that Pumpkin-Pox kid Wally?" taunted Nora.

The sound of that name stung Elizabeth deeply. It reminded her so much of poor Wallow for some reason. She had left him behind. He was most likely dead. Killed by the Googins, just like Toma and the others. And she still did not get her necklace back. Elizabeth supposed she should be thankful she escaped with her life.

"Yeah Bianca would never go for him; he's so poor and hideous. She thinks she's so pretty, and proper. I can't stand the way she acts," Raquel snipped with a disgusted look while brushing her hair, staring into her black compact.

Elizabeth thought the opposite. She wished she had met Bianca first. She seemed like the kind of girl Elizabeth would be friends with since Bianca had given Elizabeth a feeling of warm kindness. Even though Bianca's family was very well off, she treated everyone with respect and compassion that reminded her of Princess Whitecloud in Noir.

Okay, I am going crazy. I'm just upset I misplaced my necklace. There is no Land of Noir. But yet I have this new moonstone ring...

"Shhh. Here they come," hushed Nora. Bianca and Wally seemed to be having a pleasant conversation as they walked down the crowded hall together. Elizabeth noticed Bianca's perfect smile when Wally made her laugh. As they neared Elizabeth, Nora shouted out loud enough for the entire school to hear.

"Hey Pumpkin-Pox. Halloween isn't for another month, you can take your mask off." The entire hallway erupted in laughter, some even pointing at Wally.

The way Wally sunk his head looked just like how Wallow dropped his. Elizabeth's guilt was gnawing away at her heart. Her world was being torn apart. Dealing with all of her earthly troubles, she did not have any more energy to worry about some birds in a magical land that half the time, she thought was made up in her head.

But the Googin in her bag, the missing necklace…her necklace. It was the only thing Elizabeth had to console her, and she missed its warm touch. It had felt alive since the day she discovered it, but she never told anyone because she knew how insane that sounded. The necklace's comforting presence seemed like it would always be there for her in times of trouble. In the brief time Elizabeth had it, touching the necklace seemed to calm her and the right thoughts would come to Elizabeth's mind. It was like magic. Magic! Yes, thought Elizabeth; she could go back and see if Babarosa could help her retrieve the necklace. After all, she was a magic woman who said she knew all.

No way. I almost died. Elizabeth thought. Was the necklace worth more than her life?

The three mean girls cracked up in loud laughter and Elizabeth watched Wally walk off, not saying a word more to Bianca. Bianca shot a glare towards the girls and started to reach out towards Wally but before she could say a word or take a step, Elizabeth saw the same studly looking jock from her first day of school take Bianca by the arm. Elizabeth wanted to speak up and say something to these wicked girls, but her one fleeting moment of courage was gone when the bell rang, and Nora dragged her by the wrist into their classroom.

Her English teacher Ms. Thorn was in her usual attire looking like a fortune teller, trying to teach English Literature to a class full of kids who would rather be anywhere but there. Elizabeth spent the period debating if she was going back to seek out Babarosa's help. The bell finally rang to dismiss them but before she could head out, Ms. Thorn called to her, "Elizabeth come see me." Elizabeth was thankful as it gave her an excuse to not have to leave with Nora who gave her a wink on the way out as if to congratulate her for getting in trouble. Elizabeth could not think of what she had possibly done. But then she remembered how she left during the middle of the quiz the day before.

"Ms. Thorn, I'm really sorry— "

"Hush child," she commanded sternly, "I understand why you did what you did."

Panic welled up in her stomach and all the way to her throat. Did Ms. Thorn see the Googin?

"It's terrible what happened to your father and family. I just want you to know that Ms. Thorn is here for you. If you ever need anything, all you must do is ask. Ms. Thorn can help you."

Elizabeth was stunned by her kindness. Ms. Thorn had seemed so mean and uncaring. Yet, here she was reaching out to her like none of her other teachers had thought to.

"Now go quickly to your next class, lest you be late."

Mr. Betto, the history teacher, was putting the class to sleep as usual while Elizabeth tried to make sense of what had been happening. Elizabeth's head ached from the blurring of the two realities. From the Toad Queen in the land of Noir to some talking owl, was she losing her mind? Worse, she was starting to feel all these weird connections with the people at her school. To top it all off, her encounter earlier in the day with the Gothic kid Steven had given her the chills when he came up to her and the girls:

"Hiii Steven," said Nora and Tanya in unison swooning over his good looks and bad boy attitude as he strutted down the hall in his black leather jacket. Raquel looked away and huffed a breath while crossing her arms. Steven ignored them completely and looked right at Elizabeth. Elizabeth cringed at the disgust on the other girl's faces for being dissed.

"Hey Liz. Looking good," Steven said while flashing her his perfect smile before swaggering off, never missing a beat.

"Pshhh. He's poor anyways," Nora complained.

"Yeah! I told you he's not worth our time!" reminded Raquel.

Even as the memory ended, Elizabeth kept thinking about the way he smiled at her. As if he knew her. And for some strange reason, Elizabeth felt as if she knew him.

Her day dream was broken up by a loud snap followed by a squeal of pain. The overweight kid the girls always tortured was standing up crying in agony.

"Nathaniel. What's wrong son?" asked Mr. Betto in a monotone voice.

He held up a broken sling shot in tears. "Someone pulled and broke my slingshot and the rubber band hit me hard. It hurts," he said through tears with a lisp in his speech.

The entire class laughed at him and Elizabeth turned to Nora, who delivered a wink and wicked smile, letting Elizabeth know who was responsible for the act. Nathaniel sniffled and sounded like he needed a few tissues, while he rubbed his eyes with his wrist.

Mr. Betto suddenly began talking in a voice that reminded Elizabeth of someone, but she couldn't quite put her finger on it. "Whoever did this step forward. One must learn to take responsibility for one's actions. If you have caused something, you must do your best to fix the situation."

Mr. Betto turned and looked right at Elizabeth. "Especially if you're the only one who can." The words sent chills up her spine and for some reason Mr. Betto suddenly felt like Owah looking at her, telling her she was the only one who could seal the gateway between Noir and her world.

And to make her guilt even worse, Mr. Betto's entire lecture that day was about a squad of Special Forces for the military who survived impossible odds because they stuck together and did not abandon their comrades. Their mission was to save a deserter, someone who ran off to chase the selfish desire of love and was now stuck behind enemy lines. Elizabeth felt terrible because she knew deep down her only reason for going with Toma and the tribesmen of the Cookapeepooh tribe was to get her necklace back. She was just like that selfish soldier.

But what was she to do? Elizabeth was no warrior. How could she possibly help in Noir when she could not even help in her world? Her mother Susan needed her help, not some strangers she had just met in a bizarre land.

"Sometimes we are thrust into situations that require us to act, whether we wish to or not and our feelings are irrelevant, only our actions matter," quoted Mr. Betto from one of the surviving soldiers as he closed the thick, crumbling, history book.

After a guilt-ridden day, the final bell rang at last. Kids tore out in a frenzy and Elizabeth led the pack, cutting out before the girls could find her. The more she thought about it, the more compelled she felt she had to go back to

Noir, not just for her necklace but to fix what she had broken. Owah told she had power in Noir and also in her own world. Elizabeth wished that were true.

She desired the courage to stand up to Nora and the mean girls and wanted to so badly to fix her life at home because her mother was too helpless to do so alone.

Elizabeth thought about what her father would do and suddenly she felt the imprint of her necklace. It felt as if it were there and Elizabeth could feel her father's warm touch. He had always told her to follow her heart and stay true to her actions, that no matter what she should always do the right thing.

It made no sense to Elizabeth but for some reason she felt strongly that if she helped Noir, she would help her life here in her world. Was this the magic of Owah twisting her mind or her own instincts? Even if she did return, how was she going to retrieve her necklace? The Cookapeepooh tribe warriors had been wiped out, and Babarosa said not to trust them and Owah. She would have to return to Babarosa. Elizabeth just hoped the moonstone ring Babarosa gave her would show her the way.

Again, the ghost imprint burned on her chest. Father also used to always tell her, the more you gave the more you received. And Elizabeth knew this to be true. Her father always gave his wealth away to help others and it seemed that his fortunes would just double each time. Elizabeth remembered the other fathers of her old friends. Greedy, mean, misers who cared for nothing but themselves.

Elizabeth felt heavily ashamed. She was just like one of those old scrooges. All she cared about was her necklace. Already people had died for the quest to save their land.

Now Wallow and everyone else's lives in Noir would be over because of her. Elizabeth could not allow that. Her actions, her fate whatever it may be, the responsibility was now linked and the lives of others, though they be talking birds, were in her hands.

As Elizabeth passed through downtown towards the rundown neighborhood where she lived, she saw Wally through a cafe's window built into a brick wall sitting at the bar with his hands buried in his face. Before Elizabeth realized, her feet were moving her into the building and she felt the warm ghost imprint of her necklace again.

"Hey," she said.

Wally looked up with heartbroken eyes but said nothing.

"Don't listen to those girls. I think you have good shot with Bianca. Just keep being yourself and have confidence." Elizabeth surprised herself with her own words. Where had they come from? It was not in her behavior to give life advice to others.

He wiped his tears with his sleeve and sniffled, just like Wallow did after he got lectured.

"Thanks," he said with a small smile. She smiled back and headed for the door, anxious to be home.

"Hey."

Elizabeth turned back around, surprised. "Yes?"

"I'm sorry about your father. My dad passed away too…" lamented Wally.

Again, Elizabeth felt the warmth on her chest. Every time she thought about her father lately it felt as if the necklace was still there.

"I'm sorry to hear that Wally," was the best she could offer.

His head just hung as usual, just like after Nora embarrassed him in front of the girl he liked and the entire school. Elizabeth took a deep breath.

"I'm sure your father is proud of you Wally; you're the top student in the entire school."

"Wha… how'd you know?"

"I read the school newspaper."

"Oh," he replied embarrassingly, "No one reads that."

"I normally don't but it's something my father used to do… so when I saw one laying around I just grabbed it," informed Elizabeth, "Well I'll see you around, take care."

"Thanks Elizabeth. You too," Wally said with a smile.

Elizabeth took one last look back as she walked down the street. The sight of a sparrow—landing to rest its wings on a brick right above the window where Wally sat—turned her walk into a run.

Chapter 15:

Not What It All Seems

ome was the same scene as it had been in the previous acts. An empty, miserable feeling, with the rotting casserole still in the oven, her mother slaving away at her terrible jobs. Elizabeth had no appetite anyways. All she could think about was her task at hand. Determined she was to fight this time. Grabbing the sharpest knife from the kitchen, which wasn't very sharp, she wrapped it in a towel with trembling hands. Visualizing fighting Googins made her almost turn back as she creaked up the stairs. Elizabeth did not know if she would have it in her to actually stab and hurt something, but she knew going back to Noir without a weapon was certain death.

Rubbing the moonstone Babarosa had given her, Elizabeth thought it might be able to open the portal somehow. Unfortunately, she had no idea how to make the gateway work, so she just laid on her bed and clutched her weapon to her chest and dozed off. Sleep was over when the cool breeze gently stroked her awake. Except this time, she smelled the crispness of fresh fog and moisture. In the bathroom, the mirror now had branches of the tree coming through and Elizabeth could see the mist was even heavier than usual that night in Noir. The runes in the mirror frame glowed brightly. The mist cooled her nostrils and felt sinister, like the blood-red smoke, striking fear into her.

The closed eye at the top of the mirror was now partially open. Elizabeth did not dare touch it, remembering how the last time she did, the evil image in the mirror came and attacked her.

Clutching the knife tightly she gave one last thought about her mother and dove through the quicksilver glass. It rippled like a still pond and she swam through the blissful euphoria. The magic comforted and gave her hope.

The journey felt like hours, but it could have only been a few seconds. Just like being in a dream, the passage of time in the world of the soul was different. The quicksilver ocean began fading and she could see the dark forest of Vadu coming up fast. Out she shot through the gateway, like being fired out of a cannon. Elizabeth feared she would smash recklessly into the ground, but as usual, time slowed to normal as she felt her feet exit the magic. Disappointment filled her soul. Elizabeth still had not heard her father's voice since her first journey through. She wanted to stay in the embrace of the quicksilver, but the spirit of the gateway reminded her she had a quest to fulfill and dutifully she returned to reality and Noir became all she saw.

Wallow was waiting for her as she landed softly on the forest ground. He jumped up and wiped his tears with his sleeve.

"I knew you'd come back!"

"Wallow I'm sorry I left…"

He ran up and crushed her legs with a mighty bird hug. Wallow seemed content, so she said no more.

"There's so much mist tonight," Elizabeth noticed.

"Because the Queen of Mist is near at hand," Wallow whispered nervously as he looked around, "I think our battle last night has attracted her attention and she has come to dispose of us herself," he whimpered fearfully.

"What happened to the warriors? Is anyone alive?"

"All dead except Toma."

"No way? We saw him take that arrow through the chest."

"He's from a legendary bird-line of warriors. It will take a lot more than that to kill him. We must rescue him."

"Really? Even after the way he treats you?"

"Yes. He is still my tribesman. I know he would do the same. We are a team each with a role to play. He is the warrior. He is the one who must battle the Queen while we retrieve the Rune. And aside from that, this is more than just about our lives. This about the entire world of Noir and yours beyond."

Elizabeth was impressed. Wallow had undergone a transformation since last night's experience. She supposed she herself had as well. Maybe they did have a chance after all.

"So where do we go from here? There's just two of us?" Elizabeth asked.

"We just follow the river north until we enter the swamp. We will figure it out on the way. I hope…"

The walk was silent. Too silent for Elizabeth's comfort. The moonlit forest that once seemed magical now felt ominous and threatening. Furtive eyes watched them from the shadows but when she would turn to look, only darkness was to be found. Elizabeth was on edge. And just like last time, her knife had turned into a stalk of celery. At least she had the moonstone ring from Babarosa to show them the way; she still hadn't figured out how she was going to reveal it to Wallow without having to explain her meeting with Babarosa. Wallow seemed trustworthy, but could he just be a pawn of Owah's? What if Babarosa's warning about the Cookapeepooh tribe was true? Elizabeth felt bad for deceiving Wallow because she wanted to do the right thing like her father always taught her. The end never justifies the means, the way you do something is more important than the goal. But if she was able to save the tribe and get her necklace back, wouldn't that justify her actions? Everyone would get what they wanted. But what did Babarosa want?

What if Babarosa would not help her if she knew Elizabeth was helping Owah? It tore at her heart thinking about having to choose between her necklace or helping the tribe and saving Noir. The silence filled the air uncomfortably. Wallow had not said much at all. He seemed lost in his own thoughts.

"Wallow how old are you?"

"I'm two thousand twenty-two years old."

Elizabeth hoped he didn't notice the shock on her face. Wallow had the mentality of a teenager.

"And you?"

"Fourteen."

The familiar scent of sulfur tingled Elizabeth's nose as the edge of the forest neared and a stinging buzz of insects made her cover her ears. The trees became fewer and the padded forest floor turned to soft squishy meadows, signaling the start of the Swamps of Sorrow. Tall grass up to her waist and fern looking plants brushed against her. Hundreds of fluorescent rainbow-colored miniature dragons were lighting up the dark with their flames of fire, toasting the tornado-formation of armored beetles that swarmed around in a whirlwind. The buzzing sound of the insects intensified with each step into the swamp as she swatted away the ones who came too close.

Eventually the tall trees of the forest thinned out into skeletal trees that protruded sharp spears for branches. The moonlight shined through here brightly but deeper into the swamp she could only see eternal darkness. Elizabeth stared into the infinite maze of bogs with vegetation that seemed to have dried out and died long ago. The bog of swamp water closest to them stirred. The water rippled lightly and then waves rolled. Something huge and heavy broke through the water and slowly lumbered onto land. It looked like a massively powerful man with tentacles for arms, and he was wrapped in vines with green moss growing all over his body. His intelligent eyes fixated on them, but he made no move towards them. Elizabeth held her breath and she turned to Wallow. A huge crash of water snapped her head back but all she saw were the rocky waves from the creature's dive back into the bog.

"Which way?" Wallow asked.

A half broken, submerged bridge seemed to be their only option to cross. But did they even need to cross? Clueless Elizabeth was on where to go. She tried to recall any details from her journey from the Toad Queen's throne to help them. Wallow began ranting on about the number of bugs while Elizabeth focused on how they were going to accomplish their tasks.

Her concentration was interrupted by the sound of an offbeat orchestra. Elizabeth's eyes and ears searched for the source. All was still in the murky swamp. Right below her feet she saw a few crickets, using their arms as violins.

Before she could think another thought, a large slithering snake slid down a branch from above. Two heads with horns where ears should have been forked off from the thick powerful body. Elizabeth froze as its tongue flickered out towards them. It retreated as quickly as it had come and disappeared into the trees.

Off in the distance, she heard a familiar sound. Clamping Wallow's beak shut with her hand, she held her breath and tried to listen harder. She yanked him by the arm to hide behind the dried-out husk of a dying tree. Wallow pulled away and tried to take a look, so Elizabeth wrestled him to the ground in the nick of time. Dirty and banged up from their hard fall, they watched a squad of Googins, some mounted on their wombat-mounts, dragging a huge beast in a net that seemed way too small to contain it. Angrily it thrashed around, tearing up the marshy ground and causing a panic among the Googins. Its ferocious cry echoed throughout Elizabeth's entire body, sent a few Googins off scrambling, and Elizabeth could feel Wallow trembling.

When she got a closer look, it looked like a giant man covered in fur, but its eyes were those of a wild beast. The little green monsters poked it roughly with their spears, yelling in their high-pitched language while the giant beast bellowed and tried to grab at its captors.

"Poor thing. We have to help it," Elizabeth said quietly, never taking her eyes off the tortured creature.

"Are you kidding?"

"No. I know what it's like to be captive and dragged around in a net. We have to free it."

"No freaking way! That is the legendary swamp monster Bog. He will eat us both alive. We are not going anywhere near that thing."

"But those Googins are torturing it."

"The second you free him he will eat us. Besides how can we save him even if we wanted to? And it's not part of our quest. We need to find Toma."

"I can't just leave the poor thing like that."

"Okay fine. I will cast a spell to free Bog but then, we are running the opposite way."

"You can do that? You have that kind of power?" she questioned.

"Of course!" Wallow beamed with pride and thumped his chest with his fist. "I will summon a mighty creature of the forest to battle and drive off the Googins."

BOG

"But how will Bog escape the net?"

"Worry not! My magic will do it all."

Elizabeth anticipated a giant bear or mountain lion as Wallow closed his eyes and began chanting in his bird language. Elizabeth was shocked when Wallow's staff began to glow. The ground began to shake, and the tremors caught the attention of the Googins and their mounts who all froze, hearing the roar of a stampede. What had Wallow summoned? Suddenly she feared for her own safety. Whatever was coming, there was a lot of them. An entire herd it sounded like. The sound of hundreds of thumping feet got closer and the ground shook harder.

"Wallow! What's going on?" cried Elizabeth but she saw Wallow was even more frightened than she was. Elizabeth hugged Wallow and crouched against the tree trunk, hoping it would keep them safe from the stampeding horde. Elizabeth cracked an eye open.

Soft, white fluffy bunnies by the hundreds ran right past them in their hidden place, the herd heading towards the Googins, who jumped up and down excitedly. They started trying to spear the rabbits and chased them deep off into the swamps, leaving Bog behind.

"That was your mighty beast you had in mind?" Elizabeth laughed.

"Um…"

"Well I guess it doesn't matter. It worked. Come on let's free it."

"No way!"

"Fine. You stay here since you're scared."

Elizabeth left the comfort of their concealment with determined strides. Wallow sulked out behind a second later. When she got closer, Bog trashed out at her violently, a huge paw nearly swiping her head off.

"Is that how you treat someone who is trying to save you?"

"Why are you talking to it? It's not going to understand," Wallow chided.

Elizabeth simply put her hand up for silence and she tried to get close again.

"I'm going to let you out, but only if you don't eat us. Do you understand?"

"Elizabeth it's—" Wallow started.

"Yes! Bog understand!" he muttered gutturally while nodding frantically.

Hidden eyes silently emerged from the murky depths of the Swamps of Sorrow. They took in and recorded all that

was happening to report back. Fearing the wrath of his
master if he lingered too long, the eyes sunk swiftly beneath
the mucky water of the quagmire.

Elizabeth was surprised at Bog's intelligence. It
seemed that he comprehended everything her and Wallow
were saying, even though his ability to communicate was not
strong. Even after explaining their mission, Bog insisted on
coming along. He was like a big goofy overgrown child. He
had the cutest smile and laugh despite his terrifying face with
huge eyes and sharp giant rows of fangs for teeth. Bog's
brown beard matched the rest of his fur. If you could call it
that. Elizabeth thought his skin was more like the ground
itself. Two miniature trees sprouted from the top of his head
like horns and his entire back looked like miniature hills,
complete with bushes.

Elizabeth had used Babarosa's moonstone ring to
point the way to the Toad Queen. She had tried to not act
impressed but just like when she used it to get home, it lit up
a map of the world in incredible detail in the air next to them,
foreign to her but Bog and Wallow excitedly named every
place it revealed. When Bog had tapped on the Swamps of

Sorrow and the map zoomed in, he jumped up and down while clapping excitedly. The earth shook with each bounce and Elizabeth nearly lost her balance when she had to cover her ears because each time Bog's hands collided, it sounded like a thunderclap.

Elizabeth had laughed heartily, and her cheeks still hurt from her wide smile. Bog had pointed to where he said the Toad Queen was and just like before the map dissipated into a beam of light that shot out like a bolt of lightning. It zig-zagged off the trees and deep into the swamp but left behind a faint residue for them to follow. Elizabeth risked only using it for a second but at least they knew which general direction to head in. They would have to risk using it again when they got closer. Bog took the lead and seemed to know where he was guiding them, and Elizabeth hoped he really did know how to find the Toad Queen. Wallow on the other hand would not shut up about Elizabeth's magic powers. He really believed because of what happened back during the vision ceremony in the village and with the magic of Babarosa that she really was descended from the men and women with pointy hats and long branch staffs. She wanted to tell him the truth but dare not reveal where the ring came from. Babarosa had told her to tell no one, and if she did tell, then Babarosa would be gone forever. Elizabeth couldn't afford that. Babarosa was her best hope for getting her necklace back.

But how she was going to sneak off to see Babarosa? Every step they took deeper into the swamp took her a step further from Babarosa. Bog and Wallow were arguing over the best way to get past the giant insects they called Flying Death that guarded the Toad Queen's domain. They were not natural creatures of Noir; they were magically made by the evil frog to attack anyone who was not a welcome visitor.

"What about bug spray?" Elizabeth suggested.

"Bug spray?" questioned Wallow. Bog looked just as lost.

"It kills insects."

"You have such magic?" asked Wallow excitedly with big eyes of surprise.

Elizabeth laughed. "No, it's not magic, just bug spray."

"Where can we get this, 'bug spray'?" asked Wallow while Bog nodded excitedly.

"I have some at home. I can go get it."

Elizabeth's stomach was in knots. She felt awful for lying to Bog and Wallow. Elizabeth would go home and get the bug spray; however, on her way back she would stop to visit Babarosa again. The knots in her stomach tightened even more as Elizabeth feared asking for more help since Babarosa had already given her a ring to give her comfort and always show the way, but where else could she turn to? There was no way they could penetrate the Swamps of Sorrow and defeat an entire army plus the Toad Queen with just three of them. Wallow could not return to the village so what other choice did she have? And Babarosa did tell her if she needed help, she just needed to ask.

Her luck had changed for once. Elizabeth now had a guardian angel to help her but what she was going to ask seemed too much, even for a magic woman like Babarosa. However, Elizabeth knew nothing of this world and how powerful the Toad Queen was or how strong Babarosa's magic was. Maybe it would be easier than she suspected, or maybe Babarosa would turn her away. Either way, she had to try.

Elizabeth dropped the last rock to mark her trail as she neared the portal home. She wanted to use the ring's power only when she needed it, plus she feared the Googins could see the bright beam of light it emitted when it showed the way.

But Elizabeth was also worried Babarosa would not help her since she was still with Wallow from the Cookapeepooh tribe. She supposed she would have to be honest and tell Babarosa why she was doing it. It was a selfish reason and made her feel guilty. But if the tribe was using her to get the runes, then was it necessarily wrong if she was using them? And Wallow wouldn't be much help, if they were to get the necklace it would be because of Elizabeth and Barbarossa's help, along with their new friend Bog. Heavy guilt settled upon her shoulders and in her heart. She felt the blood of Toma's warriors on her hands as she began climbing into the portal. Who could she go to for counsel? Her mother already thought she was crazy and had a concussion, plus the trauma of her father's death and the move to the new life. No, she couldn't talk to Susan about this.

Elizabeth was feeling desperate and exhausted. What to do?

When she crawled back through her bathroom mirror the rays of dawn were already shining through. *Merde*, she thought. What was she going to do? Wally, Bog and the fate of Noir were waiting for her return and now it was time for school. The crunch under her feet hurt more out of surprise than pain. Branches and leaves had foliated through the mirror, but the bright sun had made them crispy. She egg-shell-walked across the littered ground, trying not to create any more of a mess than it already was.

The worlds were merging, and the Queen of Mist would come again. Elizabeth feared the next time the Queen did, she would be able to cross through. The eye at the top of the mirror seemed to be open just a little more. Elizabeth didn't know what would happen when the eye opened completely, but she knew she had best get back to Noir before it did.

For the second time in as many days, Elizabeth found herself pondering actions she normally would never consider. First cheating on the test, she neglected to study for since she was too busy playing in Noir, and now she was seriously contemplating on feigning being sick, so she could stay home. How could her mother, or anyone for that matter, understand what was at stake for not just Elizabeth but both of their worlds?

But who could she tell? Who would believe her? No one. And she would not expect anyone to believe her. If someone approached her with the same story she was experiencing, Elizabeth would think that person crazy. Before she could even crawl under her covers, her mother came into her room.

"I got a call yesterday about you running out in the middle of class. Why didn't you tell me that part? They said they understood you being new and that blow to your head from when you fell has us all worried. The school agreed, and you are excused today and I'm taking you to get checked out."

"Mom really, that's not necessary. Besides, we don't have insurance and can't afford a hospital bill."

"No, your health is important. And don't worry there's a free county clinic that your school was kind enough to recommend."

They arrived at the run-down health clinic. The once white walls had morphed into beige with permanent dirt marks that when combined with the smell of bleach, induced vomiting. The staff working there looked like they would rather be anywhere else but here.

Elizabeth had figured the visit would be quick and she could get home and back to Noir where Wallow and Bog waited. But the wait went on for hours and it was nearly lunch time by the time Elizabeth was called in. They walked down the hall until they were ushered through a door. Her mother and Elizabeth waited in silence in the tiny room. Finally, the door opened and the man that stepped through could barely fit. He stood well over six feet and was broader than the door. He fixed his scary eyes on Elizabeth as he examined her. A thick, coarse beard covered his entire face, making up for his balding head.

This place had been giving her the creeps all day. The smell was making her nauseous. And now she was stuck with this giant, mean, and probably smelly doctor. She dreaded him getting close and to take her temperature and heartbeat.

"Hello," spoke a warm pleasant voice, "I am Dr. Lake. It's nice to meet you…" he looked down at his chart, "Miss Montgomery and Mrs. Montgomery". He bowed slightly to her mother and his huge smile made him look jollier than Santa Claus himself. "What brings you in today?"

"Oh Dr. Lake, it's my daughter, I fear she had a terrible fall and suffered some brain trauma. She was talking about some magic world she enters through her bathroom mirror. I'm afraid the injury has caused some serious side effects."

"I see," said Dr. Lake as he began checking Elizabeth's temperature. "Well sometimes not everything is as it seems Mrs. Montgomery."

"Doctor are you suggesting what my daughter is telling me is true? That there is a magical world on the other side of a mirror?"

Dr. Lake let out a booming laugh that painfully reminded Elizabeth of Bog's laugh. She had to figure a way to get out of this quickly and back to Noir.

"Not at all. However, I am stating that Elizabeth's actions are most likely not related to the head trauma," concluded Dr. Lake.

Elizabeth could have sworn Dr. Lake was almost defending her.

"So, you're suggesting my daughter is mentally ill?" concerned Susan. Elizabeth could see mother's stress level rising and felt terrible. All Elizabeth seemed to do was stress her mother out, the opposite of what she always intended.

"No, not at all. A healthy imagination is, in fact, the opposite of mental illness. It shows the mind is still sharp, and young like a child's. Regardless, let me run some tests on Elizabeth and we will see," assured Dr. Lake with a smile.

Chapter 16:

Enemies Of My Enemy

The ride home was quiet and abysmal on the dirty public trolley. Her mother seemed more upset after the visit than she had been before. Elizabeth had thankfully not suffered a concussion or any brain trauma. She just needed a few days to rest. But Elizabeth could tell her mother was still worried. Worried if her daughter was crazy or not. If only her mother could see when the mirror was acting as a portal... then maybe she would understand. But Elizabeth could not risk it. What would happen if her mother really did see the truth? Then Elizabeth would have to confess she lost her father's necklace and knew her mother would never allow her to return to Noir, much less risk her life and fight in a battle. Elizabeth decided to milk her time from her head injury to avoid going to school, retrieve her necklace and restore natural order to Noir.

As her mother tucked her into bed and kissed her goodbye before she went off to slave away at the sweatshop,

Elizabeth tried to slow her heartbeat down. If her mother had noticed her nervousness, she didn't mention it. As soon as the front door bolt locked into place, she kicked off the blankets and dashed downstairs, heading for the maze of boxes in the living room. After a quick scan of some open boxes, she spotted the familiar green cap and pulled out an aerosol bug spray can. She gave it a good shake. It sounded nearly fully.

As Elizabeth went to close the box, a picture frame caught her eye. An old photo of her father when he was serving in the military made a lightbulb go off in Elizabeth's head and she began looking around until she found it buried under some other boxes. When she spotted what she was looking for, the ghost-touch of her necklace warmed her chest. Emotions ran high as her eyes read the words written on the dark green container. "Robert Montgomery, Second Lieutenant". Before tears would come, Elizabeth's hands released the two buckles and opened the lid with a metallic squeak.

Inside her father's old military footlocker Elizabeth discovered his fatigues and his old matching camouflage hat along with a canteen. Since they were going to go crawling through a swamp, she figured she had best prepare. Unfortunately, her father's old clothes were much too large, so she compromised by taking the belt of a bathrobe after she stumbled into her room and tripped over the long pants. Tying the belt snug and rolling up the pant legs was the best she could do to make the baggy clothes fit.

Elizabeth hoped the bug spray would not change as her knife had. She needed it to work. The stories of these winged creatures of death Wallow kept telling her about were giving her nightmares.

To her surprise, the mist poured out of her bathroom when she pulled the door open. The tree branches were nearly touching Elizabeth's door. The seal must be weakening by the hour, the Queen of Mist coming ever closer to entering her world. The eye was nearly halfway open now, the bottom of the pupil was starting to show. Holding her pantlegs up with one hand and the other against the wall, Elizabeth fumbled up the sink and fell through the portal headfirst. She swam through the magic quicksilver's embrace, not fearing that she would land roughly on the other side. The familiarity of the mirror's magic comforted her thoughts, and she felt no negativity about what lay ahead. The last stroke broke through the other side, the euphoria fading as her fingertips felt the air of Noir. Despite bulleting headfirst out of the portal, Elizabeth came through balanced and upright, landing gently on her feet. When she looked down, the clothes seemed to fit a lot better and were no longer pants and a shirt, just one long robe.

As Elizabeth approached the river, she could see in the pale, moonlit reflection, a regal looking Sorcerer. Elizabeth seemed one with the forest with her dark green robe and matching belt. Her ugly metal canteen was now a large glass potion-decanter full of red, bubbling fluid with a cork stopper for a lid, and it hung perfectly from her belt. The can of bug spray was now a thin sleek all black magic wand with a white tip, just like one from a magic show. Her hat had become pointed at the top like a Wizard's with a star in the middle that matched her outfit perfectly.

Thankfully, the trail of rocks she left was undisturbed, but Elizabeth knew she must make one stop before rejoining her companions.

Elizabeth closed her eyes and held the moonstone ring in her right hand over her heart. She thought of Babarosa and her need to get her necklace back, so she could go back to her normal life and help Susan. Like before, a map showing her landmarks and areas she did not know, illuminated the air above her. When she zoomed in on Vadu Forest, there was a wildflower on the map. Before she could think, her finger tapped it and the bolt of starlight showed the way. Elizabeth could feel Babarosa's presence and followed the light.

Her steps felt lighter and she did not run out of breath as she ran towards the destination. Elizabeth felt like she was becoming stronger as she tore through the woods, her feet lightly floating over rocks, roots and other hazards that before would have put her face into the ground. The starlight path ended abruptly, and it felt as if Babarosa's home was much closer than she remembered on her journey back to Lumiere.

Lumiere, now even I'm calling home that… she thought with a laugh to herself. What was wrong with her, why did she keep coming back to Noir? Some small part in the recesses of her mind and heart enjoyed this place.

Her knuckles tapped lightly on the door of the tiny tree. The door opened and closed slowly without a sound as she stepped into Babarosa's home.

"Elizabeth my dear," came the warm voice. A few steps into the giant tree and Babarosa's face came into light. She was as she was before, at her table with her crystal ball. The sound of something scratching constantly caught Elizabeth's ear. She looked around and saw brooms sweeping the ground on their own!

"Just some light cleaning young one. Come. Sit. Babarosa is glad to see you."

Elizabeth took a seat across from the magic woman and tried to remember the words she had wanted to say.

"Tell Babarosa why you have come back. I pray it is just to visit me and to enjoy each other's company but the

224

look on your face says otherwise." Before Elizabeth could respond Babarosa let out a loud laugh as she threw her head back. "I remember what it was like to be young. Emotions were harder to control, things burned inside that needed to be done. Babarosa understands. Babarosa will help you. Tell me child, what ails you? It must be a great pain in your heart for you to return to this world when it nearly killed you," Babarosa inquired as she gently stroked Elizabeth's hand with her own.

"I must retrieve my father's necklace that the Toad Queen stole from me."

"The Toad Queen?"

"Yes."

"You encountered her and lived?"

Elizabeth recounted her tale to Babarosa and when she was halfway through Babarosa cut her off. "That is enough child. I know of your plight. Babarosa just wanted to be sure you would tell her the truth. I am glad I can trust you Elizabeth. Trust is so hard to find. Those you think closest to you will betray you. But it is wrong to think and live such a way. We must open our hearts to feel love, but when we do, we expose ourselves to pain. Such is life, child."

"So, you will help me?"

Babarosa's eyes narrowed and felt menacing. Elizabeth tried to back away but Babarosa held her hand tight.

"Tell Babarosa why else you go to the Toad Queen's lair."

Elizabeth swallowed and looked down.

"Babarosa will not help if you cannot trust her, she has given you help and asked for nothing in return. All she wants is your trust."

Elizabeth took a deep breath of trepidation before she began, "To help the Cookapeepooh tribe defeat her and retrieve a magic rune that is to help seal the portal. All this will keep the Queen of Mist from taking over this world and my own."

"I see," was all Babarosa spoke in a neutral tone. Silence jumped rope under Elizabeth's heartbeats. Babarosa just stared at her with those huge forbidding eyes. Elizabeth had never felt so uncomfortable and found it hard to breathe.

"I'm sorry! I know you told me not to trust them, but I don't have any other way to battle the Toad Queen and her Googins and whatever else she has in that swamp. If there were any other way to get my necklace back I swear I would!" Elizabeth pleaded in near tears.

"Hush child. Babarosa understands. Babarosa is not mad at you. Babarosa cares, she understands your dilemma. Babarosa will show you the way."

Elizabeth looked, unsure if she heard right, "You will?"

"Of course, child. Did Babarosa not say if you tell her the truth she will always help? You have a kind heart Elizabeth. It warms mine. Babarosa wants to help you." Babarosa took both of Elizabeth's hands in hers as she leaned in.

"The Calling has begun, and The Queen of Mist is on the rise."

"The Calling?" Elizabeth questioned.

"The Calling is the start of the portal between the two worlds being ripped asunder. But the Cookapeepooh tribe care not for Noir. They just want to reclaim their ancestral home. Once, long ago, the Cookapeepooh tribe held domain over many lands. They mask their true intentions by telling you it is a noble cause. But it is because you have power Elizabeth. You are descended from the bloodline of Wizards and Sorcerers who have come to Noir's aid since the dawn of its time. But you are young, and still have much to learn. Owah would send you to an early grave. But that does not surprise me."

Elizabeth couldn't believe it. She hoped she really was some Sorcerer, so she could make a difference. She was tired of being helpless and depending on others. If only she could have magic in her own world…

"Why do you think that of Owah?"

"Babarosa is from another tribe, Owah and I had the same master teaching us magic. We studied under the great Magus. Together Owah and I would go from land to land in Noir, helping where need be, to defend Noir from the Queen of Mist and her evil underlings who threatened this beautiful world. He was my star and moon, and I, his moon and star as teenagers. We were supposed to run off together once we brought the peace back to Noir and get married. But Owah changed his mind, his heart, and returned to his warring tribe of the Cookapeepooh to be the Shaman… said it was his destiny because his ancestors visited him in his dreams and told him he was to fulfill the prophecy. He believed he had the higher calling of being the Shaman for the Cookapeepooh tribe and broke my heart. We were all about teaching peace and helping those in need in Noir. Owah left for his calling with his tribe where Babarosa would not be allowed to live as she was not a Cookapeepooh member." Elizabeth's heart felt like someone shattered it with a hammer. She gave Babarosa a squeeze of comfort with her hands. To her surprise,

Babarosa held back the tears and continued with a deep breath.

"They are a closed-minded people and allow no outsiders, this meant he would be going alone, leaving me...I asked, what about me? The vows we made? He did not care. He is a man of deceit with no honor. Do not trust him. Look at that wound on your shoulder. You saw how aggressive those little warriors are. And why did they rush you out of there, with no explanations? Yet, Babarosa here tells you all. Babarosa wants you to be well and happy Elizabeth. You are a sweet girl with a kind soul, do not let it be tainted by those who would seek to use you for their own gains. Just as Owah used Babarosa. We were heroes of the land and once he gained the power and fame he needed, he left me to go fight for his warring tribe to take back their lands. This was not the way we had lived for all those years. I was a fool to trust him."

Babarosa shook her head as she reached for something under the table. "Take this with you and plant it when you arrive at the Toad Queen's lair. It will help you retrieve the prize you seek."

Elizabeth looked down on the table and saw it was a seed.

"But tell no one! Only Babarosa understands how important your necklace is Elizabeth. You poor dear, it's the last link you have to your father. Really, it's a shame what happened. Babarosa understands pain. Babarosa cannot bring your father back but at least she can help you get your necklace back. Owah and his tribe just want to use you for your powers but Babarosa wants to help heal your heart."

"Bbbut how did you know—?"

Babarosa smiled widely and pointed to her crystal ball. "Babarosa knows all child. Babarosa knows all. Go forth now with Wallow. Plant the seed, retrieve your necklace and be gone from here. That is Babarosa's best advice for you young one."

Elizabeth gripped the seed tightly as she walked back in deep thought. A million thoughts ran through her head. Did Wallow know of the true intentions of his tribe? Or was he just a pawn like her? Elizabeth followed the markings she left behind to find her way through to the swamp where Bog and Wallow awaited. Elizabeth was initially worried that she was gone too long but when she exited Babarosa's house this time, she found herself at the entrance of the swamp, right where one of her rock trail markers was.

When she arrived at their camp, Wallow screamed out in fear. "Elizabeth!? Is that you? You look like one of the legendary bearded men who battled the Queen of Noir long, long ago!"

"Really? I look like a bearded old man?" Elizabeth said with a hard stare and her hands on her hips.

"Uh, nooo! I mean, uh just your…"

Elizabeth erupted in laughter. "I'm kidding. I know what you meant. But I don't think I'm a Wizard. I think, I'm a Sorcerer? Well not really. Not yet, at least…"

"What's the difference?" asked Wallow.

"I'm not sure; I was hoping you could tell me since you're a magic caster," she replied.

"Um of course I know! It's just eluding my mind at this moment…I'll think of it soon!" Bog gave Elizabeth a goofy grin, as if he knew Wallow was full of it. Elizabeth bit her lip and swallowed her laugh. Embarrassed, Wallow changed the subject, "So were you able to get your bug spray?"

Her response was the twirl of her new magic wand. With a little click of the circular button near the bottom, a cloud of lime-green insect poison seeped out. Wallow and Bog were in awe.

"Elizabeth magic!" shouted Bog as he clapped his hands while hopping up and down childishly, causing a small earthquake.

"Haha," she chuckled, "No Bog, it's not magic," assured Elizabeth. "Here, try it." When she tried to hand him the wand he refused. "No. Magic for magic lady only," the giant Swamp Yeti said in a very serious tone.

"I'll try it! I am a magic man after all," prided Wallow and he took the wand from her hand. "Watch me take out these little gnats as a demonstration," he boasted as he walked towards a murky pond that was so thick with growth on the surface it looked like solid land. Wallow clicked on the button and the spray shot him right in his eyes and mouth causing him to gag.

Reaching for his eyes and spitting out the spray, Elizabeth watched the wand tumble out from his hands. She screamed and dove towards it. The edge of her fingertips scraped the wand and she closed her hand. For a second, she had it, but the wand slipped right through her fingers. Elizabeth held her breath, and watched it sink into the murky depths of the quagmire, disappearing forever in the liquid quicksand along with their hopes.

"Uhhh, uhhh. I'm really sorry Elizabeth…" Wallow spoke quietly.

For the first time in her life Elizabeth was angry. Furious with boiling rage that threatened to burst the lid off the tea kettle. A cauldron of fire so hot it could melt stone. She was livid at Wallow. How could he lose their one chance to succeed?

"Now how are we going to get through?" she grinded through her teeth.

"We just need another wand," he replied meekly.

"I don't have another Wallow."

"Then you must get another."

"I can't," her voice raising.

"Where did you get this one from?"

"A store."

"So, can you just go back to this… store?"

"No, because I don't have any money to buy another one."

"Money?"

That was the last straw. Elizabeth snapped. She felt rage heat her blood and Elizabeth wanted to unleash her anger on Wallow.

"Listen Wallow! Where I'm from I may not have little green monsters on giant wombats chasing me down to kill me, but it's not all sunshine and green hills like you, Owah and the Queen of Mist think it is. It's not what it's cracked up to be. My life sucks! My father's dead. We hardly have any food. My mother is killing herself, working too much every day. And I lost the one thing I care about, my necklace! Here! In this disgusting swamp. And now you just lost my one chance to get it back!" accused Elizabeth as she rubbed where her necklace should be. Bog watched with sad eyes and he copied her, stroking an invisible necklace.

"But what about the quest, and the runes and—"

"I don't care about the quests, your stupid runes or your stupid world. Ever since I've come here it's caused me nothing but pain and stress. It's ruining my life in my world. Where things actually matter. I'm going to go back, steal a new 'wand', get my necklace and never come back here again."

Wallow's only response was tears coming down his face.

"And stop being such a big baby all the time. You'll just have to figure out how to get the other two runes yourself. I help you get this one and when I get my necklace, we part ways."

"I'm sorry…" Wallow spoke softly, his gaze never leaving the ground.

"Who cares!? You lost the wand, sorry isn't going to bring it back!"

"No, I'm sorry about your father. My father is dead too."

Elizabeth's rage cooled instantly. She looked down at her hands. They were shaking. What was she doing? She had never yelled at anyone like that.

Wallow seemed to be too sad to say anymore, his head hanging down as he just stared off into the creepy swamp.

"Wallow…" Elizabeth felt terrible for getting so angry. Everything had just caught up to her at once. She saw Bog walk up to the murky pond, look down and point.

"Bog get?" he questioned. He pointed again into the murky water. "Bog get!" he said with a smile, and dove right in. His giant body made a vile, squelching noise as he penetrated through the mucky slime, into the water.

"Wait!" yelled Wallow, "No, what is he doing!? Those quagmires are like quicksand. He's as good as dead…" Minutes passed, and all that they saw was the mucky water reforming its permanent wall of algae on the surface.

As soon as they lost all hope, Bog burst through with his head covered in green vegetation, moss and algae. He looked like the swamp monster Elizabeth had envisioned when the Toad Queen had sent her off to be eaten by him. He stood there with his big, goofy grin, holding up the wand.

"Bog! You did it!" exclaimed Elizabeth and she ran up and gave him a huge hug before thinking what she was doing. The grossness of the swamp water was not enough to deter her from the warmth of her big, new friend who just saved the day for them. She felt Bog hug her back warmly. For the first time since they began their quest, Elizabeth felt

TOMA

like they had a slim chance to achieve their goal together, as a team.

But her joy was short-lived as a rustle from the shadows ended their celebration. Elizabeth held up her wand, Wallow pointed his staff and she heard Bog growl like a feral dog. She was sure glad Bog was on their side.

From behind the stumps of fallen trees, out came a bleeding and stumbling Toma.

"Sir!" yelled Wallow and he flapped his wings while running, trying to get there before Toma hit the ground. He dove to catch him but Toma's weight was too much, and he landed with a hard thud on top of a squawking Wallow.

Instinctively Elizabeth's free hand went to the potion on her belt. Before she could even rationalize, she felt her fingers pulling the cork lid out and poured the red drink into Toma's mouth. After a few forced gulps and a violent cough, he stirred and opened his eyes. "Elizabeth?" Toma questioned unsurely as he stood up slowly. "Owah was right. You are descended from the men and women with robes, pointed hats and wooden staffs. Except you are a child. Most were all old men, with wizened beards. But you have proven your magic today. Thank you for saving the life of Toma. I will never forget this debt." He bowed deeply. Toma seemed to notice Bog for the first time. "Swamp Yeti! What are you doing with him?" Toma's axe was out instantly. Bog took an aggressive stance. Elizabeth had to throw herself between the two.

"Stop!" commanded Elizabeth. The authority in her own voice surprised her. "You will both cease fighting at once. You are comrades now. Bog is our ally. We saved his life. He is an honorable creature and he is helping us retrieve the rune."

"He has eaten many of our ancestors. He must pay for this."

"Bog no eat birdies! Bog no eat people, only berry and fish!"

"This is where the cycle of hatred and vengeance ends. Let him help you, instead of taking more life, let him help you preserve life. Besides we need him. Us three alone cannot take on the entire Kingdom of The Swamps of Sorrow." Elizabeth surprised herself with her words. Where had they come from? Was it the robe? Her pointy hat?

Toma crossed his arms in defiance. "Fine but as soon as this is done, we are no longer comrades." He stormed off before anymore could be said. Elizabeth looked at Wallow for guidance, but he simply stood there, dumbfounded and scared.

Chapter 17:

Unlikely Allies

"We must decide on an alternate course of action," declared Chieftain Sage.

"There is no proof that the mission has failed," retorted Owah.

"The scouting party found the entire force wiped out, save Toma. Wallow and Elizabeth are missing as well. Even if all three are alive that will not be enough to take on the entire army of the Toad Queen," argued Sage.

Owah felt the years of his age weighing heavily upon him in this moment. It seemed under his guidance his ancient tribe would fall, their culture destroyed, and their people annihilated. For the first time in many centuries, Owah had no idea what he was to do. Everything seemed impossible. He looked around at the other elders and war council gathered tightly in the small hut where only a single lantern scorched. Blank faces stared back in the dark room, offering no help. Heavy eyes weighed upon Owah and he felt frustrated for the first time in many, many moons.

What good had his life and accomplishments been if he could not face the biggest one of his life? So much rode on his next decision, the worth of his life, the fate of his entire tribe and culture. Though, what ate away at him the most was sending Wallow to his grave. Indeed, dark times had fallen upon them. If he could just know what came of the three who remained missing and were possibly alive, he could better decide their next course of action.

"We must think of a trump card. Something out of the ordinary that we have yet to consider," was the best Owah could offer to the room.

The silence was broken by a strong female voice from the back of the room, "What about Captain Blackbird?" Feathers ruffled as Princess Whitecloud invited herself to the table.

"No. Absolutely not," Sage declared immediately, his arms crossing with conviction.

"We need to consider all options," argued the princess.

"No. The price for his services is too great," Sage replied flatly.

"How can you say that? Our entire tribe is at stake. What cost could not be worth it?" retorted Whitecloud with aggressive steps towards Sage.

Owah felt the tension in the hut rise like the temperature of a growing fire. He closed his eyes and sent a silent prayer to his ancestors for any kind of help. When it seemed Chieftain Sage and his granddaughter were one more word away from throwing punches, the door to the hut creaked loudly as it slowly opened and the shaft of light from the lantern the visitor held caused most the birds to raise a wing to shield their eyes. Owah had not realized how long everyone had been in here.

Through the slit in the door, poked in a familiar face. Years of traveling the skies and seas, the crinkled, salted face was covered by a massive beard and a moustache so long, it was braided into pigtails on both sides. His eyebrows so bushy they were only second to Owah's. Blackbird removed his spectacle over his left eye, along with his old, beat up pirate hat, and gave a slight clearing of his throat.

"Pardon," spoke Blackbird with a slight bow and tip of the hat. "Obviously I be comin' at a bad time. I'll be back when it not be so serious around here."

"Actually," smiled Whitecloud, "This is a great time. Come on in." Blackbird looked back through the door to one of his men on the other side and gave a nod to who Owah presumed to be Blackbird's right-hand man, his First-Mate Pasqual, and closed the door.

Blackbird was never one for traditional customs, and Owah could feel the other elders' enmity towards his old friend.

"Well then. What be the cause for this joyous celebration?" mocked the Pirate Captain.

"Our entire tribe's well-being is on the line. And we fear the worst," began Sage.

Blackbird feigned a yawn, "What else is new chief? Got any firewater?" he asked while helping himself to what Owah saw was Chieftain Sage's most prized and expensive bottle.

Owah cut in before Sage erupted. "Blackbird."

"Captain," Blackbird interrupted with a point of his finger, never stopping the pour of his drink.

"Captain Blackbird," Owah corrected, "We have a task force who have met a most unfortunate circumstance. Three members may still be alive and heading towards their goal, the throne of the Toad Queen."

A loud spray of liquid was Blackbird's response as he spewed in shock, all over Sage, who Owah saw reaching for his warhammer. "What the pluck?! Put that pipe away, every time ye smoke something bad happens! What moron sent them there? And why ye be goin' to her lair? Ye trying to start trouble?"

"As I tried to tell you!" yelled Sage, "We are at war with the Queen of Mist. The portal has been opened."

"What!? Why did ye open the portal!? Ye just were walkin' through the woods one day and see it and say, 'Oh shiver me timbers mate, let's open this forbidden portal that will doom our world forever' Yeesh!" Blackbird exasperated.

"Fool! We did not open it! We had a gathering and the spirits told us where the first rune is to seal the portal. It's somewhere in the Toad Queen's domain," Sage countered.

"And so ye sent the task force before even knowing where the item is they are to retrieve? Ye dumb pluck. I'm not surprised ye would do that, but Owah?" Blackbird questioned as he turned to the owl.

"We knew the proximity and there was no time to delay…even now the Queen of Mist could be approaching the portal to Lumiere…" Owah defended weakly.

"What'd the spirits tell ye?" asked the old pirate.

"The first of which you seek

Lays deep where it reeks

Between two rocks

Staying Dry in a wet spot," Owah repeated.

"The first rune be the prized ruby that rests upon the middle of her crown, a gift from the Queen of Mist,"

Blackbird stated matter-of-factly, "Ye tree huggers couldn't figure that out because ye stay blind here, in ye own little world."

"What do you know?" raged Sage, "You left too long ago! You have forgotten your ways. You have no right to speak here in this council! You left to the world of corruption and greed, leaving your roots for gold."

"I couldn't live off berries and seeds, rum and chicks were better to my liking. Take it easy old man, or ye might be havin' a heart attack."

"Why you insolent little sh—"

"Grandfather," Princess Whitecloud interrupted, "Stop this childishness. We need his help."

"No, we don't!" raged Chieftain Sage with the pound of a fist on the table.

"Then who?" fired back the princess.

"Anyone but him!" he declared loudly, throwing his wings up in frustration.

"Hrmmph," sighed Blackbird, "That be fine, I be wantin' no part of this madness. I should have just stayed on me path to Vail and listened to me crew. Every time I visit it's always something ye pull me into! But not this time! I was just stopping in to trade some goods. I'll be on me way, thanks for the drink," Blackbird concluded with the tip of his glass and a smile too wide for Chieftain Sage.

"Get out! You worthless heathen. You will always be a disgrace to the Cookapeepooh tribe!"

"Uncle, wait!" pleaded Whitecloud, "Please! I ask you not as a leader of this tribe, but as a family member. Please put aside your pride and hear out Shaman Owah." Blackbird stood mute, halfway out the door. Whitecloud moved closer and as she spoke sternly to her uncle, "All you know, your trade, your way of life will be no more. Once the Queen of Mist enters the other world she will have the power to enslave and end us all."

Blackbird sighed heavily, "Why ye need me? I be a simple pirate. I be good. Well sure, I plunder once in a while. And... cheat every so often. But the mist don't bother me. Sure, sometimes it be makin' it hard to sail, but I be wantin' no part of the Queen o' Mist."

"Uncle we cannot do this without you. The tribe needs you. Will you answer the call?" demanded the Princess.

Blackbird kept shaking his head as he looked down at the ground, muttering to himself while he finished his drink. Owah had never seen his friend so indecisive.

"Think of the past wars of this world. Those times are upon us now," Whitecloud reminded him. Blackbird looked around the room and into the eyes of all those present. He just stood there mutely, his face an unreadable mask.

"Oh, alright fine, fine. But only for me special little girl. Not for that old flying rodent ye call ye granddad," Blackbird spoke as he strode back over to refill his cup. Owah felt his bones ache as he restrained Sage from bashing Blackbird's skull in with his warhammer.

"So, tell me, what's the plan?" asked Blackbird as he turned from pouring his drink, seemingly genuinely oblivious to Sage's aggressive behavior.

Chapter 18:

Just In Time

The dried-out husk of fur flopped over bones, fed fear into the party. Dozens of rabbit corpses littered the fetid swamp ground. They were shriveled up like raisins. In Bog's huge hands the rabbit looked even smaller as he held it up for inspection.

"Bzzzzzzzzzz," was the noise that came out of Bog's mouth.

"Bzzzzzzzzzz," he did again while staring at Elizabeth.

"Flying Death," Toma said solemnly as he leaned against his spear.

"Flying Death?" Elizabeth echoed.

"Giant insects who are vile blood sucking creatures," chimed in Wallow, "They are the creations of the Toad Queen, her nasty little guardians of the Swamps of—

FLYING DEATH

"Shhh!" interrupted Toma with great urgency. A low hum that sounded like a waterfall rumbled in the distance. Closer and closer the sound came until a horde of what looked like giant mosquitos as big as Wallow were zooming right in on them! The entire swamp was filled with hundreds and they occupied every square inch of free space, fighting each other for the first taste of Elizabeth and her friends.

"Run," ordered Toma.

The symphony of terror was closing in on them. They were fleeing blindly but with the fear pumping in her heart Elizabeth could not think of a better plan. They had ventured deep into the swamp, tracing the path of starlight that the moonstone ring had shown them earlier. Just when she thought they were getting closer to their destination they were turning back.

Wallow tripped over something and went down hard. Toma's spear whistled past Elizabeth's ear, heading perfectly towards its target. However, at the last second, the Flying Death zipped to the right, avoiding the spear. Another quick flap of the wings and it had Wallow pinned to the ground with its massive forceps. Out of its mouth a disgusting bulbous stinger that looked sharper than any knife Elizabeth had ever seen, dripped with nasty yellow looking pus.

Time and space came to a near stop. Elizabeth heard the others shout Wallow's name in slow motion and felt her hand go to her wand. The air filled with a cloud of insect death. The insect tried to escape but the power of the magic spray made it thrash violently in the air before it crashed on the swampy ground for a few last twitches before it shriveled and went still.

Their victory was short lived as dozens of the disgusting buzzing insects appeared through the dead trees of the swamp. The rest of the flying horde had arrived, and Elizabeth held the button down on her wand in desperation and closed her eyes, waving it left to right like it was a sparkler on the fourth of July. She sneaked a peek, expecting a nasty stinger to pierce her chest but she saw a huge cloud of spray in the air, holding their hunters at bay while Bog easily snatched Wallow and Toma with one arm. As he rumbled past her Elizabeth felt her feet levitate off the ground and the race was on as Bog put them on his back while sprinting wildly through the swamp. Elizabeth and Toma held on to the trees growing out of Bog's back for dear life while Wallow was tucked under Bog's arm like a football.

The horde quickly caught up and it sounded like Elizabeth had stuck her head inside a beehive. The buzzing from the powerful flapping of giant insect wings signified their inevitable death. But Elizabeth couldn't die. Not now. She needed to get home to take care of her mother. The sudden thoughts of her mom filled her with energy and

Elizabeth felt her fingers wrap around her wand. The ghost print of her necklace burned fiercely. Thoughts of harm befalling her mother surged the magic through her veins and into the wand. Her stomach was like the lid of a boiling pot of water, itching to escape and explode. Elizabeth felt the ghost print of her necklace warm her chest even more as she exhaled the magic she felt boiling in her belly. She only thought of her mother, suffering, overworked, desperate for any kind of help. Directing her thoughts towards the Flying Death horde, the spray shot out like the huge flames of a fire, licking the nearest enemies, instantly dropping a dozen or so flying monsters. Elizabeth's wide eyes were amazed but her heart feared the power.

The branches of dead hanging trees zoomed past so quickly. Elizabeth felt like she was on a motorcycle. She lost count of how many times she cringed and closed her eyes in anticipation of them crashing into something but despite his massive size, Bog ran with the grace of a gazelle. Elizabeth buried her face into Bog's back as the horde caught up to them yet again, not deterred by the deaths of their comrades.

When she finally pulled her face out of the safety of Bog's huge back Elizabeth saw Toma's face clad in iron determination. His eyes bled for the victory to protect his comrades, uphold his duty as their champion and save his tribe. Elizabeth felt cowardice for being afraid. She wished she could be as courageous as Toma.

"Almost!" Bog yelled out encouragingly. But so was the horde.

Toma began swiping with his axe at the deadly insects hot in pursuit, inches from catching them. The look in his eyes fueled her warrior instincts to life. How could she expect to fulfill her quest if she just stood by?

Elizabeth inhaled deeply and closed her eyes. This time, she thought about more than just her mother. She filled her heart with the love for her comrades, her new friends. Memories of the coffin going in the ground and her mother suffering flashed before her eyes. The ache for her father's touch swelled the magic in her belly even more fiercely than before. She could hear Toma's fierceness with every swing. Elizabeth felt tears of regret as she in this moment remembered all of his men had died fighting to protect her.

Gone. Dead. And Toma never said anything or ever made her feel like their blood was on her hands. But she felt it was.

No more.

No more suffering.

No more death.

Elizabeth felt the ghost imprint of the letter "N" on her chest and again felt a strange warrior spirit flow through her blood as she roared the fire within her to life. Out came her wand and she focused her thoughts on saving her friends. Power surged through her like never before and when she activated the wand, it felt like her insides were being torn apart. From her toes through her arms and legs, and to her neck, she felt the energy flowing unstably. It felt like minutes but was only seconds. At last the magic energy inside her sizzled out a massive lightning bolt of mist from the wand, violently striking the closest Flying Death, just inches away. The magic zapped and bounced from target to target and the lightning played hopscotch between their enemies. The lightning mist arced through every last Flying Death.

Toma looked at her with wide eyes. Wallow was stuck under Bog's arm and had not even seen what happened.

Victory vanished as the world turned upside down. The rush of defeating the horde was squished, just like the mud her face was in. Turning over to figure out how she was on the ground led to the painful discovery that her ankle felt broken.

Toma wasn't moving, he looked unconscious from the fall. Elizabeth followed Wallow's terror filled eyes.

Elizabeth screamed out at the sight of the hideous winged monstrosity. She watched in terror as a Flying Death almost twice the size as the others hungrily fed off Bog's blood. A massive stinger pumped blood as it swallowed and drank and drank, each gulp wracking Bog's veins with pain as he twitched venomously.

"Bog!" screamed Elizabeth as she tried to rise, but her ankle shot pain like her lightning spell all the way up to her hip, and she collapsed. Elizabeth gritted her teeth and began crawling, but she was so far...

Wallow watched with fear as usual. The pulsating body of the huge insect made him gag. It was as large as it was disgusting, each wing was bigger than he was. Worst of all, he knew he was next. Every drink it took was one step closer to his own fate. Wallow tried to imagine what it would feel like to have his blood drained from him, sucked completely dry like the poor little bunny rabbits he had summoned.

"Wallow!" he heard someone cry from far, far away. It was muffled but sounded like Princess Whitecloud. He looked over and saw Toma bleeding from his head, not moving.

"Wallow!" came the Princess's voice again. Bog's wails of pain made his heart thump even more painfully.

The princess. The village. Owah. His duties. His failures. His parents ashamed in the afterlife.

His eyes found Bog's. They screamed with pain every time the giant monstrosity drank. They begged for help, for mercy. He just watched as he had his entire life, despite always wanting to help. Wallow was tired of always standing by his entire life. But he had no strength. No power. What could he do?

Wallow couldn't let Owah down. And he promised the princess he would carry out his mission.

Paralyzed with fear Wallow knew he must act. He saw Bog's eyes one last time and Wallow remembered. Remembered how he watched them die while he stood there and did nothing. Since the day Wallow's parents died nothing had gone right. It had been all downhill. Tears of regret filled his eyes. Why did he just stand there and let his parents die? Why did he not help them? Why? Why!?

"Wallow! Help him! Please!" came the cry from the Princess and Wallow saw she was hurt, crawling to try and fight. For the first time ever, he felt his royal blood awaken. Power coursed through his veins. Anger puffed his chest and he let out a high-pitched shriek as the skinny fluff of feathers ran towards the monstrosity and grabbed it with fingers of iron determination and wrung the skinny, fragile neck of the giant insect.

Wallow felt things pop and move in its neck as he tried to crush the life from it. The Flying Death pulled its stinger out of Bog and tried desperately to fly away but Wallow held tight. It was repulsing, and he wanted to let go but something inside him burned. Years of bottled in emotions began mixing together like an unstable concoction. With a mighty war cry he felt his enemy's body go limp as he slammed it to the ground, squeezing the neck even harder as he smashed its head repeatedly into the mucky ground.

He could faintly make out others calling his name. The world was becoming black as the bloodlust gave him a feeling he never knew before. A lifetime of frustration taken out on a single target. Over and over he slammed the insect's head into the ground.

Hands began prying him away. Wallow tried to fight and scream. He couldn't stop. But then he heard the Princess calling his name as the darkness began to recede and the Swamps of Sorrow faded back into view. His eyes still filled with blood lust and his chest heaved with exhaustion as he looked around at the shocked faces of his friends. It wasn't the princess. It was Elizabeth. Suddenly reality flooded back into his mind.

"Wallow…" trailed Elizabeth, "Are you okay?" she asked tenderly.

He looked down and saw the mangled bloody wreck. Wallow's hands were shaking like an earthquake and he could not hold back the vomit in his throat.

"I think so, I'm not sure," was his weak reply after emptying his stomach.

"He is fine," resonated the deep voice of Toma, "Just the effects of his first kill. He has never had to take the life force of another to save a life."

Another herd of buzzing terror could be heard coming closer. This was it. They could fight no longer. Bog barely clung to life, and Elizabeth's ankle was badly injured. She stroked his fur and tried to comfort her big friend, but he just lay there, not moving.

Elizabeth's face crinkled from fear to confusion as she saw the hull of a ship gliding on the smooth leaves of the heavy ancient trees that soared above the dead rot of the swamp. The ship created green waves with the leaves as it started its descent. The hull began scraping loudly against the barren, skeletal trees of the Swamps of Sorrow. The deeper they had gone into the swamp, the darker it had gotten from the massive trees that blocked most of the moonlight. When the ship finally emerged into a clearing above them, Elizabeth saw the biggest hot air balloon she had ever seen. It was shaped like a football and looked as if it had been ripped and repaired hundreds of times, its cloth a patchwork

THE NOCTURNAL

disorganized maze of colors, shapes and stitching. In the pale moonlight she could make out different colors; it looked like a rainbow.

"Captain Blackbird!" shouted Toma.

"Ahoy young buck! We be letting the rope ladder down, hurry up now. Bunch o' angry buzzers after ya".

Toma grabbed the dazed Wallow and shoved him up the ladder, then helped Elizabeth gingerly. "Can you climb?"

"I'll try. I mean yes. Yes, I can." Using just her good foot, Elizabeth hopped up the rope ladder one rung at a time. There must have been at least a hundred rungs and her arms ached from the effort.

"Welcome to the Nocturnal," Blackbird announced as she felt feathered hands pull her onboard. Elizabeth looked down to check on Bog's progress, but she saw nothing but the swampy ground where he was.

"Wait!!!" she shouted while hobbling towards Blackbird on the top deck, making the rest of the birds on board freeze and stare at her like she was crazy, "We have to go back. We left Bog".

"I'm sorry lass, he be a goner," indicated Blackbird as he peered over the rail.

Elizabeth saw another horde buzzing around where they had been rescued from.

"No…"

"Mmm Bog you say? Legendary Swamp Yeti?" spoke a voice with a heavy English accent.

"Yes!"

"Highly unlikely young lady," the deep regal voice spoke again as Elizabeth turned to see a short toucan with a bored expression on his face. He looked light on his feet, but she got the impression he would rather have them kicked up. He leaned on his cutlass like a cane as his intelligent eyes surveyed Elizabeth.

"He's down there! He's our companion; we can't leave Bog, he saved our lives," Elizabeth argued.

"Incredulous!" sang a high-pitched voice with a French accent. A tall slender crane with a bandana wrapped too tightly around his head, emerged from the crowd of Blackbird's crew. His movements were graceful, each step a carefully chosen stroke from the brush of an artist. A long scimitar, equally as slender as its owner, hung from his sword belt. "Tell me more. Did you have tea and dine together? Made plans to have him come to your next birthday party?" taunted the crane with narrow eyes.

Loud, booming laughter erupted. Elizabeth saw a huge bald chicken hawk that was as wide as a refrigerator approach. "You's funny Pasqual!" the brute commented as he slapped the crane across his back. It was the same crew she had seen in one of her dreams!

"Yolk. How many times have I told you to never lay your filthy hands upon me!" yelled Pasqual at the chicken hawk Yolk, "Wouldn't it be nice if it really were true Wilmington?"

"Indeed," replied the Toucan, "If only Bog were really down there…I could finally retire."

"He is down there!" Elizabeth could feel herself getting angry again.

"Then let's have at it!" screeched a loud high-pitched voice from above followed by insane laughter. An owl with an eye patch dove from the crow's nest and right past Elizabeth and the others. She saw him rip two revolvers from their holsters as he began to descend past the ship. Yolk snatched him out of midair with grace that didn't match his massive bulkiness.

"You's goin's nowhere Two-Shot unless the boss tells ya," Yolk told the owl Two-Shot as he set him gently on the deck. Two-Shot took off quicker than lightning and Yolk snatched him as if he was expecting that to happen. Two-Shot kicked and struggled but Yolk just pinned him to the ground and sat on him.

"Awww man come on!!! Let me go look. Just real quick!" Two-Shot squawked at the top of his lungs.

"No. We knows you too well. You gonna run off and start trouble!" said Yolk the enforcer. Elizabeth heard the

YOLK

click of a revolver hammer and Yolk jumped up and Two-
Shot had one of his guns pressed against Yolk's butt.

"No fun…you guys used to be cool…" Two-Shot
complained before letting a maniacal laugh out as he flapped
his wings back up to the crow's nest.

"Enough!" screamed Elizabeth, "Bog is down there.
We need to help him!" Elizabeth felt something poke her leg
and she looked down. A tiny crow held a flower in his hand
and smiled up at Elizabeth. "Boom," the crow said as he
handed Elizabeth the flower, "Boom," he spoke again when
she did not take the flower.

"He's sayings nice to meets you's," Yolk told her.

"Oh… nice to meet you too," Elizabeth said as she
took the flower.

"Boom! Boom boom boom. Boom. Boom. Boom,"
the crow said excitedly.

"What?" questioned Elizabeth.

"He says he hopes the flower makes you feel better.
He noticed you's was sad," Yolk translated.

"Thank you… um…"

"Boom. His name is Boom," spoke Wilmington,
"Stay away from him, he's a bigger nuisance than Two-Shot."

"I heard that!" shouted Two-Shot from up above.

TWO-SHOT

"Good," Wilmington replied as he leaned over the airship rail and peered down, "I wish you were right young lady, alas there is no Swamp Yeti."

"I swear he is. Toma! Tell them!" Elizabeth pleaded as she turned to the tribesman. Toma stood stoically, his face unreadable and mute. His mouth moved to open, but he seemed lost in an internal struggle. Toma's eyes begged Elizabeth for forgiveness before he looked away.

"I'm sorry," came Blackbird's comforting voice again. "We must be going." The horde of Flying Death was on its way. "Pasqual!"

"Yes sir!"

"Get below and have the crew raise the dragon oars, we need liftoff. Now!"

"Yes, Captain Blackbeard!" yelled Pasqual as he disappeared in a flash down a ladder.

The buzzing horde was nearly upon the ship when Elizabeth saw giant oars shaped like dragon wings shoot out each side of the airship. She could hear Pasqual yelling orders and the oars began to flap. A few of the giant insects had caught up. Elizabeth went to reach for her wand, but Pasqual came flying up the ladder and in a single leap, he landed flawlessly on the edge of the thin rail of the deck. His eyes were laced with concentration as he swayed with perfect balance and placed his hand on the hilt of his sword. She saw his hand move but the rest was a blur. Three lightning fast stabs skewered three Flying Deaths out of the air. Elizabeth's jaw dropped with awe. She knew how fast and elusive those bugs were and Pasqual made them look slow. He wiped his sword on the rail in disgust and never looked down at the insect corpses that fell towards the ground. Pasqual's eyes carefully inspected his fine blade and when he seemed content it was clean, he sheathed it as he stepped off the rail and onto the deck in one fluid motion and disappeared below again.

A few more flaps from the dragon wing oars and the Nocturnal left the horde in the dust. Above the trees and into the bright starlight they went. It was an amazing sight for Elizabeth. She had grown up in a city her entire life and the stars were far and few. The sky had hundreds if not thousands of twinkling stars. Three half-moons lit up the ship nearly as bright as day.

"Don't worry," said Blackbird, "They be deathly allergic to the star and moonlight. They won't be a followin' no more."

Elizabeth heard the horde buzz off as they faded away from the Swamps of Sorrow. She leaned over the edge of the ship and looked down through an opening in the huge ancient trees, past the dead brush of the swamp, awaiting the horrid image of Bog's dried up body. Her eyes searched through the dead trees, but she did not see him.

Bog… Elizabeth could not believe it. Only a short time had she known the loveable creature, but it hurt her. He had died saving them. It wasn't right that she lived while he suffered death. Elizabeth looked over at Toma and thought of his warriors who were slain. How was he able to let it go? Or did he mourn and hurt deep down inside too?

Toma watched the swamp fade away. For the first time in hundreds of years, Toma was unsure. Bog did save them. That made him a comrade. And you don't leave comrades behind. But Bog also killed and ate many of the Cookapeepooh tribe. Toma stared up to the stars, hoping for an answer to know if he acted right or wrong. The thought of not supporting Elizabeth when she asked gnawed on his heart. He looked down one last time at the swamp and movement caught his keen hunter eyes. "Elizabeth!" Toma shouted.

Elizabeth looked down to where Toma pointed. The earth moved, and small trees and plants moved with it. The giant bundle of swamp marsh stood up. After a mighty shake and a few blinks Bog emerged from his camouflage. The small trees she had seen were the same ones on his back that she held onto during their escape from the Flying Death. Elizabeth saw the rope ladder still laying on the floor, next to where she boarded. The rope was so thick she could barely get a grip on. Her back ached from the weight but she somehow managed in desperation to get it up on the rail. She shoved it over but knew there was no way it would reach the ground from their current altitude. When Elizabeth looked over the rail, her worries vanished. The rope kept growing longer and longer as it fell, making it all the way down to Bog and stopped, inches from the ground.

"Heys! You's not supposed to touch that!" yelled Yolk as he stomped over, followed by Wilmington and Pasqual. Elizabeth stood firm and felt her hands ball into a fist as Yolk reached for her. The ship suddenly tipped violently, and Yolk went head first over the rail. Elizabeth looked down and saw Bog climbing the rope ladder with one hand, Yolk in the other.

"Sacre bleu! What is a mountain doing climbing the ship? Quickly cut the ladder!" Pasqual ordered.

"But then you shall need to acquire a new brute to do your dirty work," Wilmington said calmly.

"Forget Yolk! We need to save our own hides!" Pasqual argued.

"Oh my. Look down," Wilmington told Pasqual. As Bog climbed the marsh began falling off his body. Arms and legs began to take shape.

"Encule! What in the world is that?" Pasqual cried.

"I told you! It's Bog!" Elizabeth snapped at the pirates. The massive Swamp Yeti tossed Yolk on the deck and he landed roughly on his head. The airship nearly capsized when Bog stood on the rail and jumped on board. Thankfully down below the oar crew flapped the wings on the other side just in time to straighten the Nocturnal out. Stunned silence and jaws to the floor filled the scene. Even Blackbird had no words. Yolk stood up and shook his head until he regained his senses. He ran up and gave Bog a huge hug.

"Thanks! You's saved me!" As he crushed Bog with his gratitude, his hand smashed a bush growing on Bog's back. "Uhhh, oops. Sorry!" Yolk yelled as he slowly backpedaled away from the Swamp Yeti.

A chuckle from Blackbird finally broke the silence. "He be worth a lot more if we take 'em in alive."

THE FORMIDABLE FEATHERED FIVE

Elizabeth shot him the glare of death. "No. He's my friend and you will not."

Blackbird laughed even harder as he took his hat off and fanned himself. "Easy young lass, Blackbird just be jestin' with ye. If he be a friend o' yers he be a friend o' ours. Right ye scallywags!?" Blackbird shouted to his crew.

"Aye Aye Captain!" was the response from the entire airship, except for two. While the rest fell in line with the Captain's orders, Pasqual and Wilmington exchanged a knowing look that ended with a slight nod.

Chapter 19:

Inner Strength

"Aye, another fine mess that pluck has gotten the tribe into," griped Blackbird, pacing back in forth, his boots clacking off the wooden planks of the galley floor while stroking his huge, braided beard. He finally settled into his throne of a chair with a resigned sigh and kicked his feet onto the table. The intricate, geometric shapes and colors on the tablecloth looked… well magical to Elizabeth somehow, like the runes in her mirror. Gold hilted swords, jeweled scepters, and treasures of all sorts littered the floor and table tops in the Captain's quarters. Five arched windows made up the back wall, affording a beautiful view of the moonlit sky. Thick, heavy carpets covered the area they were seated in, along with an ornately carved wooden desk. Fresh fruit and water had been served for her to eat.

Blackbird had been very kind and accommodating to Elizabeth and felt the comments Wallow made to her before they boarded the Nocturnal couldn't be further from the

WILMINGTON AND PASQUAL

truth. He seemed to have integrity and honor, despite being a pirate.

It was the same feeling and vibe she got from all of his crew. When she first came aboard, Elizabeth saw all different types: crows, cranes, kingfishers and even the chickenhawk Yolk. These were hardened birds no doubt, but they had pure hearts of loyalty. This was as clear as day to Elizabeth. Blackbird had explained how they were mercenaries, so their reputation was strongly misrepresented in Noir. Wallow rolled his eyes during the entire conversation, obviously not buying a word. Elizabeth was curious as to the past of Blackbird and the Cookapeepooh tribe, but there were more pressing matters.

Blackbird stretched in his throne. His mood was as bleak as the old, peeling, cherry-stained wood cabinets and arches that lined the walls. Paintings of other ships and even one fighting off a giant sea monster hung haphazardly throughout. Burning candles were everywhere, some grouped up in candelabras. The gloomy dimness—along with the smoke from Blackbird's pipe—made the fruit less appetizing. It smelled like her grandmother's car when she was a very young girl.

"Well then, I suppose let's get ye all back to the village and we can be a plannin' from there," offered Blackbird.

"So, this is the infamous Swamp Yeti?" questioned Wilmington as he circled Bog who continued to poke away, with a massive finger, the dozens of pirates in awe who kept trying to touch him.

"Yes," was all Toma answered.

"Interesting. Quite interesting indeed. What do you think Pasqual?"

"I think he's my ticket to getting my old life back." Pasqual lowered his voice to a whisper but Toma's sharp ears caught it, "Think of how much money we could make, especially with no Blackbird."

The snap of a branch interrupted their conversation as everyone froze. Boom held a small tree from Bog's back. "Boooooom…" Boom said slowly with a sad look on his face. "Boom," he told Bog as he handed him back the broken tree.

"Shows over! Back to woyk or you's gonna be shark bait walkin' the plank!" Yolk ordered.

As she emerged onto the deck, the cool breeze so high in the air refreshed Elizabeth like nothing ever had before in her life. The crispness filled her nostrils and pores, leaving her feeling born anew, a fresh mind and perspective on the world like an infant. The Nocturnal sailed the night sky as she reflected on her journey. The incidents of near death replayed in her mind. They had narrowly escaped. Would she go back again? Elizabeth knew the answer before she even asked the question.

The moons and stars of Noir lit their way brightly as they made their way back to the Cookapeepooh village. The Mudsepy River flowed below them as they left the deadness of the swamp behind. Noir looked so different from up above. She could see the lights of the trading town Saint Bernard Bay that her and Wallow had passed by. In the thick of Vadu Forest, one tree stood taller than the rest. Elizabeth felt the familiar touch of the quicksilver and knew that was the ancient tree with the portal back home. She had escaped death yet again. Why was she going to roll the dice again? Just for her necklace? What else drove her on? Elizabeth was no hero, no warrior. Sure, she wished she could help, just like she wished she could in her own world. But was Elizabeth even fighting on the right side? Babarosa's words loomed heavily on her mind. How could she know who to trust?

In the distance, light burned dimly through a massive fortress of trees and she heard the familiar beat of the Cookapeepooh drums. A mountain to the north looked like the tip of a tower poking through the mist. The mist was so thick it looked like a barrier the Nocturnal would not be able to fly through. Elizabeth stared at the tower, and as it faded away from view, the fog parted slightly, and the moonlight revealed a castle built into the mountain. It was gone quicker than it came. One blink of the eye and it vanished. Was she imaging things?

Elizabeth reached out and touched a cloud as they passed through, the mist moving at her touch. Did she stay because she wanted to believe she had power here? Because life here was better than back in her world? In Noir people depended on her, looked to her to help them, something she was not used to, something she never wanted. And a force called her back to Noir whenever she left...just like Princess Whitecloud had said.

As Elizabeth walked over to check on Bog, she saw Toma speaking with some of the crew. They seemed to be getting along. Warriors with warriors she supposed. Wallow was still off in the corner staring at the sky. He had not been right since the encounter with the giant Flying Death.

Bog's whimpering took her attention away and she saw he was curled up in a ball, trying to use a stack of crates as a safety blanket. Despite his massive size and fearless battle prowess, he was as dangerous as a daisy at this point. He shivered in fear from the heights they sailed but Elizabeth was also worried he was still recovering from the giant insect attack. She had taken a sip of her healing potion and it fixed her ankle and she gave the rest to Bog. But Elizabeth knew it would not be enough for his size and injuries.

"You okay?" she asked while checking his temperature by caressing his forehead. He felt very warm.

Bog shook his head like a child with a tummy ache.

"You want to move downstairs or stay here?"

He mumbled something inaudible.

"What's that?" she coaxed.

"Here," came the pouty reply as he buried his head under a crate.

"Okay, well here's some water and a purple apple."

Bog looked up at the food and moaned while making a yucky face.

"Bog," Elizabeth said sternly. She felt like her mother. "You eat your food and drink your water, or you won't be strong enough to help us fight." When he made no move she snipped, "Now."

He quickly scrambled into action and gulped down the water in one swig while swallowing the apple whole.

Elizabeth laughed and patted him on the head warmly, "I'll get you some more." She couldn't explain why but now she knew she had to go check on Wallow. The journey so far had changed her. It had changed all of them. Things had gotten rough. She could have been killed. The danger was real. And it would only get worse. They would have to stick together as a team if they were going to survive. And Elizabeth knew not all battles were physical. She was not the strongest fighter in their party, but she could support her comrades in other ways when they needed it.

A still statue in the moonlight, Wallow just looked completely out of it and did not even turn to her approach. The way he looked reminded her of someone back home.

"Wallow." Still, he made no move. "Wallow I saw your face. I can't pretend to say I understand your pain and what you are going through. But I want you to know I'm here for you. You can tell me how you're feeling."

"I just need some more time," he replied, his gaze still off in the distance.

"What happened back there?" Elizabeth asked as she leaned her arms on the rail to join him. The Nocturnal flew high and the world below was now just a miniature, where entire buildings could fit in her palm.

"Nothing," he muttered coldly.

"You can tell me."

"Leave me alone!" he squawked.

Elizabeth fought back the fear that crept up her stomach.

"No. No, I won't leave your side. You're my friend."

Wallow finally turned to her.

"You can talk to me Wallow."

His mouth closed when it got halfway open. Elizabeth thought he wasn't going to speak as he fought back tears, but he surprised her when he continued. "When I saw Bog's eyes…they were just like my parents' eyes when I watched them die. And ever since then, I knew I would always be too weak. Too weak to fulfill my destiny, to be a great magic bird and the next Shaman of the Cookapeepooh tribe, to have the courage to tell the girl I love how I feel about her. I am too weak to do any of that," he spoke with the shake of his head.

His gaze stayed on the ground and she expected him to cry, but his steel composure surprised Elizabeth.

"Wallow…" she said softly but he either didn't hear, or he ignored her as he continued on.

"But when I heard your voice, I thought it was Princess Whitecloud. My love for her, my pain for my parents, it mixed together, and I lost it. I blacked out. I don't remember what happened," he said as he sniffled back the tears.

Elizabeth put her hands on his shoulders and made him face her. She looked him dead in his eyes and told him, "You saved Bog, you saved his life Wallow."

"Yeah…I guess I kind of did," he admitted.

"I didn't see someone who was afraid or too weak. I saw someone giving everything they had to protect their friend. I wish I was as strong as you Wallow," Elizabeth confessed.

Wallow closed his eyes and took a deep breath. Elizabeth felt a wave of energy surround him, but it was gone as quickly as it came. When he looked at Elizabeth, his presence felt stronger and suddenly overwhelmed her, making her take a step back.

"Thank you, Elizabeth. That means a lot to me," Wallow said with an air of confidence and poise she had never seen before.

Peace had found its way on his face and Elizabeth knew her work was done. The harshness of the reality that lay ahead sobered her mood quickly. "This journey isn't over yet Wallow. You and I will have to fight again…and possibly take someone's life."

"I will be ready. I have awakened my warrior blood, just as Owah always said I would." He looked down and then with a powerful voice she had never heard before, "And this time I promise I will protect you Elizabeth. Owah and

Chieftain Sage have tasked you with a quest only you can complete. It is my duty to see that you do so, even at the cost of my own life. I will not hesitate and run any longer. I will make my parents proud."

"I'm sure they already are," she said with a tear.

"Elizabeth, what's wrong?" Wallow asked, confused at her sudden turn.

"Nothing. Just proud of you, that's all," Elizabeth lied with a smile as she stroked a necklace that was not there.

A crow from up in the crow's nest let out a loud squawk and Elizabeth saw the sails on the giant masts pull up as the airship hovered down to land in the village.

Chapter 20:

A Simple Fix

The mist was so heavy Elizabeth could push it out of the way; it felt like snow stuck to the air. Even with oversized lanterns full of firefly colonies, visibility was limited to a few feet. As they climbed down the airship they were greeted warmly by the tribe. Elizabeth saw Whitecloud ask Toma something. He shook his head but showed no emotion. Whitecloud covered her mouth with her hands in sorrow then embraced him fiercely, burying her face into his burly chest. Toma's face fell into her hair and he returned her embrace. Guilt filled Elizabeth's heart for the death of Toma's brothers-in-arms. Wallow stood tall and walked solemnly, giving a slight nod to Owah as he headed for their war room. Owah feigned a stone face and nodded back but Elizabeth saw the relief in his eyes. Elizabeth had left Bog on the ship…better he stays there for now based on what Toma had told her about how the tribe felt towards him.

"You look very wizardly," Owah observed.

"Looks can be deceiving."

Elizabeth studied Owah. She found it hard not to trust him but Babarosa had warned her. She felt the seed brush against her chest in the inner pocket of her Sorcerer's Robe. Elizabeth feared Owah would somehow know, with those piercing eyes and his shaman magic. What if he already did?

"Can you teach me?" she asked the old owl.

"Child, it is I who should be asking you," he said with a laugh.

"I don't know what I did back at the ceremony. And the only magic I have are from items I brought over from Lumiere." Elizabeth's head dropped, her gaze to the ground. "I have no real magic. If I really am descended from powerful Wizards and Sorcerers, how am I to learn?"

"Let us decide our next course of action. Then we will see about showing you how to unlock your magic. You stopped the Queen of Mist...no one has that power. But come quickly, they await us."

They huddled into Chieftain Sage's gathering hut and Elizabeth quietly spectated from the shadows, watching Blackbird and the Chieftain argue back and forth. Blackbird insisted the mist itself was the Queen's army and only a matter of time before Mist Monsters started spawning.

Chieftain Sage mocked him and told him to stop believing in fairy tales. Thankfully, Owah finally ended the bickering.

"Either way, you will both agree the first immediate step is to defeat the Toad Queen and cleanse the Swamps of Sorrow. We cannot battle the Queen of Mist directly until we complete the gathering of the Runes of Noir. And, defeating her three underlings once and for all will be a huge blow to the Queen of Mist's efforts."

"Yes, but those magical creatures of the Toad Queen are powerful. Those Googins are weaklings without them!" declared Sage.

"Hmmph," taunted Blackbird, "Scared?"

"What!? How dare you!?" blurted Sage with fury, as his eyes nearly popped out of his head. Blackbird flapped a wing at him dismissively and turned to Elizabeth.

"I know ye' already told me ye' is all out of that magic that took down them winged nasties. But we be in a pinch me lady. As you can see the leader of this tribe be more brawn than brain. Right now, ye' is Noir's only hope." He leaned in closely, inches from her face and scratched his head, "Any way ye' can think of to get s'more?" Blackbird asked gently.

"Well… I could buy more but um, well…" Elizabeth trailed off, eyes to the ground embarrassingly.

"Say no more," assured Blackbird with a wide sweep of his hat, "Take this gold and ye' can be buying enough to supply our army."

"Our army?" erupted Sage, "Since when are you part of this tribe?"

Blackbird rolled his eyes and stuck his tongue out, not bothering to turn around to acknowledge his brother. Elizabeth had to bite her lip to not chuckle.

The feathered hand of charity reached out. The pouch felt heavy in her hands. Elizabeth opened the drawstring and her eyes went wide.

"This is much more than I need. Here. I only need one gold coin," she told him as she pulled one out and handed the pouch back.

Blackbird shook his head, refusing to take it. "Nay, we dun' know what we may end up needin'. Hang on to it fer now."

Elizabeth didn't know what else to say. Supplies were needed to win the war. But still, the pouch was full of so much money. Elizabeth couldn't help but feel a little bad for some reason. Was it because she feared to take some for herself to help her mother? Blackbird and Sage took her silence as acceptance.

"Then it's settled," declared Sage, "Elizabeth will return to Lumiere and retrieve more magic to defeat the enemies of the Cookapeepooh tribe."

"Ye' think it's that easy. Ye is losin' ye mind in yer old age," laughed Blackbird as he strolled over and poured himself a drink from Sage's liquor cabinet. "Lizzy ye do yer part and the war council here be planning the rest."

"What do you know of a war council, you dishonorable pirate?" roared the chieftain. "You're nothing but a disgrace to our tribe. You think you are part of the war council?"

Blackbird continued to sip his drink casually. He smacked his tongue in refreshing satisfaction. "Part of? No. Never." His gaze swept across the room of elders, "I will lead it," the pirate captain declared with a smirk and the raise of his glass.

Sage bellowed with laughter, "You know nothing of war." Sage took an aggressive step. "Get out."

"Grandfather! He saved everyone!" argued the princess.

"Aye. He be right. I ain't no general. But I know how to stay alive. I know how to win. Ye got ten o' yer best warriors killed already. Ye sent yer best hope and aspiring Sorcerer to her death. Yer lucky I bailed ye out. Ye got no clue what yer doin," Blackbird indicted sharply with a thump a finger against Sage's chest with each accusation.

Owah's huge wingspan separated the two right as Sage reached for Blackbird's neck, "This is not a matter of who is right or wrong, nor is it of the past. Every second we waste fighting amongst ourselves is a second we lose to prepare. My Chief, let us heed the words of Captain Blackbird and all the council here. We must prepare the best plan possible."

Sage shook with rage and just stared hate into Blackbird, who winked and blew him a kiss.

Chapter 21:

A Surprise Gift

Elizabeth tripped over the oversized army fatigues as she fell through the mirror, her foot caught in the sink and she hit the floor hard. Unlike when she entered into Noir, the magic of the portal did not aid in her landing back into Lumiere. Furthermore, the journeys had become decreasingly less euphoric each time, and Elizabeth still had not heard her father's voice since her first voyage through. Was the portal's magic weakening as the Queen of Mist gained power? The eye on top of the mirror was now halfway opened. Quickly she tore off the fatigues and shoved them under her bed in case her mother was around. Thank goodness it was Friday. She would have the entire weekend to save Noir.

She recited her story in her head one last time of how she came upon gold coins and prayed her mother would buy it. Elizabeth hated lying but even if she spent just one of Blackbird's gold coins, it would be enough to let her mother quit one of her jobs. Then at least they could attempt to build a life. Elizabeth knew the bug spray wouldn't cost more than a hundred dollars, even if she bought two shopping carts worth. Each gold coin had to be worth thousands each. But she felt bad even taking one coin for her mother's sake. Elizabeth decided she would just sell one coin, buy the bug spray, keep the change and return the rest to Blackbird.

Once again Elizabeth found herself doing things for survival she never would have considered before. Tough times threatened to take the last of her mother's sanity. It had not even been a month and her mother's energy was completely sapped. There was no way they could continue on. Elizabeth wanted to help so desperately it hurt.

Elizabeth kept telling herself that it was not stealing. It had been given to her. But the money was to prepare for the war in Noir. But what about her life in Lumiere? If she wasn't healthy here, she couldn't fight in Noir, so if she took just a little bit, just what was necessary, it would be alright? Yes. Yes, somehow, she would repay it to Blackbird. Elizabeth knew she had to take the money for her mother's sake, lest her father's soul watch them struggle miserably another day.

It was not her proudest moment, but Elizabeth had come to learn since her father died, that you had to do things to survive you otherwise would have never done. Circumstances force your hands to do deeds you know are wrong. But what was the alternative? Starvation? Death? Elizabeth could not watch her mother suffer another day.

Without another thought Elizabeth opened the pouch of gold from Blackbird. Her heart stopped when she poured the coins out onto her bed. The wooden nickels clunked together in a pile.

Of course. Everything changes when it goes from Noir to Lumiere.

Tears of frustration poured down. For a few moments she dared hope that life could finally be a little more tolerable. She finally thought she had a way to help her poor mother. She was aging and dying by the day. Elizabeth could see it in her eyes and face.

"Lizzy."

She had not heard her mother come up the stairs.

"What's wrong?"

"Nothing mom… I just wish there was more I could do to help support us."

"Oh Lizzy," said her mother with a heavy heart, "Come here," and swooped her daughter into her arms.

"You're such a sweet girl to even have such thoughts. I'm so lucky to have you," she said as she kissed her lightly on the forehead.

"I think it's the other way around mom. You're killing yourself around the clock. It's not fair."

"Well guess what? I have a surprise for you."

Elizabeth wiped the tears from her eyes and looked up.

"I took tomorrow off, and we have tickets to a show at the theatre! Our favorite, just like when your father was around," Susan said warmly.

Elizabeth's heart dropped. How could she refuse? She could feel the call from the mirror burning a hole in the back of her head. How could she neglect Noir? But her mom had already taken the day off work and gotten the tickets. It was her first full day off since they moved. Elizabeth just had to go.

"Wow! That's great! I can't wait," Elizabeth feigned. Her mom bought the act.

"We will leave first thing in the morning and catch the red line. We can stop at Monty's for lunch, and then off to the show we go! Then I thought once we got home around sundown, you and I could just talk, you know some mother daughter time, sound good?"

Elizabeth was torn. That did sound lovely. She missed her mother dearly and had not seen her at all since they started their new life. It had been so hard without her father and Elizabeth hadn't realized until now how little time they had spent together. But that would take up the entire day. And she still had to figure out how to get bug spray.

If somehow Elizabeth was able to obtain it today before the store closed, she could go back tonight or first thing tomorrow night after her mother went to bed, if the portal would even open. It was a weak plan but since she couldn't control the gateway, it was the best she could come up with.

"Yes. Yes, mother it does," said Elizabeth, forcing her best smile. The one her mother returned was genuine and it broke her heart even more. Wasn't she supposed to be supporting and helping her mother? And here was Elizabeth's one chance to do so and she was looking to cut her time short to go running back to some fairy tale land? What was wrong with her? Elizabeth was a confusion of hurt emotions.

Elizabeth dug through every box, between the cushions of the disgusting couch, but could find no money. Seeing that her mother had passed out from exhaustion in her work clothes, Elizabeth knew what she had to do. With a sigh of deep regret, one by one went her stuffed animals off the shelf and into her backpack. She loved them all so much because her father had given her one every year for her birthday. They were rare collector's items and she knew she could get a good price for them. More than enough to buy the bug spray and save Noir. But not enough to save her mother like gold coins could have, but at least enough to help out with some bills and necessities they still needed for their home.

Her chest burned for her prized necklace. It was worth selling her stuffed animals to get back her last link to her father. If Elizabeth had to help the Cookapeepooh tribe with their war to get it back it was worth it. But she couldn't help feeling something for her new comrades. It was sad to think she had more friends in Noir than she did in her own world, her real life.

The mist was seeping into her bathroom and reminding her time was short. She left a note for her mother, saying she went to the library with some friends and locked the door on her way out. Elizabeth knew she had to be quick if she was going to make it before the swap meet closed.

Elizabeth felt foolish for holding onto her expensive animals when they could have helped her mother long ago.

She made her way through the streets, towards the trolley station. Careless drivers sped down the narrow streets and hopeless eyes from the alleys stared at her with about as much life as a zombie.

"Elizabeth?" questioned a familiar voice. She turned expecting to see Wallow. Instead of the familiar feathered face in the magical land bathed in starlight, it was a tall lanky teenager with an unfortunate case of severe acne.

"Oh, hey Wally! How are you?"

"I'm alright. You?"

"Good."

"Where you headed?"

"To the store. Well the swap meet first then the store," Elizabeth said wistfully.

"You'll never make it to both before they close," Wally predicted.

"I know but I have to try because I won't be able to tomorrow," protested Elizabeth.

"What's the urgency?" Wally questioned.

Elizabeth hesitated. How could she explain it?

"Let's say I have a huge insect problem, and I need to get a ton of bug spray."

"I know that too well," he laughed.

"What do you mean?"

"Come with me," Wally assured her.

"But the stores are closing…" Elizabeth complained.

"Don't worry, I have more bug spray than you could ever use. Our building has a huge problem."

It was not a long walk through the poverty-stricken streets to Wally's apartment building. The dirtiness of the smog that filled air made it hard to breathe, as more and more polluting automobiles spewed smoke out of their exhausts like dragons in a fantasy world. It seemed every thought now reminded her of Noir. But how could that be? The worlds were so different, so far apart.

The sun seemed to be setting but it was hard to tell, the sky nothing but a grey blanket of smog. Wally's apartment was even more run down than hers. Elizabeth thought she had seen it all but here the squalor was nauseating. It smelled like vomit and unflushed toilets. The old yellow cracked paint only made the feeling intensify.

"Watch out that step is missing," Wally instructed her as he led her up the building. Up three flights of stairs then into his apartment they went, the creaking door slamming loudly behind them. It looked just like her home. Barren. Cold. Empty. Not just cold from the frigid air, but a hollow emptiness that chilled the soul and heart. A cold that no fire or heat could warm. Her scan of the empty green painted room found no pictures or anything of that sort. It almost seemed as if Wally lived here alone…

Wally walked to the kitchen, which was just a small section of what appeared to be the entire unit. There were no bedrooms or doors for a bathroom.

"Please take what you need," his voice snapping her out of her detective daydream.

Wally opened the pantry and instead of salt and pepper and canned goods, Elizabeth saw everything from mouse traps to cans of bug spray.

"Wally I can't. Besides I need a lot."

"Please take all of it then."

"How much?"

"I said you could take it all"

"No, I mean how much money?"

"Oh. Free."

"I can't."

"Elizabeth please take it," Wally begged. "I want to help you. You've already helped me so much."

Elizabeth was taken aback. She hadn't realized until now how much her chat with him at the cafe had meant to him.

"Thank you, Wally. I really appreciate it. This means a ton, not just to me but to a lot of people," she assured him appreciatively.

Elizabeth began sorting through the pantry. There was everything from mosquito repellent, to spray cans, to little traps. Elizabeth couldn't decipher it all, so she just grabbed the bottles of the same brand she took the first time into Noir.

"I'll take all this insect spray… and what's this bottle with the skull on it?"

"Rat poisoning."

"Perfect."

"You have rats too?"

"Wombats…but this may do the trick," Elizabeth said, unsure how to explain to Wally her theories on how items turned into magical artifacts in the Land of Noir. Elizabeth thought she had figured out how the crossing of items worked, and this experiment would either make or break her theory.

"I'll help you carry this bag to your place," Wally offered as he began putting all the contents into a plastic shopping bag.

Her arms ached already, and they were only down the first flight of stairs. Wally only had one bag and it ripped when they overloaded it, and now Elizabeth felt like she was hugging a huge tree as she carried an armload of canisters. They hadn't even made it out of the building and her back was already aching. Elizabeth had no idea how they were going to make it home. They finally made it to the bottom floor and she could see the door back out to the street.

"Hey," sounded a deep, gruff voice, startling Elizabeth. A large man with thick jet-black hair and a moustache to match leaning on a black wired cart made her nearly drop her spray cans in fear.

"Joe!" yelled Wally.

"Hey kiddo. How you doin'?" asked Joe with a warm smile that seemed out of place on his mean face.

"Good, just helping my friend. Do you know Elizabeth? She just started attending Iberville High last week."

"Yeah I seens her aroun'." He held out a huge thick hand. "Nice to meet ya Elizabeth. Here," Joe said as he began taking his things out of the cart. "Put ya stuff in here. Just bring it back, Wally knows where to drop it off when ya done."

"Thank you. Thank you, Joe," was all she stammered out, still in shock by his kind demeanor.

"Of course, sweet-hawt. Take care ya self out there."

Elizabeth took two steps with the cart full of a successful mission when Joe's voice stopped her in her tracks, "Hey." She turned and saw him go in and clank some things around in a hallway closet. It must have been where he was when they had walked through the hall. Joe emerged with a large scuba tank looking container with a hose attached. "I needs this bug sprayer back too, it's for the building. But looks like you got a war coming on your hands with all that stuff, so you take it for now." Joe dropped the cannister roughly into the cart, nearly overflowing it.

The last rays of sun clung to the day as they made their way back to Elizabeth's apartment. The rough sidewalk buckled the cart harshly, each hard thump wrung all her bones with discomfort. A few times some canisters had fallen out because the cracks in the cement were so terrible. To her surprise, no one gave her a second look. Elizabeth supposed in the area she lived in a girl with a cart full of bug spray was not the strangest thing her neighborhood had seen that day. The fetid smell of trash and smog in her nostrils told her they were close to home.

"Wally since we're friends I need to tell you something. I don't really have an insect problem. I need all of this because I have to help… I have to help save the Land of Noir. It's a long story but I opened the portal by accident and now I'm the only one who can seal it. I know it sounds crazy but it's the truth."

"Elizabeth. You don't have to lie to me. I promise I won't tell anyone, and I don't judge. You saw where I live…"

"Wally, I swear…"

He laughed loudly. "Elizabeth it's cool. I live with bugs too," he said with a laughing smile.

Elizabeth was staring into the mirror, waiting for the portal to summon her back to Noir when Susan opened her door.

"What's that smell? You been spraying for bugs in here?"

"I think it's this new perfume one of the girls at school let me use. I don't like it, but I didn't want to be rude."

Susan laughed warmly. "Oh, that's my Lizzy, ever so sweet and caring of others. Funny that you say, your school left a message that they are going to be spraying for bugs at your school. Anyway, I was thinking we could watch an old movie together tonight."

"Oh… I was just going to go to bed early. I'm really tired and want to be rested for tomorrow."

Elizabeth's heart broke when she saw her mother's face.

"Yes of course dear. I know it's not been easy for you with our new life."

How terrible of a daughter must she sound like? Her mother's week was thrice as long as hers. Yet here she was, lying that she was too tired to spend time when they finally had it. Elizabeth looked into her bathroom. She could feel the armory of ammunition she had under her bed, waiting to go and save the day at Noir. But it could be hours before the gateway opened again so she decided a quick movie might actually be just right. She really did want to spend time with her mother; Elizabeth had just been so caught up in her quest to get her necklace back that she wasn't thinking straight.

"I mean I guess we could watch one and I'll just fall asleep to it with you," Elizabeth suggested. Her mother's face lit up and Elizabeth felt guilty because all she could think about was her necklace, Babarosa, Owah, Wallow and the rest of the tribe, but she knew she made the right choice.

"Ohhh, that sounds wonderful. It will be just like old times…" Susan trailed off, obviously lost in bittersweet memories of her father. Before her mother burst into tears, Elizabeth embraced her firmly and held her close. She felt her mother's tension ease and her breathing return to normal.

Again, Elizabeth surprised herself with her own strength. Her adventures in Noir had changed her permanently. Most of her experiences had been horrific and traumatizing, but this moment made it all worth it. She had power that she did not have before, was this what Owah was talking about? How would it be once she went back to school on Monday? Or would she even live that long? The thought made her consider not going back as she walked with her mother hand in hand. Why risk going back? Life was precious and fragile. And yet, so many lives in Noir depended on her…how could she not answer the call and return? How could she live the rest of her life with their deaths on her conscience?

As they laid down on her mother's bed to start the flick, Elizabeth mentally prepared herself for the battle at hand. If she died in Noir, would she die for good? Maybe she would just reappear in Lumiere. No. Every time she was injured she brought those wounds back home with her.

Her mother looked happy for the first time since they moved. She smiled warmly at Elizabeth right as the movie began. Why was she feeling the call to return to Noir? She tried to convince herself it was for the necklace, her last link to her father. But something inside made her yearn to return to her quest. Was this her destiny? Forces that beckoned to her? The promise of Owah to teach her how to unlock her power? Was that who she saw in her dream when she first got the mirror, her ancestor of the past, a Sorcerer? Where did her magic come from, her mother's side? Her father's?

"Mom… can you tell me a little about our family history. Not the stuff I already know… but…"

"I'm not sure I follow Lizzy?"

"Well I mean, was anyone ever like, you know, royalty, or had special powers?"

Her mother laughed, obviously thinking it was a joke.

"Yes dear. I kissed a toad once and he turned into your father. Oh, look its starting! We haven't watched this since…"

Elizabeth squeezed her mother's hand and gave her strength. "I love you mom." Susan squeezed her appreciation back but had no words.

Elizabeth couldn't watch the movie, she just looked at her mother, wondering if this would be the last time she saw her. Just a few hours of sleep and she would sneak out of her mother's room and into Noir.

Chapter 22:

Uncertainty

Panic crept through the curtains as the sunrise blinded her freshly awoken eyes.

Merde!

The heaviness of the bed covers crushed Elizabeth with defeat. A quick snap of the neck and 6:30 glared on the alarm clock. She maybe had time to go to Noir… just for a little bit.

Careful not to disturb Susan, she ever so lightly sat up, inch by inch. Nothing but deep peaceful breaths rose from Susan's chest. Elizabeth held her breath and slowly began turning her feet off the bed and onto the balls of her feet. Pushing off with her palms, she shifted her weight to her feet without hardly a disturbance in the mattress. Quickly she crept out of the room, silent as a ninja, making no noise.

Yes! Success!

"Lizzy? Good morning sweetie," said her mother sleepily and she rolled over just as Elizabeth's last step was nearly out of the room. "Be a dear and get the coffee going for me?"

"Yes mother," she resigned.

Elizabeth tore down the stairs, banging cupboards and drawers loudly as she tried to sprint to the finish line. But the more and more she thought about it, there was no way she could enter Noir before they left. Her mother would be looking for her surely. And what if she was gone for several hours? Elizabeth still was unsure how the passing of time worked when she was in Noir. With a heavy sigh, she sulked up the stairs in defeat with her mother's morning brew.

She was surprised that there was no mist seeping out of her bathroom. Elizabeth got dressed and used her mirror to straighten out her hair with a brush. The runes had no life and when she put a finger to the mirror, it was as plain as her mother's cooking.

The high-pitched struggle of the electric trolley engine putted them through the midday traffic. Every time they went up a hill, it felt like it was going to explode. It made whirling robotic noises out of a Science Fiction movie. Despite the windows being closed, the excessive amount of exhaust smoke from the old metal boats spewing fumes out as they drove past the trolley was making her nauseous every time she took a breath. Elizabeth tried her best, which seemed to be working, to smile and look like she was listening to her mother. Susan was in the best mood she had been since they moved. Elizabeth should have been happy. This is what she wanted for her mother, but maybe because she knew it was temporary and that tomorrow her mother would go back to her terrible struggling life, Elizabeth could not enjoy the moment. They passed by an intersection she recognized. A right turn would have led them to the lake market. Elizabeth intended to go there to sell her stuffed animals and help her mother out with some much-needed extra cash. Those gold coins may have turned into wood, but she knew those animals would provide real money.

Strange. Why did the necklace not change when I crossed into Noir? And why does Babarosa's ring not change when I come home? She thought as she stared down at the moonstone ring, which her mother noticed.

"That's a pretty ring, who gave you that?" Susan questioned.

"From a friend at school, just borrowing it," lied Elizabeth.

"Well I'm glad you're making friends already!" Susan warmed with a huge smile. If only her mother knew the truth.

This day just totally sucked. Elizabeth couldn't enjoy their time together because all she could feel was the weight of responsibilities on her shoulders. Blackbird and the tribe said she was the one who was needed to save Noir. How could that be? They had an army, Owah had magic. She had a few spray cans. Then there was Babarosa telling her to not trust the tribe. But Elizabeth realized the more time she spent with them, the more she had begun to like them. Susan finished her story, which Elizabeth hadn't even been listening to. Her mother laughed joyfully with a beautifully perfect smile, the brightest one Elizabeth had seen since her father died.

The trolley stopped, and Elizabeth felt her hand being pulled. "Let's go sweetie. Are you feeling alright?" Susan asked with a hand to Elizabeth's forehead.

"Yes mother, just hungry." Which was only a half lie. She was genuinely starving.

Anger blocked her hunger as they approached Monty's Tavern. Elizabeth could only imagine what sort of slave drivers ran this place, paying her what surely was well below minimum wage. Elizabeth really felt that Henri betrayed her father; she would not let the same happen again to her family. She wore a scowl on her face as they entered, determined to stand up for her mother.

"Susan!" came a delightful voice as they entered. Elizabeth saw an elderly woman dressed in a floral blouse with white hair, straining to stand with a heavy lean on the bar.

"Hello Delly! This is my wonderful daughter I've been telling you about, Elizabeth." Elizabeth feigned a slight bow and hid her fangs as best she could. She would not be fooled by false kindness. Her mother was the kind to be taken advantage of and Elizabeth was sure that behind closed doors, Delly treated her completely different.

"Oh, my goodness, well isn't she a beauty! Please come and join me, you're just in time for lunch. We just cut the prime rib."

Elizabeth's stomach gurgled like a draining sink. They followed Delly out of the main dining hall and into a private room with a booth of comfortable thick leather. Delly smiled warmly at her, genuine. Elizabeth tried her hardest not to, but she couldn't help but like Delly. She reminded Elizabeth of her grandmother.

Without even asking a waiter brought three steaming plates of prime rib heaped with garlic mashed potatoes, roasted mushrooms, and some grilled zucchini on the side. Elizabeth was about to dive in and then realized there was no way they could afford to eat so lavishly.

Elizabeth leaned over and whispered into her mother's ear, but apparently not low enough.

"Come now young one. This lunch is on the house," interrupted Delly. "Your mother is such a hard worker; Susan is so amazing with our customers and she is just an absolute joy to have here." Delly pulled something out of the front pocket of her blouse. "Here are the tickets for the show today. I want you and your mother to have a great day."

"Ttthank you..." stammered Elizabeth, lost for words.

"You're welcome dear. It's my pleasure. I just haven't been able to make myself attend the theater since… since Monty passed."

"I'm sorry— "

"Eat my dear," interrupted Delly. "This is a day of celebration and pleasure. We can talk about my husband another time," she spoke with a sad smile.

The meal tasted even better than it looked. When her plate was near empty, the waiter came back with another and traded it out. Delly never lost a beat in her conversation with Susan and just gave her a smile and a wink. Apparently Delly had been gone to Europe for the first few weeks when her mother started working here. It had only been a few days but mother and Delly seemed like old best friends. After nearly finishing her second plate Elizabeth was caught off guard.

"Elizabeth, what's on your mind dear? You've been on edge since you got here? You can be honest and tell me," inquired Delly with a worried brow.

"Nothing," she tried to lie with a smile. "The food was amazing, thank you so much for the wonderful meal, and the theater tickets, but most important of all, thank you for being my mother's friend. It's been so hard for her and..."

"Lizzy!" Susan fretted with embarrassment.

"I'm sorry," submitted Elizabeth, her face looking into her plate.

"It's okay dear," soothed Delly. "I know it's been rough for you and your mother. I'm glad she is here, things will get better."

"What makes you so sure about that?" challenged Elizabeth. It was time to call Delly's bluff.

"Elizabeth!" flushed her mother with anger.

"I may still be a kid but I'm not dumb. I know math, I know deduction. I helped do our budget. I know how much comes in from here and how much from the sweatshop."

"Sweatshop?" puzzled Delly.

"Yes. Sweatshop. My mother works sixteen hours a day between here and there because you both pay illegally low wages."

"Elizabeth... stop..." pleaded Susan.

"Susan is this true?" Delly asked with shocking disbelief.

Susan just buried her hands into her face.

"I had no idea. Susan why didn't you tell me? And what's this about illegal wages? I pay all my employees well over the minimum wage and with her tips from customers—"

"Ha? Really?" interrupted Elizabeth, she felt her anger rising. "You pay my mother four dollars an hour and she says she has to give her tips to the manager since that's the policy for all new servers."

Delly's delicate white skin turned brick red. "Susan, please tell me this is not true?"

Her mother just sobbed into her hands. Elizabeth felt terrible, but she knew she had to stand up for her mother. But Delly seemed genuinely taken aback. Guilt flooded her veins and the delicious lunch suddenly wasn't sitting so well.

"I'm sorry... I didn't mean to ruin lunch," spoke Elizabeth softly, as she twirled her fork through the food on her plate, but it did little to ease the discomforting tension.

"No, not at all dear. It's my fault. I let my own heart blind me. I have been getting complaints about Arnold, but he's been working for us for nearly twenty years. He's the one who hired your mother and did her paperwork."

"There was no paperwork. My mom showed up and started working, he just pays her cash."

"Lizzy, that's quite enough," instructed Susan, "You've already made a big enough scene. Delly I'm really sorry."

"No, I'm the one who is sorry. I will straighten this all out by tomorrow when you come in. You both go enjoy the show."

They had the best seats in the house, dead center and high enough to see the orchestra on the wings in their balconies majestically striking string and blowing wind. The riveting performance so far had erased her mother's mind of the lunch conversation. But for Elizabeth it taunted her, nagged her conscience. Two rival houses were at war in the Renaissance era. The House of Gaia and the House of Sorrows were plotting on how to destroy one another. Gaia wanted to preserve the nature of the world, Sorrows wanted to build over everything and make it modern. Noir was on the verge of destruction and here she was enjoying herself at a play. But she knew for her mother's sake she must. Her mother needed this more than anything. She needed a good day, a day away from work and to just forget about life for a while. Her mother beamed her brilliant smile at Elizabeth as one of the actors on stage sung merrily and danced about. Elizabeth returned the smile.

The play concluded with a fierce battle between the House of Sorrows and the House of Gaia. The actors fought with such venom it looked genuine. Elizabeth watched soldiers pretend to be stabbed and fall to the ground with death cries. After her last trip into Noir, Elizabeth knew the next time she went it would only be worse. The deaths would be real; the blood would be real.

In the end, the House of Gaia won out and preserved the land from the dark clutches of the House of Sorrows, but with great losses. The hero survived the battle, but the curtain closed with him crying over the corpses of his comrades. It felt prophetic to Elizabeth, as if she was glimpsing into her future. When she looked up at her mother, they shared a genuine look, the first one Elizabeth had given her the entire day. Susan looked so happy to see her daughter so enthralled in the play, seemingly forgetting about their harsh reality and tough life at home. If only her mother knew the truth. Or did she? No, it was just coincidence that they attended this play.

Why were connections between Noir and her world becoming stronger each day?

Her mother fell asleep on the trolley ride home with happiness on her face. Elizabeth began to mentally steel herself for the battle ahead. She would have to play her part and face danger and even possibly death. The rise and fall of her mother's chest made Elizabeth realize this could be the last time she saw her. Elizabeth suddenly felt the need to embrace her. She hadn't realized how hard she was squeezing or that she was sobbing into her mother's shoulder until Susan cupped Elizabeth's face in her hands.

"I'm so sorry sweetie. I promise things will get better. I know it's been really hard for you since your father passed,"

Susan whispered gently as the trolley rumbled home for the evening.

Chapter 23:

Eclipse

"Yes," complained the annoyed amphibian voice. "Yes, your majesty. We shall." With the wave of her hand, the Toad Queen dispelled her magic mirror and the Queen of Mist's image faded.

"Good riddance! I canneth stand her foul presence much longer. Captain Draccus!"

"Yes, my Queen?" slithered the Googin voice as he urged his wombat-mount towards her.

"How goeth the scouting mission into Lumiere? Hath thou secured an agent to help me cross?"

"Not yet my Queen," he scratched subserviently.

"What!? What in the croaks is taking so long?! Do I need to find more competent leaders?"

"No, your highness. We have not been able to get another Googin through, and the one who did has been taken captive or killed." He opened a small book and showed the blank pages to the Toad Queen, "His twin to his magic journal remains empty. Something has happened."

"Maybe the idiot you sent just doesn't know how to write!" screeched the Toad Queen, losing her proper speech as she always did when angered.

"The Cookapeepooh tribe has been watching our every move, their army is now gathered near the gateway. We will not be able to get through until we defeat them."

"Pffft. Really Draccus? You're telling me you can't crush a few overgrown birds?"

"We will bring you victory my Queen. Or we will die trying."

"Hmph," the toad queen huffed, "We need to end this quick. Or I'll lose my shot to get into Lumiere before the Queen of Mist. I'll send a little insurance with your troops."

The Toad Queen hopped over to her wooden guardian statues. They stood out proudly compared to the deadwood that rotted most of the swamp. She approached the two giant twin alligator statues.

"Je vous convoque Dechirer!" The huge wooden alligator slowly began turning green and life pulsed through its body. Dechirer opened his mouth widely, revealing rows of huge teeth. "I hope you are hungry my pretty. There are lots of chickens for you waiting to be eaten," laughed the Toad Queen menacingly. A guttural grunt and a huge lick of his tongue over his jagged teeth was Dechirer's response. He hungrily eyed Draccus, backing him up a few steps. The Toad Queen patted him affectionately over the head, eliciting a toothy smile from the massive alligator as she wobbled over to the next statue.

"Je vous convoque Macher!" The wood glowed brightly as it turned midnight blue. Out came Macher, not as big as her twin brother Dechirer, but sharp intelligent eyes surveyed the lair. "My Queen. It is an honor to be summoned. How may I serve?" Macher asked dutifully.

"'Tis time to enter Lumiere. Our enemies block the way," the Queen informed her with a wicked smile.

"Understood," Macher said darkly, her bright red eyes glowed menacingly and their reflection in the water looked like two fires burning. The Toad Queen made her way to the giant snapping turtle statue and waved a webbed hand over its face.

"Je vous convoque Vivaneau!" The wood began to glow and blink, but the lazy turtle tried to resist the reanimation process, preferring to stay in magical hibernation. Frustrated, the Toad Queen waved her hand again. "Ungrateful vermin! I summon thee!" After a few more moments of struggle, Vivaneau poked her head out of her spiked shell and stretched her long neck. "Oh bother. What do you want?"

VIVANEAU

"How dare thee! Address me properly. Servant."

Vivaneau rolled her eyes, "How may I serve you, my Queen?" she mocked.

"Insolence! I should have Dechirer tear you to shreds!"

Vivaneau raised an eyebrow, "Him? He's nothing but a coward."

Dechirer growled and stomped over to the snapping turtle, who was nowhere near as long as the gator but certainly thicker.

"Come on big boy. Try me," taunted the turtle, unimpressed, "Just hope Toadie over there can cast a spell to fix your broken teeth."

"My Queen," interceded Draccus, "The Cookapeepooh tribe marches as we speak. We must complete the battle preparations."

"Battle? Oh gosh, you mean I have to actually do something?" whined Vivaneau as she stretched her limbs all the way out of her shell, flexing her reptilian muscle. Dechirer eyed her hungrily within striking distance but she peddled right past him as if he wasn't even there. "Fine, but when you get to Lumiere you take me with you. A girl like me needs the hot sun to warm her bones."

The Toad Queen regained her composure and held her anger in check. "Ride with me into battle and crush my enemies. When I enter Lumiere and rule Noir, I will let you retire to the world of sunshine."

"That's the best thing I ever heard out of your insect eating mouth. Deal."

"Why how dare—" the Queen started, her hands moving to cast a spell.

"We must make haste," ordered Draccus as he bravely separated the Toad Queen and Vivaneau with his wombat-mount. "The Cookapeepooh tribe has assembled their main forces at the border of the swamp. We will engage them there, feign defeat so they chase us into the swamp and let the Flying Death take care of those pesky birds."

Vivaneau plopped down. "Great plan. Doesn't look like you need me at all. I'll stay here and guard Toadie err our Queen in case they send an attack team ahead."

"Those dimwits couldn't come up with a plan like that. Besides, Indra is my guardian, not you," the Toad Queen indicated with the point of a webbed hand towards the giant snake statue. "Now submit before I summon her and feed you to her as a snack!" The mention of Indra made Vivaneau lay on the ground while Draccus and some Googins attached a saddle and put a harness over her mouth. The Toad Queen climbed on her back and Vivaneau groaned in protest, "Packing on a few pounds for the war eh?"

"How dare thee!" the Toad Queen screeched as she yanked as hard as she could on the reins, "Now march!"

Vivaneau took her first steps behind Captain Draccus and towards battle with a deep sigh. With a heavy heart, she turned and took one last look at the tiny turtle statue next to Indra.

Chapter 24:

The Beginning Of The End

By the time she crawled through the gateway to Noir, the forest was littered with the army of the Cookapeepooh tribe. The few thousand warriors prepared to face battle settled the reality of war in quickly. Lanterns burned brightly, and low-pitched chatter moved quickly in the air.

"Elizabeth!" Wallow shouted. "Perfect timing!"

Sage shoved Wallow out of the way. "Good, I see you have brought your magic, um magic lady," he commented as he saw her arms full of wands and a huge wedge of cheese.

"Yes sir. Where is Blackbird I have his—" Elizabeth started as she made a grab for the bag of gold.

"Never mind him," stated Sage. "What have you brought to help us defeat the Queen's magic? All we ask is for a neutral field to fight those Googins."

Elizabeth handed two wands each to Wallow and Owah. "Here. These are wands like I had before. It's easy magic. Just focus your thoughts and when ready, squeeze this button. I'm sure you understand Shaman Owah."

"Yes, quite my dear. Thank you for this. Although Wallow I hope you…"

"Yes, Shaman Owah! I have awakened my warrior spirit, just as you always said I would," Wallow said proudly.

"Bwahaha!" roared Chieftain Sage. "I'll have to see that to believe it.

"It's true! Right Elizabeth?" Wallow moaned.

"Well yes, Wallow defeated a giant Flying Death," Elizabeth said flatly, afraid to anger the Chieftain.

"Impossible!" retorted Sage.

"I did! With my bare hands!" huffed Wallow with pride.

Elizabeth looked around, quick to change the subject, "Where is Toma?"

"About to take off with the recon unit ahead for a surprise attack," said Owah.

Elizabeth began ripping apart the huge block of cheese. Get these to him and his men. We need them to get close enough to bait the wombats. If they eat this cheese, they won't be fighting anymore." The birds all gave her a puzzled look, but she shook her head. "Trust me. No time to explain if they are leaving now."

DRACCUS

Sage squawked, and a raven came flying over. "Tell Blackbird to bring his sorry hide here before they take off." The raven responded with a salute and shot off like a rocket.

"One more thing." Elizabeth reached through the portal and pulled out the large scuba tank looking spray canister Joe had given her. Through the quicksilver it came and nearly snapped her arm from the weight as a huge cannon plopped down on the ground.

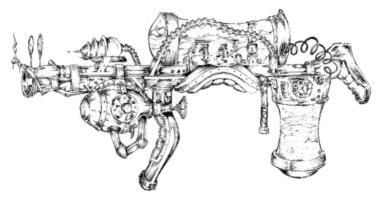

"Holy Earth Mother!" exclaimed Chieftain Sage as he jumped back, narrowly avoiding his feet being smashed. "What is that?" Elizabeth wasn't even sure herself. It looked like an alien blaster that was more fit to be mounted on a ship than to be held by someone's hands. Two transparent tanks flowed with insect spray, one huge one in the middle that rested on top of the cannon's barrel, accompanied by a second tank at the butt of the gun, connected to the rear handle. The contraptions and tubes looked like the design of a mad scientist, yet the weapon was crafted of wood and had the touch of nature's magic.

"It's the same magic as these smaller wands, so it'll take down Flying Deaths. I don't know how many shots it's going to have, so we need to use it for the perfect opportunity," Elizabeth suggested to the group. Wallow spoke first, "Attach it to Blackbird's airship, he can blast down the hordes of Flying Death from above once our warriors breach the swamp."

Sage shook his head, "No, we will take it on the ground. We cannot leave it to that rogue to be there for our warriors," he told Wallow as he took a step towards the cannon as if to take possession. "Besides what business do you or a pirate have in deciding what we will do with our ground troops? You both fight from afar. Well, you don't fight at all," sneered the Chieftain smugly.

Before Wallow could fire back the crushing of branches introduced Blackbird's arrival and the Nocturnal. "This better be good, we was already on we way…Elizabeth! Hello, my dear," spoke Blackbird as he bowed from the deck up above. His eyes went wide at the sight of the cannon. "Perfect! I see you have brought a gift for me ship. Sage make yeself useful for once and help haul that thing up. It's about the only thing ye gonna be good fer."

"No, we are taking it with the infantry."

"That be the stupidest idea ever. Take ye pride off for once, stop flexing ye muscles so blood can flow to ye brain and think for once in ye life."

"I dare you to say that down here on the ground to my face!" challenged Sage with the draw of his famed warhammer. The ship landed, and Elizabeth began handing the cheese up to Blackbird's crew. "Give a few pieces to your men. If you get the wombats to eat it, I'm not sure what will happen, but they should be out of the fight." Elizabeth cringed at the thought of it killing the wombats. When she was crossing through the portal, she hoped the cheese would save them somehow and not harm them. Elizabeth couldn't forget how the wombat looked at her when she and Wallow were running the night they took a long tumble down the cliff. It looked as if it was being controlled against its own will.

"The cannon next."

"No. How can you be leading the recon team for a sneak attack and then be by our sides to bring down the Flying Death?" asked Sage.

"Trust me, as much as I like torturing ye, I'd never let ye die or ye men either. Ye say what ye will but I am still a member of the tribe. These be my people too. Now up with that cannon!" Blackbird demanded as he indicated with the waving of his fingers as if to say bring it here.

"Catch," Elizabeth told him as she threw the bag of gold up. He caught it with ease and juggled it a few times in his palm. "Ye din't spend a single coin?"

"Nope. Your gold turned to wood in my world," laughed Elizabeth.

"Well here then. It's me lucky wooden nickel," Blackbird spoke as he flicked it high into the air with his thumb. Elizabeth tracked it and at the last second, barely caught it with both hands. "Fer good luck in the battle and yer days ahead of ye," Blackbird told her with a wink.

Toma felt the mist get heavier as wildlife became scarcer. In stealth they flew like ninjas in the sky aboard the Nocturnal. Somehow Blackbird could cloak not only their visibility but also their noise. Deeper into the Swamps of Sorrow they went. Since he had lost all of his men in the last skirmish with the Googins, Toma chose to join the assault team with Blackbird's crew, as was his choice to always be first to challenge death. It was this battle where he would seal his fate as future chieftain…or meet an early grave.

I am the water that douses the fire of evil. My bloodline has chosen me to be a protector of my people. At all costs. By any means necessary. Sacrifice of my life is as normal to me as eating and breathing.

Descended of royal blood he one day would fully transcend into the revered bird form coming from a strong bird-line of warrior lineage. He was only halfway through his transformation to his final form. And with Chieftain Sage having no male heirs, Toma was most fit to marry the Princess to keep the royal bird-line strong. Failure was not an option. It never had been.

He looked down upon the unsuspecting Googins below. They yelled at their wombat-mounts and tried to furiously fight them for control. Before coming aboard, he and Boom from Blackbird's elite crew had planted the magical cheese Sorcerer Elizabeth had brought back from Lumiere along the border of the swamp in hopes of giving their friends on the ground the edge. And just as they had hoped, the wombats were sniffing out the free food. Boom had also planted several bombs which Toma had to keep digging up and return to his strange new comrade.

Toma gave a nod to the rest of the crew and took a deep breath as he lowered himself down the rope, dangling dangerously in the air, a fall would be certain death. The airship flew in deeper, carrying Elizabeth and the others to the Queen's lair as he stayed behind. The feel of the marsh on his feet felt even colder. Alone in the heart of the enemy ranks, he saw hundreds of Googins lined up, each squad with an officer mounted on a wombat responsible for commanding them. Sprawled on his stomach on the murky swamp ground, Toma inched his way towards the cavalry of the Toad Queen's army. He had to get those wombats closer to the eucalyptus cheese. Even if it meant he was the first piece of cheese they would go after. Once he did that and scattered their ranks the Cookapeepooh tribe would attack. He could hear their war drums getting closer with each inch he gained, dragging his elbows and pushing with his knees through the muck.

The chattering, fast paced Googin speech came into earshot. Toma could smell the fetid wombats. When he saw the Googin closest to him he nearly snapped his spear with rage. It was the same one from the ambush. The grey one, the same Googin that had killed several of his men and led the attack on them. Toma watched one of the other mounted Googin, a green one, ride up to him, whipping the reins hard on the wombat to get it to listen.

"Captain Draccus," scratched the mounted green officer, "We cannot attack with our wombats like this. Send back the giant alligators, they are scaring them."

Toma's warrior senses homed-in on his target. He did not hear Draccus' response. All he focused on was the perfect throw. Revenge for his fallen comrades and a chance to take down their commander. Like a shadow he danced in the moonlight and let his spear fly. Even from that great distance, he knew it was a perfect throw, the razor-deadly tip whistled straight to pierce Draccus' throat. At the last second, the other officer moved in front by pure chance and the spear knocked him from his mount, instantly killing him as the shaft went all the way through its chest. Immediately the dead Googin's wombat-mount turned to Toma, its nocturnal instincts much sharper than the panicking Googins.

Toma moved like a fox as he trotted through the swamp and the pursuit was right behind him. Not the smartest way to get the wombats closer to the cheese, but he could not control his rage when he saw that Googin Draccus. Harder he ran on and back towards the grassy ground of the forests. Past the first few pieces of buried cheese he ran, but the cavalry of the Toad Queen's army was still in full pursuit.

A huge war cry of his tribe went out as he led the mounted pursuit north, away from where the two armies would clash. The more officers he lured away, the more chaotic the Googins would be. The Cookapeepooh tribe would have the upper hand. He looked to his left and in the distance saw the vanguard of the tribe charging, old man Sage in the lead with his warhammer out, mouth wide open with a cry for the defeat of his enemies. Unnoticed by the Googins, the rest of the Cookapeepooh army quietly crept in the vegetation, camouflaged by their grass helmets while the loud vanguard with drums distracted their enemies to allow them to strike from the shadows unseen. Deeper into the woods they went as Toma was able to zig and zag between trees quicker than the wombats, allowing him some space to think. He heard one crash into a tree and a squeal of pain filled the air. Branches tore through him and a trail of blood followed his escape but on he pushed. Gone completely were the sounds of the battle and deep into the forest he found himself, only pursued by one rider. Draccus. His heart beat from exhaustion and his eyes desperately searched for a solution. He literally stumbled into it as his foot got caught on a gnarled root, hidden under the grass.

Toma dove headfirst into a tree but managed to squeeze through a tiny hole, barely large enough for him to fit in. He smashed hard into the rough wood and the giant chomping maw of the wombat tried to jam its way in. Vicious hate filled eyes screamed angrily as its jaw snapped over and over, Toma thrashed against the rough bark inside, avoiding sharp fangs by inches, drool falling on his arms from the near bites. It screamed and struggled but its frame was much too bulky to fit.

Toma reached for the piece of magical eucalyptus cheese he had taken just for a situation like this and threw it down the gaping chomping mouth of the wombat. After some painful spasms and wild screams, the wombat began shrinking. Draccus was forced to jump off and when the transformation was complete, a koala bear smiled.

"Toma!" the koala yelled with joy. Her eyes turned to fear as she saw Toma's axe flash right past her ear, just in time to parry the thrust of Draccus' spear intended for the koala. Time froze, and the forest became suddenly still as Toma gently moved his friend out of the way and crawled out of the tree, his axe still holding the spear at bay.

"Hmph. Pathetic. You're the captain of your army and yet you chased and abandoned your entire force," taunted Toma as he circled Draccus, twirling his axe in one hand.

"A good leader always has those capable below them to carry on in his absence," came the even reply from Draccus. "I could say the same for you. You're the leader of your forces, yet here we are, a mile from the battle. I recognized you. I knew who you were. I came to strike a blow for the Googin army by bringing you back on a skewer to eat," Draccus declared, his eyes never leaving Toma as they continued to circle one another. The forest remained still, an arena just for these two warriors.

"A fight it is then. May the better warrior win," Toma affirmed with a deep bow. Draccus leapt in at the opportunity, which Toma had been anticipating and easily blocked the thrust, eyes still on the ground. "But a coward like you is no warrior. Even though my warrior blood thirsts for revenge, yield now and I will spare you Draccus," Toma spoke as he stood, brushing the spear aside with his axe.

"You will fall, just like your weak men."

A mighty swipe from his axe was the response and the battle ensued.

Chapter 25:

The Point Of No Return

On the border of Vadu Forest and the Swamps of Sorrow, wombats by the dozens chomped greedily on the cheese while their Googin masters failed to control them no matter how hard they yanked on the reins. Chieftain Sage, a fearless heroic warrior in his younger days, let out the war cry of the Cookapeepooh tribe and charged in with his huge warhammer. Hundreds of tribesmen and dozens of birds followed him. The Googin's columns were staggered and disorganized from the chaos of their officers trying to get their mounts under control. The charging Cookapeepooh tribe's spears crashed like violent waves upon rocks. Shields cracked and smashed. Cries of pain filled the air.

Hundreds of tribesmen seemingly appeared from thin air, rising from the grass behind the Googins. Well-placed thrusts ended many a Googin. Sage and the vanguard smashed forward, and the stealth hunters of the tribe had easy pickings as the Googins retreated right into spear tips.

The initial onslaught of the tribe was fierce. The tribe pushed deeper into their enemy's lines, driving the Googin army's front line back into the swamp.

Sage led the charge still, wounded in several spots. He didn't look his age. He ran with the strength of a younger bird. Finally, the officers had abandoned the wombats as they began their transformation. The Googin officers called for a full retreat. Into the air Sage's wings flapped and he took flight after the officers. He landed with a heroic smash, instantly crushing two Googins. Another stopped its retreat to stay and fight and Sage easily slapped the spear aside and thrust his hammer, dropping the officer to the ground with ease.

A huge cheer went out as they completely decimated the cavalry of the Toad Queen and wombats began turning into koala bears, friends of the tribe and the forest. They joined in on the rout of the Toad Queen's front lines as they pursued the fleeing green creatures into the Swamps of Sorrow. The disoriented Googins were completely overrun by the organized and disciplined but extremely angry villagers. They fought for their homes and families, to push back on those who had come to harm their way of life.

"Owah! Wallow! To the front! Be ready to take down the Flying Death. These cowards are sure to rely on them!" Sage yelled as he turned halting a stop to the charge. "Reform the line! Do not chase recklessly! There are dangers in the swamp. Stay in tight formations." Sage raised his warhammer and let out a loud war cry. His army responded with the same cry and raised their weapons. Owah and Wallow emerged to Sage's sides as Owah closed his eyes and chanted. A huge red flare lit up the night sky. Seconds later a similar one responded, deep in the swamp.

"To the fire signal! Blackbird shows the way to the Queen's lair! This is the day her evil ends! This is the day we bring peace back for our tribe!" A huge war cry was the response, making the Googins tremble in anticipation.

Onward the tribe charged. Chants filled the air, war drums beat heavily. They were met by hordes of Googins, and the war for the Land of Noir began its second battle.

The Googins had reformed a tight wedge in between two huge lakes, room with only enough for four Googins to stand shoulder to shoulder. There was nowhere to flank them. Head on Sage met their charge, smashing the front four with one huge swipe, sending them lost forever in the bog. Arrows pierced his thick skin and slowed him as he swiped through the next line. But one Googin ducked and buried his spear deep into Sage. Sage grabbed the spear with one hand and swiped the attacker into the water with his hammer in the other. He pulled the spear out but stumbled to a knee. Dozens of tribesmen charged in and protected their fallen leader. Mighty thrusts of spears found Googin flesh but the Googins fought back ferociously. For every one that fell, another replaced it. They could not force the Googins back. Tribesmen slipped in the unfamiliar swampy terrain and the Googins continued to shoot arrows and throw spears from hidden spots in the trees, halting the advance of the Cookapeepooh army.

Tribesmen fell by the dozens, pierced and hacked by Googin weapons. The swamp kept their footing unsure and their movements mucky and slow. The Googins took the narrow strait and forced the Cookapeepooh army back.

A gate of branches wrapped in flesh eating vines materialized and dropped onto the ground, halting the counter charge of the tribe as the Googins continued to attack with projectiles. The tribesmen hacked at the gate, but it held strong as the vines began taking bites out of the warriors.

Owah closed his eyes and lay his hands upon Sage. He chanted quickly. Energy flowed from Owah into Sage. Sage's pain left his face but Owah's filled with agony. The wounds closed but Owah fell over in exhaustion.

"Master!" concerned Wallow. Owah waved him back with a mighty wing. "I am fine, just my age," he cracked with a smile.

Chieftain Sage summoned his energy. Wind gathered, and lightning sizzled through him as he flew high into the air, narrowly dodging arrows and right over the Googins bottlenecking the narrow strait, over the magical gate and into a large open space, smashing his warhammer into the ground.

Huge yellow shockwaves of energy rippled in the air from where his hammer hit, rocking the enemy and sending them flying, but those waves healed and soothed his wounded warriors, renewing them with vigor.

Like a wild animal, Boom came sprinting from the rear lines with a live bomb! "Boom. Boom. Boom," he repeated insistently. He dropped the explosive right at the gate and took off running, laughing like a maniac and shouting "Boom!" over and over again. The bomb detonated, and the deadwood logs and vines exploded into small pieces that splashed into the lakes along with the Googins blocking the strait, clearing the way.

The tribesmen charged in and the few bird warriors there flew overhead and joined Sage. From the rear, Sage and the birds held the Googins at bay while the tribesmen charged into the narrow strait between the lakes. Out into the wide-open muck poured the Cookapeepooh tribe, driving the Googins even further back. Cheers rose as they brought down the archers in the dead trees from above with expert spear throws. The Googins retreated with their tails between their legs in defeat to the next narrow strait and reformed their wedge. The tribe charged in with triumph on their chests and smashed through the Googin wedge easily and again poured out from the strait and onto wider land. The smell of victory faded quickly when swarms of Flying Death came buzzing in. Another gate of deadwood and flesh-eating vines materialized behind them, trapping the tribesmen.

By the dozens Cookapeepooh warriors fell to the vicious stingers, their life being sucked from them while still alive. Those who ventured to close to the magical gates were eaten by the carnivorous plants. The flying warriors of the tribe valiantly swung their swords, but the horde overwhelmed them. For every Flying Death that fell, ten more took its place. The aerial defense of the army fell from the air one by one, immediately punctured by dozens of hungry monsters and sucked bone-dry seconds after hitting the ground.

The screams were horrible and enraged Chieftain Sage. He tried to swipe at the giant insects, but they moved too quickly. He ran up to smash in the brains of one that had a tribesman pinned down, sucking his blood out. He raised his hammer but felt a sharp stab into his back as he fell face forward. Immediately he felt paralysis take over his body as he felt his blood being leeched. After a few drinks, he felt the insect go limp. When he turned over in shock, Wallow stood

there, wand out as he continued to spray and shoot
down the Flying Death around them, freeing and saving the
lives of their warriors. Owah had a wand in each hand, his
blasts nearly three times the size of Wallow's.

The song of his ancestors played in Chieftain Sage's
head. He heard the call of his forefathers and stood.
Weariness drained his bones, but he heard the song and
charged in. Violently he smashed into the Googins who
sought to regain the battlefield. He swung his hammer back
and forth, over and over. He single-handedly smashed
through the second magical gate that had his army separated,
and the rest poured onto the battlefield with a deafening war
cry. The reptilian little monsters kept coming at Sage, trying
to stab and cut him but they were no match.

The few surviving flying warriors rallied with the help
of the Shaman and his apprentice. But there were too many
and they couldn't protect everyone. The tribesmen were
fighting bravely but the Flying Death were too much. Wallow
and Owah cast their magic and dropped the insects by the
dozen but more and more kept flying in. Retreat was not in
Sage's nature but if this kept up, they would lose.

A massive explosion sounded off in the dark skies
and in the distance, he saw a huge ball of white looking fire
getting bigger and bigger. The ball came closer and closer.
"Fall back!" he yelled as he stumbled back to retreat. The

meteorite of white crashed into the ground and exploded, filling the air with smoke. A huge sphere of energy grew larger and larger until it swallowed the entire battlefield. Sage waited for the pain, but none came. Instantly the Flying Death sizzled into husks and fell to the ground, twitching venomously as they thrashed, trying to fight for another second of life, littering the entire battlefield. There was no ground to walk upon, just hundreds of Googin and insect corpses.

Blackbird must have fired that giant cannon. That darn fool actually came through…

"Boom! Boom!" Boom yelled excitedly while clapping his hands.

Both sides had halted and tended to their wounded. Victory was near at hand, but the Flying Death appearance allowed the Googins to regroup. Only one more strait to take, and there would be no more bottlenecks for the Googins. But the fight was going to take longer than Sage expected. He had hoped to join the fight with the Toad Queen, but they weren't going to be able to catch Blackbird at this rate.

"Come on Elizabeth," Chieftain Sage muttered under his breath, "We are counting on you."

"Yes, we are…" whispered Owah as he limped up next to Sage.

"Owah. You and Wallow must fly ahead, you must aid Elizabeth." Instructed the chieftain as he leaned heavily on his warhammer. The skies should be safe, if there are any Flying Death left you and Wallow must defeat them with your magic.

"No," Wallow shook his head, "We can't leave you and the warriors, what if more come?

"Give me a wand," commanded one of the birds who had flown over. "You can't use it, you do not know magic," Owah told her. The bird pulled her helmet off.

"Whitecloud! What are you doing!?" exclaimed Sage.

"Fighting," the princess stated with her arms crossed in annoyance.

"You return at once to the safety of the village!" ordered her grandfather, his eyes nearly bursting out of their sockets in disbelief.

"I will stay here with you and protect us from the Flying Death. I have studied warfare under you and magic under Shaman Owah. Do not deny me this because I am your granddaughter and you fear for me. You are here to lay your life down for your people. Why must it be any different for me?" she told him with iron conviction, the warrior spirit burning in her eyes. Owah handed her a reserve wand from under his robe.

"Sage there is no time. We must be off. Please protect the princess." And he and Wallow flapped off above the trees. Before Sage could find his words, the Googin lines parted and cleared a path. The ground rumbled and quaked with each step of whatever was coming through. The Cookapeepooh tribe held their breath.

A huge snarl announced the arrival of Dechirer, the terror of the Swamps of Sorrow. The Googins stayed far back as Dechirer entered the battlefield, his eyes locked right onto Sage's. The alligator was at least twenty feet long. It would take nearly ten tribesmen to equal his length and twice that to equal his strength.

The ground started shaking again and in came an identical alligator except its scales were blue. If it wasn't for her sinister, crimson-red eyes, Sage thought she would be cute. She wasn't as bulky as her twin brother, but she looked a lot meaner as her predatory gaze shifted between her potential meals.

"Hold your ground!" snapped Sage over his shoulder. He could feel the fight being drained from his army as they inched away with each step the alligators took.

The last in tow was the Toad Queen herself, mounted on the back of a massive snapping turtle. Her jewelry gleamed in the moonlight as her pompous face surveyed the battlefield with a smirk. She yanked on the reins as the turtle resisted and nearly bucked her off. The Toad Queen regained her composure after sharp words to her mount and narrowed her eyes, her face smug as usual. She hadn't changed a bit after all these years. The pounds of caked-on makeup proved her vanity hadn't slipped.

"Well, well, thou hast grown older and uglier than I hath ever imagined. I'm surprised to see thee here. I thought thou would hath been buried long ago," the Toad Queen croaked.

"Not until your reign of terror on my people ends. You have threatened our way of life and invaded our lands. When you have been defeated once and for all, then I will rest with my ancestors," Sage retorted.

"Hmph. Old fool. Today is the day thou join thy ancestors!"

"As long as you're defeated, that's fine by me," Sage replied.

"Thou canneth defeat me, I am flawless."

"You break the mirror that reminds you of your ugliness," Sage told her.

"What!? How dare thee!? I am the fairest in the land."

"On the outside yes. But where it really matters, the inside, you are not," Sage counseled like the wise bird he was.

"You sound like my mother," the Toad Queen spat.

"Sounds like you should have listened to her. Your emptiness you feel, that makes you lash out at others, so you can feel better about yourself, is all your own doing. You seek answers from the outside, for questions that come from within. Only until you can cast away your hate, can you love."

"Silence! Words of the weak. Only the winners get to preach and write history. And your tribe's time ends today. Dechirer! Macher!" ordered the Toad Queen, "Feast on them!"

Dechirer and Macher rushed in with frightening speed. Sage met them head on. He smashed his warhammer into the ground, splitting open the marshy ground. Chunks of earth flew into the air, and the ground rose up like a wave, slowing the two alligators down. Sage took flight and came smashing down on Macher before she could recover from his Earthquake Smash. He heard the rush of the tribe surround Dechirer as he narrowly avoided the massive snapping jaws of Macher, teeth nearly as large as himself, missing him by inches. He could smell her hot fetid breath with every miss. Soon Sage would tire, and those fangs would find their target.

A flash in the sky zoomed past Sage's vision and Macher reeled back in pain. Whitecloud pulled her staff out of Macher's eye and twirled it under her arm as she landed gracefully on her feet. She stood in a cat like stance and every time Macher went in for a bite, she easily danced out of the way and scored a hit every time with a hard smack from her staff to the nose or a poke to the eye.

Sage stood with his mouth open as he watched the Princess single-handedly keep the giant gator at bay. Regret filled his heart at all the times he had held her back. She was a magnificent warrior and he should have had more faith in his own blood. His pain from the loss of Whitecloud's parents had made him overprotective. Sage had stifled her from anything combat related because he could not go through what he went through again. He would die a thousand painful deaths before he would experience the pain of loss again.

And here she was, protecting him. For the first time since the loss of his son and daughter-in-law, Sage felt hopeful for the future. Their spirits lived on through Whitecloud. She was his granddaughter. She had his blood and his strength. How could he be so blind and not see this? All these years of a rocky relationship and arguing when all he wanted most was to be close to her.

For the first time that day, Sage had a reason to survive this battle. Winning wasn't enough. He had to win and live, so he could make things right with his granddaughter. He could not go into the next life with these regrets in his heart. He must tell her how wrong he had been.

The Toad Queen surveyed the field of victory she was about to reap. Her pets were slowly trapping the pesky tribesmen against the giant bog, their doom inevitable. The scent of wildflowers caught the Toad Queen's nostrils and her cold blood boiled with anger.

Babarosa! You old hag! You think you can sneak into my lair while I am gone?

"Vivaneau! Return Home. Now!"

"Huh? We just got here…"

"I said now, you disloyal servant!"

"Not if you're going to talk to me like that…" Vivaneau said flatly as she plopped on the ground.

"Insolent fool!" the Toad Queen shouted as she dismounted. "Once this war is done, your punishment will be more severe than you could ever imagine!" With the wave of her webbed hands, vines came down from the trees above and wrapped around Vivaneau's limbs.

Sage saw the Toad Queen yell at her turtle after binding the animal with magic vines and hop off frantically into the darkness.

Good. They must be close to her lair! Sage thought.

"Ha-Ha," taunted Dechirer. "You got in big trouble."

"Shut up Dechi. How old are you? Grow up," snapped Vivaneau.

The Cookapeepooh army slowly began creeping towards escape while the giant beasts argued with each other.

"I bet your punishment will be letting us dine on turtle soup," Macher said, her red eyes glowing brightly.

"Macher. Behind you." Vivaneau warned.

"Like I'm going to fall for that. I expect better from you Vivi."

"Boom! Boom! Boom Boom!" came the war cry. Boom emerged from the crowd laughing wildly with a live bomb in his hands! Sage watched the fuse burning away as he headed right for Macher. The blue alligator turned around and smiled before opening her jaws wide. If the fool didn't yell out he could have surprised her. Now he was just running into certain doom.

Boom gave one last loud cackle and used the burning fuse from the bomb to light two fuses on each one of his ankles. Boom dove into the air as explosions went off around his feet and he flew like a firework through the air. Macher

351

tried to chomp him but she was too slow, and Boom sailed right past her deadly teeth before they could close. Smoke poured out of her nostrils, the behemoth reptile sneezed mightily and out came Boom tumbling head over heels.

Macher's evil red eyes were suddenly full of fear and she ran for the murky lake and dove in. A huge explosion sent massive waves crashing onto the swampy floor. Up floated the wooden statue of Macher, dancing in the waves. A loud cry of victory rang out through the Cookapeepooh ranks but it was short lived.

"Sis! No!" cried Dechirer, drowning out the celebration. "Now I'm angry! You're all going to pay!

Sweat dripped from both warriors. Their chests heaved, their eyes locked.

"Not bad for a little, grey turd. Almost enough to get my respect," reprimanded Toma as he raised his axe above his head. "Tell me, why do you serve that spoiled toad?"

"Why do you care to know bird?" Draccus spat, blood running down his mouth from teeth that had been knocked out.

"One last chance for you to bargain for your life. This battle is going to end in my people's favor. Unnecessary bloodshed must be avoided. You will convince your warriors to lay arms down peacefully. Unless you are to fight until you are killed to the last man."

"You talk as if you can even kill me. Or that your side even has a chance. Even now as we speak the Queen's summoned champions are feasting on the flesh of your brothers and sisters. You'll never make it through the Swamps of Sorrow and all that lay within. You were fools to attack us. You fell right into our trap."

"If what you say is true, then I cannot waste any more time. Your last chance to yield, Captain Draccus."

Draccus kneeled to the ground. "Ha. There's a smart little Googin," taunted Toma, "Now lay down your— "

In a quick flash Draccus' arm flung muck right into Toma's eyes and stabbed him right through his stomach with his spear. "Now you die you stupid bird!" grinned Draccus. The grin withered into a frown as Toma gripped the shaft of the spear with his free hand as Draccus was trying to pull it clear. Toma smiled into the Googin's eyes, "Goodbye Draccus. May you fare better in your next life." A swipe of the axe intended to sever his head descended upon Draccus' neckline. He abandoned his spear and ducked. The axe severed the tip of an ear and buried itself into the top of his skull. Draccus staggered away, trying to yank the embedded axe out.

"Toma!" concerned the watching koala.

"No, Ka. Stay back. This is between him and me." With a heave of pain, the spear came out. Quickly he removed his headband and tied it over the open gushing wound. Draccus stumbled to the ground, unable to pull out the axe. Toma advanced and thrust with the spear. Draccus desperately pulled his scimitar from his sword belt to parry. He struggled against Toma's onslaught of thrusts as he lay on his back. He fought with grim determination, but his strength was failing him. Toma feinted a thrust to his eyes then pinned Draccus' arm to the ground with a mighty pierce through his sword arm. To Toma's surprise, he did not cry out in pain.

"Finish me bird. Be done with it. But know you fight a losing battle. Even if you win out the day, you will never defeat the Queen of Mist. That's why we serve the Toad Queen. Survival. Our people would be extinguished, just like your tribe will be once she decides you are worth a second of her time."

"Better to fight for what is true than to be submitted into evil," said Toma, "I understand your choices but that does not make them right. Though you fought valiantly, I cannot respect one as you. My men are dead because you fight for evil. Just like the Queens you serve. You will not be given a warrior's death. That would be too good for your kind. You are my prisoner now." Toma picked up the scimitar and began hacking vines that hung from the trees. "Ka. Help me." To a tree they bound Draccus and Toma pulled the axe out of his head. Still Draccus made no noise or indication of pain. "You're a tough one, aren't you?" Toma asked with a grin as he tied a cloth around Draccus' head to stop the bleeding. "Don't die on me, I'll be back for you." Silence was Draccus' answer.

Toma turned to the koala bear, "Can you get me to the Queen's lair? I need to catch up to my comrades."

Ka climbed up a tall tree. "Follow me."

Toma laughed, "You know I can't fly, I'm only half falcon for now... These wings are just for show."

"You expect me to carry you?" Ka grumbled as she climbed down.

"I think it's the least you can do after we saved you and the rest of your tribe," he teased despite having a hole in his stomach and several other painful wounds.

"Fine. Just don't tell the princess."

"What?" asked Toma with embarrassment. "Ka it's just a ride."

"Sure. That's how the story always starts. Just a ride…"

"Will you two hurry up? You're going to make me vomit," hissed Draccus.

"Shut up. Or I'll tear you to shreds," Ka threatened as she traced a thick sharp claw across Draccus' neck. "You enslaved me and my people. If it weren't for Toma, your blood would already be on my hands."

Toma climbed onto her back and up she went, swinging from tree to tree with great haste.

Chapter 26:

The Smell Of Defeat

The airship sailed through the bright moonlight just above the skeletal branches of the trees. The ride had been fairly silent aside from the massive cannon blast they had fired into the battlefield after they spotted hundreds of Flying Death racing towards their comrades. Elizabeth hoped it had found its mark. She clutched her wand, wishing she had more power. Blackbird's elite crew, minus Boom, would be doing most of the fighting. Blackbird had admitted it himself, even in his younger days he was not much of a fighter. But he assured Elizabeth he had a few tricks up his sleeve and would support from above when the final showdown happened.

The four pirates sat quietly. Pasqual sharpened his blade on a whetstone, his stick-like crane features matching his long thin sword. Yolk was eating a bag of chips with his mouth wide open and chomping loudly, crumbs spilling all over his burly chest. Two Shot kept running around and ripping his revolvers out and pretending to shoot enemies while laughing like a hyena. Wilmington flapped his wings once and levitated off the ground. He clacked the heels of his boots together then vanished.

Into thin air.

Elizabeth blinked a few times then looked around, but he was nowhere to be found.

"Don't mind me," Wilmington said as he reappeared next to Elizabeth. "Just getting away from that crazy one."

Elizabeth wished she could be as calm as them. They seemed so prepared for what lay ahead. She trembled inside at what was to come. It would be easier to just stay on deck with Blackbird. But she couldn't do that. She was glad Bog was still with her. He was hiding below so the heights wouldn't scare him, but she knew she could count on him when the time came. What of Wallow, and Toma? And the rest of the warriors? Were they winning? Were Wallow and Toma hurt, or even lying in the marsh lifeless? The images made her shudder and her fear worsen.

A feathered arm on her shoulder startled her, eliciting a little scream. Curious feathered faces looked at Elizabeth. "What's on ye mind?" asked Blackbird as he stood beside her, looking down into the swamp. "It's okay to be scared. We is all scared. Scared to bloody death. Trust me," the old captain laughed.

Elizabeth did not believe him. She appreciated his efforts to make her feel at ease. "I'll be fine. I'm just not battle seasoned like you and your crew. I wish I could be calm like them."

"Oh, trust me young one, they is a quaking in thur boots, they just ain't showin it. No matter how many times one steps into battle, there's always fear. Me father once told me that courage is simply being scared but going into battle anyways." Elizabeth found it hard to believe. Each of the pirate birds had retreated into their own world, they seemed in complete control of their emotions. Suddenly the pirates snapped up into attention, weapons drawn. They posed perfectly still, ready to eliminate the threat that was approaching the Nocturnal. Elizabeth followed their eyes and saw two solitary figures flapping furiously to catch them.

"Hold ye arms boys and girls. It just be old man Owah and that lil lost fur ball of his. Hurry ye picaroons!" Blackbird shouted down. Owah and Wallow flapped onboard, exhausted from their plight.

Two Shot let out a loud laugh. "You landlubbers are lucky Captain said something, I had me finger on me triggers!" Two Shot screeched as he poked Wallow with a revolver.

"That must be hard," Wallow replied flatly.

"Aye, it was hard to not shoot ye!"

"No. I mean it must be hard to aim two guns with only one eye," Wallow told him as he pushed the revolver away.

"Me only may have one eye, but I gots two shots. You wanna test it magic boy?" Two Shot threatened.

"Enough," Owah silenced with one word. The two separated but kept their hateful stares on one another.

"The Formidable Five, minus one," Wallow commented as he looked around the Nocturnal for Boom, "No surprise there."

"Hey," replied an offended Yolk, "What's that supposed to mean?"

"Pirates have no loyalty; you wouldn't know what it is like to have a true comrade," Wallow fired back.

For the first time, Elizabeth noticed a slight glint of danger dancing in Pasqual's eyes that she had never seen before. He took two long, pronounced strides across the deck, nearly covering half the distance of the ship with those lanky legs. "Leave the past where it belongs. Always live for the present. Try it once and then come thank me." Elizabeth felt the force of a powerful wind nearly blow her over. When she opened her eyes, Owah stood in the middle of the conflict and he seemed to have grown about a foot taller. No words were needed. His eyes said more than his mouth ever could. Wallow gave Pasqual one last hateful stare before wandering off to be alone somewhere.

Elizabeth felt reassured by Owah's presence. His magic was strong and would be needed to defeat the Toad Queen. As long as everyone did their part, she should have her necklace back and be safely home. Would she ever return? Would Babarosa be angry with her for helping the tribe? But then why did she give her the seed? Elizabeth fumbled for it in a hidden pocket in her Sorcerer's Robe. It was pulsating with life, not cold and empty like it was before. Perhaps the closer they got to their destination, the more the magic awakened.

Babarosa hadn't exactly said what the seed would do, just that it would aid Elizabeth in getting her necklace back. That was all that mattered, right? The reason why she had ever come along this crazy journey? Otherwise she could have been safe back in her home. Her shambled home, but it was home nonetheless. Elizabeth had lost her father but still had her loving mother. She wished she had new friends back home like she had in Noir. Elizabeth was having trouble believing what Babarosa said about Owah and the tribe. Or was it all just an act by them? Why would Babarosa help Elizabeth? She was like a guardian angel to her. She surely saved her life from the Googins. Twice she had given her magic artifacts to aid her in this foreign world.

Elizabeth saw Owah studying her face. Could he read her thoughts? She was so confused, tempted to tell him of her meetings with the strange magic woman. But if she did…Babarosa would know. Babarosa saw all. Maybe the magic wouldn't work if she did tell Owah now, and then she wouldn't get her necklace back. But wasn't helping save Noir, and her world of Lumiere from dark clutches more important?

"Are you prepared for what is ahead Elizabeth?" inquired Shaman Owah as he leaned heavily on his staff. He looked exhausted as if he could barely stand. His face ached not just from the flight, but from something else. He was fatigued in his soul. Was this the price of casting magic? Would she be drained in a similar way? Elizabeth tried to think back to how it was when she had used the wand. It had taken no toll until she invoked her emotions through her heart and turned the bug spray into chain-lightning. After she had released the shot that took the horde down, she felt completely empty and drained.

"I think so…" she replied unsure of herself, too many thoughts of what was right or wrong clouding her mind.

"We are ready master!" exclaimed Wallow. "Elizabeth and I have fought and survived. We know what it will take. I will protect her, and you master, I promise." Elizabeth hoped that would play true. Wallow had definitely undergone a transformation since their last visit to the swamp. Would it be enough in a full pitched battle? Against the Toad Queen?

"Owah, just how powerful is the Toad Queen? Can your magic defeat hers?" Elizabeth questioned.

"Yes, of course he can! The Toad Queen is no match for Shaman Owah!" declared Wallow. Owah shook his head.

"Perhaps. I know not the extent of her power. And we are heading into her domain, where she will be at her strongest." *Great, that wasn't very reassuring*, thought Elizabeth.

Owah suddenly looked at her suspiciously and sniffed the air. That smell…I know that smell… wildflowers… but how? Elizabeth— "

"Get ready ye land lovers, we be approaching her lair," interrupted Blackbird, saving Elizabeth from having to reveal the truth. Owah left her to go speak with Blackbird.

Elizabeth took a look at her comrades and felt the ghost of her necklace burn on her chest. She knew her father would be with her. She stroked where the necklace should be, and she saw Bog emerge from below and he copied her, rubbing his chest as if he were wearing a necklace while he smiled his big, goofy childish grin at her. Elizabeth returned the smile. Bog was her friend, no matter what he looked like or what people said.

As the airship slowed and descended into a large clearing that was all too familiar for Elizabeth, a glint from the gold and jewels of Toad Queen's treasure room caught her eye. Among the dragon's hoard of wealth piled in a huge heap, the Toad Queen was alone, painting on makeup in front of her mirror. It seemed too good to be true. Out came the wooden dragon wings from the side of the Nocturnal as they flapped the airship with haste to the ground. What horrors lay in store? Before she could think upon it more, she saw the pirate birds climb down the rope ladder and hold on tightly as it began expanding rapidly towards the ground. Elizabeth's stomach knotted, and she had trouble controlling her bladder.

Another horrific toe-curling scream rang out as Dechirer chomped down his mighty jaw like a massive iron gate falling with haste. Feathers danced in the air and slowly floated to the ground as he swallowed another snack. Sage hobbled on one leg, his other one lost in the jaws of the angry alligator. Spear nor sword could penetrate Dechirer's thick scales. The Googin forces continued to cheer and had retaken the battlefield, the Cookapeepooh tribe driven back to the forest borderline. The Googins made no advance, simply content to let Dechirer do their dirty work. He slowly and methodically marched, in no rush, eating whatever got in his path. Vivaneau simply watched in boredom but Sage swore he saw regret in those turtle eyes when her gaze met his.

"Vivaneau! This is where you have been all these years? You serve evil now?" Sage confronted, his anger returning as he hopped a step forward. "You served good all those years with Owah and Babarosa. You made this land a better world. Why? Why do you serve the Toad Queen?"

"Those were better days and different times old friend," sighed the turtle, "Things are different now. I do what I must..." she said with a hint of sadness in her voice.

"I do not understand," he lamented with the shake of his head.

Vivaneau looked right at Whitecloud, "Yes, yes you would."

Sage looked over at Whitecloud, his granddaughter. Was that it? Did Vivaneau have a young one now?

"And why are you tied up?"

"Don't worry about her," Dechirer growled as he took a step towards Sage.

Sage could not lose another soldier. "Fall back! Flying retreat."

"Sir we can't," spoke a bird warrior, "There aren't enough of us to fly and carry the others."

"Drabbit to hell," muttered the old chieftain. "Take the rest of the force and fall back. Send a signal to Blackbird so he knows we have failed, and he is on his own…" His own words stung him deeper than any of his wounds. Victory had seemingly been at hand. But what could they do against such a powerful enemy? Worse, Vivaneau hadn't even joined in on the fun yet. Even if Owah was here, Sage doubted it would have made a difference. They were just too old. Where did they go wrong? Did the softness of peace lower their guard? Did they believe the tribe was strong enough to survive another war? An old fool he was. His brother was right. He hoped they would succeed where he had failed. Destroying the Queen, getting the rune and escaping before the enemy army realized their Queen was under attack was their last hope.

"Sir, we will never make it back. That alligator will easily catch up once we start running."

"Don't worry. He won't be chasing for a good long while." Sage grunted as he squared up towards the alligator and tested his wings. Even if he could run and retreat, Sage would still have made the same choice. He cared more about his people than himself. Although he knew deep down inside, it was more due to the fact that running just was not in his nature.

"Sir?"

"Go! Now!" he gritted through pained teeth.

"Grandfather wait!" pleaded Princess Whitecloud. Her voice almost made him reconsider. Almost.

Sage turned with fire in his eyes, "Do not question me. You go now with the rest of the tribe! Go!" he shouted with rage.

"Fall back, retreat to the village!" yelled the bird warrior while grabbing Whitecloud and dragging her away as she fought against him.

Chieftain Sage summoned the last of his strength. He had always hoped for a warrior's death. He had grown bored with the last part of his life. But to know he would die, and his people eventually be overrun, this was not the outcome he desired. A warrior wishes to die fighting, knowing he protected those he was sworn to protect. Sage could only delay the inevitable. Or perhaps they would escape, abandon their homeland and start the village elsewhere, far away from the Toad Queen's grasp. Yes, that was the best he could hope for. He had wished he gave that order…

"Time for the main course…" growled Dechirer as he stalked slowly towards Sage. Behind him the Cookapeepooh tribe made a full retreat. The Googins shouted and began rushing in. A huge snap of its gaping maw stopped them dead in their tracks. "Do not interrupt me…" warned Dechirer.

"But but, the Cookapeepooh Tribe is getting away!" argued one of the Googins. Dechirer turned to face the foolish speaker. Quicker than Sage could blink Dechirer covered the distance with incredible speed and swallowed the Googin whole. "Anyone else have something to say?" muttered Dechirer while he chewed noisily.

"Oh, hurry up Dechi," complained Vivaneau. "I want to go home." The giant alligator turned to the turtle. "Quiet, or you are next," he threatened with the flash of his teeth.

"Try me fat boy," encouraged Vivaneau as she tried to break free from the vines. "I dare you to free me. But I know you're too scared because Toadie isn't here to save you like she always does." The two behemoths stared each other down. The Googins stood dumbfounded with their mouths open, eyes darting back and forth between the alligator and turtle.

This was his best chance.

Up into the air Sage flew and he dived down head first. He channeled everything he had, his entire life of training and anger into what he knew to be the final stand of his long life. Right before he got to Dechirer he did a front flip, putting all the momentum from his flight into his warhammer swing. He chanted a quick spell and flames roared to life on the hammerhead as it smashed down and caved in Dechirer's face, destroying one of his eyes. The alligator roared in anger mixed with pain, and smashed Sage with a venomous whip of the tail that crushed the air out of him as he flew nearly twenty feet, crashing roughly into a tree. Sage left a streak of feathers as he painfully slid down the tree trunk. He gasped for air, but none would enter his lungs as he blinked, trying to stay conscious. Each time he opened his eyes the blackness filled his vision more and more until he could no longer see. His skull felt cracked, his back and ribs broken. Sage felt a smile part his lips. He had given it his all. What more could he have done? At least he smashed that alligator's face in and blinded him in one eye. Something for Dechirer to remember him by for the rest of his days. Sage said a silent prayer to his ancestors as he prepared to join them. He waited for the heavy footsteps of his predator, and his last thoughts were of his granddaughter.

The dead trees in the Swamps of Sorrow flew by in a whirl. Toma felt his heavy breaths, his wounds deeper than he cared to admit. Draccus had been a worthy opponent. He never expected a Googin to be able to fight that well. He did not have much left, but he would give it his all once they got to the Toad Queen. Ka panted with exhaustion, but she did not slow. Toma wondered if she would fight, or would she return and escape with the rest of the koalas?

His fingers grazed the edge of his axe as he began to steel himself for the battle ahead. He relished at the chance to cut the Toad Queen's head off with a mighty cleave. She had caused so much anguish, so many deaths of his people.

"Ka,"

"Yes?"

"Thank you. Thank you for taking me."

He could feel her grin even though he couldn't see it. "Like you said, it's the least I can do for you after freeing my people."

Toma shook his head. "Do not thank me, thank Elizabeth from Lumiere. She crossed the gateway with great magic to break the curse the Toad Queen held over your tribe. She is descended from the men with great beards and long-haired women with tall branches. If things go bad… please if you can… save her, take her with you and leave us. This is not her fight. She is but a child. Her ancestors were grown adults. Her heart is pure, and she does not deserve death because of our failures."

Ka said nothing and continued swinging from tree to tree. So far, they had encountered nothing. The sounds of battle were far off now that they were deep into the swamp.

There was only silence, the churning of murky bogs and the buzz of insects.

"I cannot promise that Toma," Ka spoke at last between tree swings, her powerful muscles straining with every pull.

"I understand," returned Toma, "You must return to your tribe, to your young ones."

"No… it's not that. I might not live to see Elizabeth to safety. I'm going to end the Toad Queen once and for all. Or die trying."

Chapter 27:

Threads Of Fate

Cloaked in invisibility, the Nocturnal quietly drifted towards their final destination. Even Blackbird's usual luster had fallen grim as he steered the airship to land right in the heart of the Toad Queen's lair. Still the Toad Queen seemed oblivious to their approach as she caked on more makeup and jewelry, tossing some pieces aside in disgust until she was satisfied with the right necklace or ring. Elizabeth had gone over the plan a hundred times in her head but as they began their descent, all parts of the plan slipped from her mind. Her knuckles whitened from gripping her wand so hard. The pirates were already on the ground and Owah and Wallow were perched on the rail, ready to join them as soon as the battle began. Another rope ladder waited for her and Bog. Elizabeth looked up at the big swamp creature and she took his hand, giving it a little squeeze. He looked down, broken from his trance and smiled at her. She had grown attached to the gentle giant in just the few short days since his rescue.

The show at the theatre played in Elizabeth's mind again and again. She couldn't explain it. It was like she was living in a movie she had already seen, and she knew how it was going to end. It was selfish to pray for Bog to live more so than the others, but she couldn't help the way she felt. Elizabeth hoped they all would survive. But this was war. This was real. In her foolish, naïve mind she thought she was here to take back her necklace. But the reality was, her comrades were here to kill the Toad Queen. Was her death worth the price of a necklace? But the Toad Queen had stolen it from Elizabeth and then sentenced her to death. Did that make what she was doing right? The seed pulsed warmly, and she hoped her choice to get the necklace back and help the Cookapeepooh tribe was the right one.

The journey had taken her through so many wounds, physical and emotional. The impossible had been done; here she was seconds from confronting the Toad Queen and getting her necklace back. Elizabeth closed her eyes, she summoned forth thoughts of her parents and her desire to protect her friends. The ghost imprint of her necklace burned hotter than it ever had before as she felt her magic gathering in the pit of her stomach.

THE TOAD QUEEN

As the airship came below the branches, the Swamps of Sorrow welcomed them with open arms. Dead trees sprouted like stalagmites from the Mudsepy River, which widened a good thirty feet at this point and the Queen's lair was the one place where soft grass grew on the river bank, disguising the muck. The Toad Queen was still unaware, Blackbird's cloaking magic carrying them in stealth. Elizabeth's hopes began to rise. If they all attacked at once they could overwhelm her. The Toad Queen opened a small sliding dresser door below her mirror. Out came something shining and bright that she placed over her head. The familiar letter "N" stabbed at Elizabeth's heart.

This was finally her chance to get it back. The Nocturnal glided over the Mudsepy River and her allies were counting down with their fingers from three for their launch. Huge splashes rippled the water and out shot giant vines, just like the ones Elizabeth saw her first day in Noir trying to eat the flying fish. Like octopus tentacles, they wrapped completely around the airship and began dragging it down.

Menacing laughter emanated from the Toad Queen's blubbery neck. "Dids't thou really think I would not notice thee? Thy magic is child's play, thou art a street corner illusionist compared to me," The Toad Queen mocked as she made her way from her treasure room and down the steps to the narrow path that served as the drawbridge of her castle.

375

Elizabeth gripped the rope ladder but as she looked overboard the ship was still in the middle of the river. She had no way to join in the fight. Blackbird's elite pirate force leapt into battle, flying like missiles right towards the giant frog. The Queen just stood there smiling. Yolk and Pasqual crashed into an invisible wall and Two Shot's bullets deflected harmlessly off of the force field. More vines shot out of the river, snatching up the dazed Yolk, Two Shot and Pasqual, holding them upside-down by their ankles.

"Hey! Let go of me!" yelled Yolk as he hung helplessly. Pasqual started hacking at a vine with his sword, but another shot out and wrapped his arm up. Wilmington looked like he was walking on water, dodging a pair of vines that were desperately trying to snatch him up. He looked bored as he effortlessly stayed a step ahead of his predators. Wilmington looked at his watch and kicked his heels together. He vanished, and the vines retreated under water.

Owah came flapping down from above and chanted quickly, waving each wing in a sweeping gesture. The air hummed, and Elizabeth could feel, rather than see, the invisible force field dissipate.

"Didst thou think I would forget about thee, Mr. Owl?" croaked the Toad Queen. She reached for her crown and pulled out the huge ruby in the middle and held it up with her webbed hand and twirled her wrist. The moonlight reflected the red light and Owah's wings stopped flapping. The Toad queen let out a wicked laugh as he crashed roughly into the ground.

From the shadows Wilmington emerged and hacked down the vines holding his comrades. Instantly bullets flew at the Toad Queen, preventing her from finishing off Owah.

"This is getting much too dangerous for my liking," Wilmington said, vanishing after a kicking of his heels together.

Elizabeth felt Bog swoop her in his arms. Overboard they went, and he slid her onto his back as he belly-flopped into the water. She screamed, fearing the water would sweep her up when they splashed into the river. Despite the wicked current, Bog easily swam towards dryland. It was like riding on the back of a turtle as she hopped off onto the riverbank.

Steps from closing in on the Toad Queen, Yolk and Pasqual froze when a hissing noise and the slithering of scales deafened the battlefield. Faster than lightning, a snake the size of a school bus headed right for the duo. Black scales with blood red stripes gleamed in the moonlight as it snapped viciously at its prey. Two massive fangs dripping with venom, each tooth the size of Elizabeth, flashed every time she went for a bite. Her eyes were blank and all white, yet somehow bled intelligence as she shot out her forked tongue towards the backpedaling pirates. Resting coiled up patiently as she took a pause, her massive torso ripped with powerful reptilian muscle and her terrifying presence had the entire war party awaiting her next move. Her body was so thick it looked as if no weapon could ever pierce her natural armor. The hiss of the giant snake pierced Elizabeth's eardrums in pain as she resumed her merciless onslaught.

The Queen continued laughing as she neared Owah, who was still on the ground not moving. Vines rose from the waters and tied his wings around his body and another one emerged to clamp his beak shut. "There. Thou shall not be trouble anymore," huffed the Queen as she placed the magic ruby back onto her crown. "Indra! Finish them my pretty," she coached her pet snake.

Elizabeth and Bog began creeping towards the Toad Queen. If they could take her by surprise…

"Where is that wretched hag!? I can smell her! No one is taking my Ruby!" the Toad Queen shouted, as she sniffed the air. Elizabeth felt the seed pulsating to life.

The Nocturnal strained against the vines, and the airship was slowly, but surely coming down. Blackbird was cursing up a storm, trying to break free but it wasn't going well. Elizabeth looked at the giant snake. Her wand suddenly felt fairly useless. She was depending on Owah to carry the fight; she didn't have any other magic. Indra pressed forward as the birds backed up until they were at the water's edge,

INDRA

where they quickly took flight into the air. Indra shot out into the air, nearly closing his mouth on Yolk, but a fierce thrust from Pasqual pierced through the side of the snake's mouth. Blackbird threw something from the ship and when it hit the giant snake it exploded like a firework, blinding the reptile while she writhed furiously on the ground, trying to get the powder out of her eyes. Bog saw his opening, leapt onto the snake's back and climbed up the neck, trying to choke the life out of it with his massive arms.

The pirates attacked while Indra whipped like a hurricane but could not shake off Bog. Down into the river they went out of sight.

"You again…" spoke the Toad Queen in a dark voice. "This time I will finish you off personally." Her arms raised into the air as the amphibian chanted dark words.

"Not on my watch!" Wallow yelled as he charged from the skies, wings flapping furiously as he fired a blast of bug spray. His aim was short and while laughing at his failure, the Toad Queen inhaled some of the spray and suffered a coughing fit.

"You wretch! How dare thee!" she coughed. The Toad Queen's mouth opened wide as a beam of flies erupted from it, buzzed loudly and struck Wallow square in the chest. The flies splattered into thick, green slime, his feather's and limbs all glued together, unable to move as he fell to the ground.

"Wallow!" screamed Elizabeth, as she ran over towards him.

"Worry not for him, thou art next!" the Toad Queen spoke as she raised her arms to cast. Elizabeth instinctively grabbed Wallow's staff, held it up and closed her eyes. She heard the buzz of the flies racing towards her. An electric current shocked her bones from the staff, but she held on. When Elizabeth opened her eyes, she saw the Toad Queen's face struck with disbelief.

"Impossible!" gaped the Toad Queen. "You lowly insect. Try this one on for size!" Elizabeth struggled to stand as the Toad Queen raised her skinny little arms up by her ears and began chanting. Elizabeth pulled the seed out and held it up, praying it would do something. The Toad Queen threw her arms down like a composer in an orchestra and from the toad's webbed fingers shot a ball of massive hornets. The seed did nothing as the blast sent her airborne and she felt it fly from her grasp. It felt like a thousand needles were in her stomach as she rolled over, tasting the bitterness of the swamp grass, staring up at her grandmother's necklace hanging from the bulbous neck of the Toad Queen.

The cries of battle awoken Sage from his slumber.
Had he already passed on to the next life? It made no sense;
his army should have been long gone and safe by now. The
dizzy world slowly came into focus and he saw his tribesmen
charging towards Dechirer along with a dozen or so koala
bears. Dechirer chomped down and ate tribesmen and bear
five at a time but his huge maw could only hold so much.
They overran him like a swarm of bees, and the koala claws
tore into Dechirer's other remaining eye while the
Cookapeepooh warriors wrapped ropes around Dechirer's
body.

But it only was a momentary victory as the gator
thrashed about in a whirlwind, sending everyone flying. The
Googin's charged in to cut down the scattered tribesmen.
Shields broke, and spears splintered. They were outnumbered
but his tribesmen were downing three Googins for every
Cookapeepooh that fell. It warmed Sage's heart that they
would fight until the end. They had gone against his orders to
fight. The same thing he would have done in their shoes. Sage
was proud of them, but it saddened him that they would be
killed to the last one.

Dechirer stomped around blindly, massive tail whipping tribesmen and Googin like toys, flinging them left and right. Some flew into the murky depths of the water, while others lay still after colliding into trees. Sage rose to stand, but his body was completely broken.

The Googins had completely surrounded the remaining Cookapeepooh warriors and koalas. There was no escape. Sage liked their odds though. Dechirer had lost his vision completely and Vivaneau was still tied up in vines. The giant alligator roared in pain and began swiping furiously with his tail.

"I'll get all of you!" the mighty alligator shouted.

Dechirer's next tail swipe crushed through a dozen trees and they all collapsed, including the ones with the vines that were chaining Vivaneau. The turtle shook the now limp vines off, "Ahhh, never thought I'd say this but thanks Dech—" a mouth full of gator tail cut Vivaneau's speech short.

Dechirer's swing whacked Vivaneau across her face and sent her sprawling. Up she came, faster than a turtle should be able to, and Dechirer let out a wail like a baby crying for his mother when Vivaneau clamped her powerful bite down on his tail. She whipped her neck around and used Dechirer as a club, smashing Googins by the hundreds all around the swamp, into bogs and trees. The Googins broke rank and fled back into the swamp. A quick cheer from the Cookapeepooh tribe and koalas went up before they surrounded the two behemoths. Dead silence ensued. They knew the odds were slim. But still, they would fight.

"What was that for?" cried Dechirer once she finally let go.

"You smacked me!" Vivaneau yelled as she rubbed the huge welt on her cheek. "Besides Sage was right. You're a monster. Just like that ugly toad. I'm outta here. Smell ya later, alligator."

"Wait! I can't see, take me back to the lair," begged Dechirer.

"You are a dummy, aren't you? I'M NOT GOING BACK!" the turtle screeched. "EVER."

"Oh really? Then what about little Vivi?"

Sage's heart dropped. So, it was true. He wished he could stand or at least shout but even his throat felt crushed. He had no voice.

"That's what I thought. Now take us back to the lair," snarled the blind alligator, "Otherwise when I do get back there, I'm sure the Queen will let me have Vivi as a snack. Turtles are delicious."

"Are you threatening my baby?" she asked, cold as ice.

"You threaten treason!" retorted Dechirer.

"That's not what I asked," Vivaneau growled as she took a step towards the blind gator.

"Bugger off," grumbled the gator, "I'm going to eat the rest of these little men, then go back to have turtle soup for dessert."

Vivaneau roared as she sunk her sharp claws into the ground and made a mighty leap, landing right on Dechirer's back. She snapped her huge mouth open and clamped down, hard, on Dechirer's neck. Dechirer thrashed like a beehive was on his head, trying to break the death grip she had on him. Over and over they rolled but she would not relent. Dechirer howled like a wolf at the moon and Vivaneau growled like one.

"Help her!" commanded Princess Whitecloud. The tribesmen rushed forward, jumping and throwing their weight on the alligator, for everyone he tossed off, two more took their place. His mighty strength began fading as he choked to death. Dechirer twirled like a cyclone in one last desperate attempt. All the tribesmen flew off, but Vivaneau would not relent her grip. Sage saw the eyes of a protective mother and almost felt sorry for Dechirer. But the evil alligator deserved it no less. Slowly, his little legs stopped kicking and he moved no more.

Silence filled the swamp. No one moved a muscle. Vivaneau finally looked up, breathing heavily, eyes full of venomous rage. Sage held his breath, which wasn't hard considering both of his lungs were collapsed for certain. The remaining tribesmen held their weapons up but made no advance. Vivaneau looked at them and back down at the now wooden alligator statue. Sage needed to speak, he knew he could convince his old comrade to help them. Again, he tried to stand but everything felt broken. The voice of the Cookapeepooh tribe was silent.

"Boom, Boom!" came the familiar war cry as the pirate began his run towards Vivaneau who awaited him with prepared eyes.

"Stop." Whitecloud's voice froze the ruffian in his tracks. "Vivaneau. I am Whitecloud, granddaughter of your former comrade and chieftain of the Cookapeepooh tribe. Let us help you with the rescue of your child. We are on the same side in this war. Our enemy is your enemy, and that makes us allies."

Sage felt tears of joy warm his face. He knew he could leave this world in peace. The tribe was in good hands with his granddaughter as the new leader. Tense silence hung in the air as the giant turtle looked the tribe from left to right. Still she made no movement nor spoke. Finally, Vivaneau turned around and started walking. "Come on. Follow me," she told the remaining warriors and off they dashed with a mighty war cry into the swamp to confront the Queen.

Sage felt a smile creep against his face as the familiar embrace of his father and ancestors began to pass over him. He closed his eyes and felt his soul start to ascend into the next life. Peace would finally come to his old weary bones. His people would defeat their enemy. Whitecloud would lead the next generation. Sage could pass onto the next life fulfilled. Higher and higher he went into the sky, until he swayed in the clouds.

"Grandfather? Grandfather!" came a distant voice. He felt himself falling and the clouds faded away until they were specks in the sky. Sage felt the healing touch of magic flow through his body. "Grandfather! Grandfather please don't die," begged a pleading voice, so sweet, so caring. He felt the tears running down her face dripping onto his. Who was this person? Where had his ancestors gone? He wanted to go back towards the light, towards peace with no pain. He had lived long, fought many battles. He wanted rest. But something gnawed on Sage. His mind screamed at him to not die, to wake up. He blinked his eyes open.

"Whitecloud…" Sage scratched, through his collapsed vocal box with a small smile.

"Oh Grandfather!" Whitecloud said with joy in her heart as she hugged his broken bones way too hard.

Ka swung them into the Toad Queen's lair and let go
of the vine. Toma landed on the ground, quickly assessing the
situation. Wallow was covered in slime, his feathers a sticky
mess as he lay unconscious. Owah was entangled by thick
vines while Yolk, Two Shot and Pasqual tried to avoid being
eaten by a giant snake as long as the entire Cookapeepooh
village it seemed. Bog emerged from the river, panting heavily
to catch his breath as he stared at the giant snake.

With his axe Toma made quick work of the vines
around Shaman Owah and caught him as he fell over. Owah
looked drained, the color gone from his face. No time to
wonder if he was alive, Toma ran towards the giant snake
battling the pirate birds. It snapped with speed so fast he
knew not how the birds could keep avoiding its bite of death.
Every time the snake would lunge at one, the other two
would attack and then quickly escape. They played with fire
but there was nothing but mute confidence in their eyes and
movements. As Toma pushed off the ground with a mighty
leap, he saw Elizabeth trying to stand up. A powerful chop
dug into the side of the snake, but it thrashed violently,
sending Toma sailing into the air, leaving his axe lodged in its
thick scales.

He hit the ground hard but came up armed with the spear he took from Draccus, ready to sink into the reptile's flesh but Indra seemed to have not even felt his axe as she continued to try and eat her other opponents. A flash of light caught his eyes. Ka swung from some vines right towards the Toad Queen, the koala's razor-sharp claws descending on her targets bulbous neck. The frog shrieked and instantly the giant snake whipped around. It happened before he could even blink. One second, Indra was fighting by the river and in the span of half a heartbeat huge fangs punctured right through Ka, green venom dripping into her body as she slid from the fangs. "Ka!" Toma yelled, as he aimed a throw for the giant snake. Yolk and Pasqual came down hard, attacking violently, while Two Shot fired his revolvers over and over. Instantly Indra was upon them, snapping at the elusive birds who somehow were able to always stay an inch away from being eaten. They moved as a singular unit, as if their minds were linked.

With Indra distracted, Bog bull-rushed towards the Toad Queen. The ground shook from his mighty steps. She thrust her webbed palm out at Bog and spears of deadwood pierced him over and over again, but the Swamp Yeti would not go down. At least a dozen tree branches had penetrated his rock-solid exterior and his breaths labored heavily as he kept moving forward. Toma raised his spear, waiting for the perfect time to pierce the archenemy of his people while running to Ka's side. The window of opportunity opened, and he felt his breath go still and arm rock back, but Bog stumbled right into view, blocking his clear shot at the Toad Queen.

Elizabeth rose from her grave and hobbled towards the Toad Queen. She flicked her wand out and shot a spray, which the Queen avoided but that distraction allowed Bog to crush her with a bear hug. Toma couldn't help but laugh at the noise the arrogant frog was making. She was not used to suffering, only making others suffer. Bog was crushing the life out of her. His laughter was short lived when he made it over to Ka.

"Hang tight! We're going to get you onto Blackbird's ship. You're going to make it," Toma reassured, as he removed his shirt to tie down the wounds.

"Promise me… promise you'll look after Luna and Selene," Ka sniffed, the color draining fast from her face.

"Don't say that Ka!" Toma pleaded as he started sucking the venom out from her bite. Ka cracked a little laugh, "Oh my, definitely don't tell the princess about this…" Toma ignored her and set to the task of syphoning and spitting the venom out. He felt his mouth burn and the world began spinning.

"Just stop it you fool; I'm a goner. Hold me close for my last breath. And promise me… promise Toma…" Toma shook the koala bear over and over, "Ka! Ka!" He buried his face into her body to hide his tears.

"Indra!" the Toad Queen managed to huff out, her fat head ballooned up even more from being squeezed. Quickly, Toma shot to his feet, spear ready for vengeance, focused on the giant reptile. Anticipating the snake to strike, he poised to throw. But Indra was just too quick. His eyes could not even detect the speed of her movement. One second she was snapping at Blackbird's crew, the next second Indra had a fang through Bog.

"Dagnabit Wil!" Elizabeth heard Blackbird curse. "Where be that dern thing!? We had 'em all ready before we be taking off! Wil! Where ye be?!"

"Right where you told me to be," came a smug voice from the helm. Wilmington puffed on his pipe while steering the wheel with his feet. He lounged comfortably in a chair with his hands behind his head, looking up into the stars, unaffected by the chaos below. The vines pulled the

Nocturnal closer to a watery grave and Wilmington just inhaled another puff.

"Why would ye be still at the helm at a time like this!" Blackbird yelled.

"What? You told me to hold the bloody helm, so that's what I'm doing."

"But we be needin' ya, we is goin' down," Blackbird pleaded.

"Why didn't you just say so?" Wilmington asked with a sigh.

"Do I really gots to be sayin' so in this situation?"

"Be right there…"

Elizabeth lay there as Bog ate spear after spear of deadwood. Every time he nearly had her in his powerful grasp, The Toad Queen escaped and stuck another spear in him. She saw Toma running over to the fallen koala bear and saw the hopeless struggle with the three pirate birds and Indra. They were only distracting and holding the snake off until someone else could defeat the queen. Elizabeth had to do something.

Elizabeth saw that Wilmington had not moved an inch while Blackbird continued desperately to keep the airship from going under. She saw Owah struggling to breathe, much less fight. There was no more help coming. Elizabeth summoned her courage and fought through the pain as she stood. With a scream like a wild animal, she lunged towards the Toad Queen and let loose her wand. The oversized frog ducked and ran, cursing at Elizabeth about the taste and smell but to her demise found herself in Bog's bone crushing hug. Elizabeth saw the frog's eyes grow bigger and bigger as she squealed in pain.

"Indra!" the Toad Queen managed to gasp, her face nearly blue. Elizabeth heard the sound, but only saw a flash of light before her eyes. Victory was seconds away until Indra had a giant fang pierced through Bog. Bog's face was unreadable as he let go of the Toad Queen who wobbled over towards her castle. Toma and the three pirates hacked, shot and stabbed the giant snake until it released the Swamp Yeti who fell to his knees, his hand over the huge puncture in his chest.

Elizabeth hobbled over to Bog as he laid on the ground, each breath sounded like his lungs were filling with water. He looked up at her with a small smile and held a massive hand out; her hand was lost in its size. Elizabeth felt the ghost print of her necklace burn hotter than it ever had before. Thankfully she had remembered to fill her father's canteen before she came back to Noir. Elizabeth pulled out the glass vial full of bubbling red froth, pulled the cork off and poured some directly into his punctured wound. It sizzled like hot oil in a frying pan, and Bog moaned in pain as it disinfected the deadly poison of the snake bite. Then she poured the rest into his mouth, causing him to choke a little as she emptied it down his throat. Immediately life returned back into his eyes.

The Toad Queen hobbled up the bridge, wheezing for air as if she had never run a lap in her life. When the Toad Queen turned to look back with eyes wide with worry, Elizabeth caught the sight of the necklace and her emotions boiled. She thought about her father. Her mother. She surveyed the battlefield and saw Wallow and Owah, barely alive. Toma was wounded severely in several places. Elizabeth closed her eyes and she saw the Cookapeepooh warriors. She remembered Toma's men who gave their lives protecting her, and the rest of the army out there battling the Googins, so they could defeat the Toad Queen.

Elizabeth felt all of their life forces began to gather in the air around her. She could feel the presence of Owah, Wallow, Sage, Whitecloud and hundreds of others she did not recognize. They gave her their energy and she let her heart flow out into the universe.

Elizabeth opened her eyes and felt incredible power within her. She wanted to save them all. She needed to. Not just her mother but the inhabitants here in Noir as well.

Directing her focus on the cause of all these deaths, the Toad Queen, energy began gathering at her fingertips and surged through her body. Elizabeth felt a radiating force enclose her, as small rocks and branches on the ground around her began to levitate. The Toad Queen reached a webbed hand towards Elizabeth and began to cast a spell. Elizabeth countered and shot her arm out, the flow of magical energy Elizabeth directed smashed violently against the dark beam of energy the Toad Queen fired from her palm. The two spellcasters stood locked in battle, Elizabeth's beam of light versus a beam of darkness.

Lightning-like pain shot through her outstretched arm, and into her heart. Elizabeth felt the sorrow and anger of the Toad Queen's heart, but she held her arm strong, pushing her magic of love against the magic of hate. Back and forth they pushed, one side trying to conquer the other.

Elizabeth took a step forward and with her free hand, activated her wand. It sprayed like the breath of a dragon. The Toad Queen tried to hop away but it engulfed her. She screamed and choked when the cloud vaporized into the air; the Toad Queen broke out in hideous rashes and pimples all over her face. She moved faster than she looked capable of as she went crashing through her treasure room. The shriek she gave when she looked into her mirror was louder than all the ones before. The giant welts began melting over her face and oozed into her eyes. "You little wretch! I'll kill you for what you have done!" screeched the Toad Queen, as she started blindly casting swamp magic everywhere. Sticky slime, fireflies, hornets and deadwood spears shot in all directions, some even hitting Indra.

The ground rumbled like an earthquake and a familiar war cry filled the air. The remnants of the Googin army stumbled in being chased by a giant snapping turtle, followed by a hundred or so tribesmen and two dozen koalas. "Attack that snake lasses!" shouted Blackbird, "I got ye cover." Blackbird threw a small, round object. It exploded on impact: a direct hit on the snake who slowed down considerably.

In charged the tribesmen and spears pierced Indra by the dozens. Yolk jumped on top of the snake while Two Shot started firing wildly, laughing like a wild maniac. Shots hit Googin and ally alike.

"Watch ye fire! Ye be shootin' friend o' foe?" Blackbird yelled out.

Two Shot lifted up his eye patch, "Guess I should be using both me eyes…" he said in a normal voice that sounded nothing like his usual self. With a mighty thrash Indra flung Yolk off and scattered the tribesmen. Yolk plopped hard onto Vivaneau's back. "Ouch. Get off, you're too heavy man!" she complained as she bucked like a bronco, trying to eject him. Yolk held on like a bull rider as the giant turtle danced around the swamp, cursing at Yolk while he laughed and yelled with glee.

Indra began eating the scattered warriors one by one. The slow effect from Blackbird's attack had worn off. Yolk continued hanging on for dear life while Princess Whitecloud met Indra head on. Her movements were swift, loud smacks from her staff told her she was scoring hits. But they did nothing to the massive snake other than anger it. Whitecloud's luck ran out. She stood inside the gaping maw of the snake, her staff implanted into the bottom of its mouth, up to the roof. The wooden staff began to bend and splinter. It snapped loudly in half as Indra bit down. Feathers filled the air but Whitecloud had managed to escape. She lay wounded on the ground as a giant forked tongue flickered out and teased its prey.

Indra opened her mouth to have her next meal. Whitecloud closed her eyes and prepared to face death. "This is your last warning! Get off or else!" Vivaneau yelled as Yolk continued to play his game while the fate of Noir hung in the air. A loud crunch popped Whitecloud's eyes open. The giant turtle had crushed the deadly snake's skull and it began transforming back into wood.

Vivaneau stopped as she took notice. Combat ceased, and silence filled the air. "Yeahhh! We did it!" Yolk shouted triumphantly, raising his arms in the air and pumping his fists. "Get. Off. Now," Vivaneau threatened in a scary voice. She crouched low and rocked her body, sending Yolk flying through the air right towards the Toad Queen.

The Toad Queen stumbled down the stairs and back out to her drawbridge while frantically waving her arms, her webbed hands flopped sloppily, as she tried to execute a spell in desperation. Elizabeth felt the familiar tingle, and the air vibrated with a hum as the force field went back up. Yolk crashed into the invisible wall that surrounded the moat of the castle and slumped down but popped right back up to his feet. Blasts from the Nocturnal, spears of the tribesmen and bullets from Two Shots revolvers did nothing. Yolk pounded fiercely against the invisible wall futilely with his massive fists.

"Boom!" came the familiar shout. Explosions rocked the force field, but it did not break. Yolk started grabbing Googins and folding them into snowballs. He mightily hurled one after another but the Googins kept bouncing off the Toad Queen's magic wall. Frustrated, Yolk backed up a few steps. He compacted his next Googin snowball even tighter as he charged forward and let the Googin fly. It rebounded off the wall so far, Boom had to duck to avoid getting crushed.

"Further than the last one, huh?" Yolk laughed. "Boom, boom!" was the response from a laughing Boom. Pasqual continued to effortlessly make shish kabob after shish kabob skewers with the Googins that fell on his sword.

Back in her treasure room, the Toad Queen tore through her jewelry boxes and equipped more rings, earrings and necklaces. Suddenly she looked back in panicked fear. "Impossible!" the Toad Queen blubbered out in disbelief. Elizabeth felt the air sizzle and the force field begin to dissipate. She turned to follow the Toad Queen's gaze. Wallow struggled to stand as he held Owah's staff high in the air. Once the magic wall had been dispelled, Wallow collapsed, the strain of the magic too much for his weakened state.

The Toad Queen clumsily tripped over the messy hoard of loot and went rolling down the stairs. Dazed, and struggling to stand, she heard the quick rush of feet with a ferocious roar. Bog beat his chest like a gorilla as he crashed into the Toad Queen, tackling her into the quicksand like quagmire that flowed around the castle.

"Unhand me you wretched creature! You'll kill us both! Stop at once!" demanded the Toad Queen, as Bog wrapped her tightly in his arms while they sank deeper and deeper into the liquid quicksand.

Elizabeth knew Bog could survive the murky waters of the swamp, but she needed her necklace. And the rune. "Toma!" she shouted, running towards the edge of the quagmire.

"Already on it!" A spear whistled past her ear and struck the crown with a perfect throw. Up into the air went the spinning crown, the giant ruby glinting in the moonlight every time the crown completed a rotation. Sprinting to follow his spear, Toma leapt without hesitation onto Bog's shoulders and snatched the spinning crown just as it hit the murky water. As he turned to leap back to safety, a sloppy fat wet tongue wrapped around his ankle. "Thurrr comin withhh usss!" slurred the Toad Queen. Toma kicked fiercely but the Toad Queen's saliva was green, just like the slime that she used on Wallow. Toma's foot was glued to her tongue.

"Toma!" Wallow shouted, somehow making his way towards Toma despite his severe injuries. "Thurrr not goin' thhhany where!" she said the best she could with her tongue wrapped around Toma's ankle. "Thhho one dusss thhhis to me! Thhhur all going to pay! Thhhur going—" the free foot of Toma smashed into the frog's open mouth as she and Bog were sucked under. The quagmire was up to his knees when he tossed the crown to Wallow. "Take it brother, complete our quest." He gave one last nod to Elizabeth and the mucky quicksand swallowed him whole.

"Come on Boggy. Come up, just like you did last time," Elizabeth whispered, while taking a look at the crown. The red ruby shined between two diamonds. The thick surface of the quagmire began to stir and out popped the

Swamp Yeti with Toma in one hand and her necklace in the other!

"Yes! Bog! Let's get out of here," Elizabeth cheered, limping towards the lip of the murky moat.

"Swamp Yeti, I guess you're not so bad," smiled Toma as he slapped Bog on the back. Owah leaned heavily on his staff as he hobbled over towards them. Indra laid defeated in the river, transformed back into a log the size of a redwood tree trunk. The rest of the tribe came over, cheering as Bog swam them over towards the shore. They began cheering Toma's name, but he silenced them with the rise of his hand. "Yeti, Yeti!" he started, and the crowd took to it. Soon the entire army was shouting Yeti, bringing a big smile to Bog's face. Owah put his oversized wing over Wallow's shoulder. "You did well. I am proud of you. So is your father." To Elizabeth's surprise Wallow didn't cry, he simply nodded with a stone face. "Thank you master. I still have much to learn."

"Wise words," said Owah, "You will in due time, due time."

Thick vines shot out of the murky depths and wrapped around Bog. He threw his arms up just in time and the vines missed Toma. Bog thrashed and tried to move but could not budge an inch. As he began sinking he held up Toma and the necklace as high as he could. "Sir!" shouted

Wallow as he took flight, covering the short distance and grabbing the necklace and Toma. He strained with the heavier warrior's weight, but managed to drop him on the muddy ground, along with the necklace, before flying back for Bog. Wallow grabbed hold of both Bog's wrists, but his grip couldn't even come close to wrapping his fingers around them. He then tried grabbing his fingers and Wallow pulled with all his might. Everyone watched in horror as Bog continued to sink, further and further. Wallow screamed and strained loud enough to wake the dead, but it was no use.

Elizabeth stared helplessly into Bog's eyes, as even more vines wrapped around him. The journey was supposed to be over. They were so close to going home. Bog stared back into her eyes as if to say he was going to be alright. But Elizabeth knew he wouldn't be. This was goodbye. Bog's eyes disappeared forever under the murky water.

Wallow pulled and pulled, but Bog's fingers slipped into the quicksand of the quagmire. The bubbles he made slowly faded and the quagmire returned to its stagnant state, as if nothing had ever disturbed it.

"Nooo!" wailed Wallow as he floated above. "Come back…" he whispered. Head down, he flapped his wings back to shore in defeat. Minutes passed. All watched in hopes that Bog would emerge. Minutes turned to ten minutes and Owah shook his head. All the tribesmen bowed their heads

402

and the whole swamp was silent. Victory felt empty for Elizabeth.

Elizabeth fell to her knees, holding her necklace. Was it really worth it? Not the price of her friends, not at the cost of so many lives. But she couldn't think that way. They died for the rune Owah now held. Maybe Babarosa was right. Look at what it had cost them. But it was needed to seal the gateway and keep both worlds safe from the Queen of Mist. The gateway she had opened. Since coming to Noir, since begging for that stupid mirror, Elizabeth had done nothing but ruin lives.

The vines holding the Nocturnal turned hard and crumbled into dust. "Put the wounded on me ship. We need to get them back to the village," Blackbird ordered as he landed roughly on the riverbank. Elizabeth was still stunned. It was over. She had lived. But Bog...

"I'm sorry Elizabeth, sorry I couldn't save him..." trailed Wallow, as he came to sit next to her.

"It's not your fault Wallow. You tried your best. None of us could have saved him. And you got the rune and rescued Toma," Elizabeth said, but her words felt as empty as her heart.

"I failed, I failed to protect you and everyone else. I am not worthy of Master Owah's praise," Wallow conceded, as he picked at the ground with his staff.

"You attacked the Toad Queen head on while I stood there paralyzed with fear and doubt. You retrieved the rune, the entire point of the mission and everyone's sacrifice. That's pretty huge!" encouraged Elizabeth, but Wallow still hung his head in shame. Elizabeth saw a huge turtle nudging her face against a wooden statue of a smaller turtle that was nearly identical.

"Vivi…I was hoping the spell would be broken once that wretched toad died. I'm sorry baby," Vivaneau lamented with a tear. Some of the tribesmen came over and rubbed her shell, others bowed to the statue of her child.

"It's been a while old friend," spoke Owah, as he made his way towards Vivaneau.

"Owah? You're still alive? Man, you must be at least… ten thousand by now?" Vivaneau joked, but her smile withered quickly when she looked back at her child, frozen forever as a piece of wood.

"Young enough still to save your child," he muttered as he raised his wings to the air and flapped a gentle breeze. The old, dead swamp wood began fleshing into a turtle. The tribesmen gasped their amazement as a baby snap turtle came to life, springing into her mother's arms.

"Momma!" she cried, as Vivaneau scooped her up and held her close, "Don't worry child we're safe now.

Thanks to your uncle Owah, say hi," Vivaneau told her baby as she turned to face her old companion.

"Does this mean we get to leave this stinky swamp?" Vivi wondered.

Her mother laughed so hard she had to close her eyes, "Yes dear one. Home, back to the rivers and lakes where we belong."

"Yay! Thank you uncle Owah, you're the best!" cheered little Vivi.

They began the task of loading the wounded onto Blackbird's airship. Elizabeth met some of the koala bears, learning that they were the wombat- mounts for the Googins. Their gratitude warmed her momentarily but once she was alone, she kept staring at the stagnant lake, looking for Bog. Elizabeth waited at the edge, not wanting to leave. Just like at her father's funeral.

"Alright ye scallywags! Follow me back to the village. We be mournin' for the dead then, for now it's time we be goin'," Blackbird commanded. "Get up here old man Owah, ye can barely walk, and you too young lad, I seen you take some blasts from old Toadie there." Elizabeth felt everyone begin to move but she could not. Finally, she put her necklace on. Its warmth replaced the ghost touch that had burned in its absence. Immediately she felt the soul, the presence of her father. Getting the necklace back seemed like it would make her world great again. It had done far from it.

Going back into Noir at first had been about her necklace. Her only link to her father and her old life. It was what drove her to continue her quest in Noir. But she had learned that the present, and people were more important than the past and ghosts. Her father lived on through her, not through a piece of jewelry. Yes, pictures and items are nice to remember people by, but over the last few days she realized that even though the necklace was gone, he was still in her heart. Elizabeth had decided she would sell it and give the money to her mother. It was the right thing to do.

Where had she gone wrong? Was it her choice to accept Babarosa's help? But if she didn't she never would have escaped the Googins. Was Babarosa wrong? The Cookapeepooh tribe seemed to be fighting for the right reasons. Besides, the seed Babarosa gave her had done nothing in the final fight. Her eyes searched for it, but it must have rolled away, buried in the battle.

"Elizabeth! You too you little Sorceress, git on board. Let's all hear it for our hero from another world!" Blackbird demanded as she walked in embarrassment with her head down, knowing she had not done much. The deep cheers of the Cookapeepooh tribe sounded like a pack of gorillas.

Owah handed the rune up to Wallow, who leaned over the rail of the ship and grabbed the massive red ruby, "Put this somewhere safe. We are still in enemy territory." He turned and faced Elizabeth with a smile as Wallow began heading towards the Captain's Quarters. Owah sniffed the air and his smile turned quickly into a frown. With furrowed eyebrows he stared back towards the Toad Queen's throne. Elizabeth followed his eyes and noticed the swampy ground was erupting muck and dirt near where the seed had fallen.

The little volcano grew and grew until the earth began to shake. Out burst the head of a giant Venus Fly Trap, sending mud flying everywhere. It had nothing on its face, save its gaping maw with sharp teeth. Up it shot like a rocket into the sky. When it stood full height, it towered high above them, at least fifty feet in the air.

Owah took flight towards it and flapped a huge wing. Waves of air sliced at the giant plant, but it dropped to the ground, completely flat, avoiding the magical attack. It flicked its tongue out towards the Nocturnal and started sidewinding towards the ship. With a waving motion, the Venus Fly Trap threw its head forward and its thin, stem body followed just like a snake. It slithered between the flying spears of the Cookapeepooh warriors but Owah was ready with a second attack. However, it took Owah by surprise when it burrowed underground and went under the ship. It coiled up on the other side, towering over the tall masts of the Nocturnal. Its tongue flicking out again as it eyed its prey.

"Wallow look out!" Elizabeth warned in desperation, but it was too late. The Venus Fly Trap dived like a hawk and Wallow turned as it opened its giant maw and swallowed him whole. Out it spit Wallow, sending him somersaulting continuously on the hardwood deck until he crashed into a stack of crates, drenched in saliva, the ruby missing from his possession. The Venus Fly Trap recoiled instantly and disappeared back to where it came from in a heartbeat. Tribesmen dug furiously, led by a dazed Wallow, but after digging several feet there was no sign of the thieving plant. Stunned silence sank in.

Owah stepped forward to investigate and stopped short of the hole they had dug, "That smell...it's her again. This is Barbarossa's magic...but how could she know?"

Pasqual and his crew watched with disinterest as the Cookapeepooh tribe mourned the loss of the rune. They couldn't care less. They were pirates. To them, it didn't matter who ruled and was in power. They were always free because pirates didn't live by the rules of society. They went where the winds took them. And for the first time in hundreds of years, Pasqual was finally going to sail those winds.

"Listen mates," Pasqual whispered to the others as Boom, Yolk, Wilmington and Two Shot leaned in for a closer listen, "The biggest booty in Noir is within our grasps."

"Yeah you're right! I can see Yolk's butt!" laughed Two Shot.

"Silence you idiot. Booty. Treasure! You fool," Pasqual corrected sharply while taking a quick glance around to be sure no one was listening.

"No more following this overgrown bat. He has lost his mind and brought us too close to death, too many times! As soon as we get the chance, we will return for our treasure. Time to cash in and sail the moons on our own boys."

All eyes followed Pasqual's greedy gaze to the quagmire, where the Toad Queen had met her end. A tiny bubble popped on the surface.

Chapter 28:

Faded Hope

There were no celebrations, just mourning the loss of the dead and the first rune. The very thing they had given their lives for and Elizabeth was responsible for it falling into enemy hands. The wounded lay in the huts, organized chaos was in full swing as tribesmen and women ran back and forth, hauling water, bandages and healing concoctions made from the herbs of the forest.

"Grandfather, stop. It's not her fault. Elizabeth did what she thought was best at the time, you cannot fault her for that," argued the Princess as she stood by Elizabeth who had nothing to say. What could she? She was as bad as their enemy now. Best she leave and never return.

"Why did you just not tell us?" asked Owah, for the tenth time. Elizabeth knew she had to finally answer. She had been duped by Babarosa. Fell right into her trap. How stupid could she be? It seemed so obvious now. She was mad at herself for not trusting her instincts. She knew Owah and the

411

Cookapeepooh tribe to be good. She had been deceitful before, so now all she could be was honest.

"The truth is… I am no hero, no Sorcerer or warrior. I only wanted to get my necklace back," she spoke as she held the golden letter "N" in her hand. "I am just a selfish person who didn't care about you at all. I just took every precaution to ensure I would get it back. Babarosa told me to not tell anyone or she would not help me. She said she understood how important my necklace was. I realize now it's nowhere near as important as saving Noir and the lives of those we love." Elizabeth finally looked up and addressed the elders. "I can't do this anymore. There's been too much death. I am sorry I failed you and betrayed you. My mother and I are struggling enough at home; she needs me there. I am not who you think I am; a can of bug spray does not make me a Wizard. I am so sorry, I am not the hero you need."

"Good riddance you traitor! This is why we do not rely on outsiders," scratched Sage, his voice barely working.

"Grandfather! Quiet!" ordered Whitecloud and the stare she shot him cut him harder than any of his battle wounds.

Owah sighed heavily as he leaned on his staff, "You are what you believe you are. If you do not believe you can, we cannot force you." Owah walked over and put his grandfatherly wing over her, just like he had done when they first met. "I will miss you sorely Elizabeth. You have great power and even more potential. All can be forgiven. Babarosa is a deceitful one. She can twist and manipulate like no other. I will regain the first rune of Noir from Babarosa as we search for the second. Should you decide to return, you are welcome here," he declared, as he turned to Sage who was about to object but a hard whack from his granddaughter silenced him quickly.

Blackbird stepped in and put a feathered hand on her shoulder. "Ye may not think ye a warrior or a wizard, but without ye we be losin' the battle. It was ye who brought us the cannon, the cheese to save our koala bear friends. Lot o' creatures be indebted to ye, young lass," Blackbird concluded with the wave of his hat and a low bow. Elizabeth remembered then and she reached into her robe and handed him his lucky wooden nickel. Blackbird declined with the shake of his head. "Nay, I want ye to have it. To remember how brave ye was and how ye helped me tribe survive and win. When ye is ready, I shall give ye a ride to the gateway," he offered, with that pirate smile of his. She would miss Blackbird.

"Take her now and close the door for good on your way out," huffed Sage as he limped off in anger, leaning heavily on two canes. Whitecloud came up and gave Elizabeth a sincere embrace while she whispered into her ear,

"Don't listen to Grandfather, he's the only one that feels that way. I wish you didn't have to go…you're a great person and I know we would be best friends. Here," Whitecloud said, and she removed her necklace made of animal teeth and placed it on Elizabeth. "Something to remember me by. You're a huge inspiration to me. Thank you for fighting for my people."

"Thank you…I'm sorry again," was all Elizabeth could muster as she hugged her back. She signaled to Blackbird that she needed a minute as she walked over to Wallow, who was staring blankly into a fire. It was the same look he had the night on the airship. Except this time, she was the cause. Her betrayal of the tribe, trusting in his master's nemesis and losing the rune that they had fought so hard to gain.

"Wallow…I'm sorry. Sorry, I let you down."

"No. No, that's not why I'm over here. I let him die, just like my parents. If only I had trained harder, become stronger, I could have cast some spell or done something different. Bog was our friend. He died for my people and yet, here still I stand. Regret fills my heart. I cannot go on. I will tell Owah tonight that I am no longer his apprentice. I am not worthy. Farewell Elizabeth," he spoke as he walked off.

"Wallow, Wallow! Wait!" she shouted as she ran after him, "You can't do that. Your tribe needs you."

"No, they need someone strong. Someone worthy. Please leave me be." And with a flap into the air, Wallow disappeared into the tree houses.

Chapter 29:

Monday Blues

The weight of her necklace felt heavier than usual as Elizabeth fought her way through the overcrowded hall. Everything felt numb and bleak, as if a part of her had been taken. She thought she would be happy to be gone from Noir and its dark tragedies but the more she lived in her world, the more Elizabeth kept seeing people and places that reminded her of the magic land beyond her mirror. Normal life… just seemed so "normal". She was almost killed several times, watched lives expire before her eyes, lost friends and comrades she had loved and failed to protect.

So then, why miss such a place? Was it because what Elizabeth experienced there made her feel more alive than anything here? Laughter rang out in the hall, but she felt no joy. She was mute and empty. Not even the improvements at home lifted her spirit. Why was that? She should have been elevated, overjoyed. Her mother's fortunes had finally turned but it brought her no happiness.

When she had returned after bidding her farewells to Blackbird and the crew and crossed back through the quicksilver gateway for the last time, her mother had been waiting for her. The mist had seeped through her room and out into the hallway. When Susan demanded to know what was going on, Elizabeth didn't know how else to explain so she told her mother the truth. Susan was stunned but when Elizabeth pulled out Blackbird's wooden nickel and placed the gold coin into her mother's hand, she either had to believe her daughter or think she was a thief. For some reason Elizabeth was sure that Blackbird knew it would turn to gold. He was like the uncle she never had.

The house was now fully furnished and the fridge completely full of fresh fruit and vegetables, milk, eggs, orange juice and just about anything else they would need to live a happy life. After Elizabeth's "incident" with Delly, it had been discovered Arnold was stealing from the restaurant for years. It broke Delly's heart but thanks to Elizabeth, the truth was revealed. Now Susan was the manager, making enough so they could actually save up and move to a better neighborhood eventually.

Elizabeth offered up the necklace and told her mom they could sell it and move now. Her mom insisted Elizabeth keep the family heirloom and deep down inside, Elizabeth was glad. She told Elizabeth the gold coin would go into

Elizabeth's savings for college and her mother wouldn't touch a dime, which she and Elizabeth argued about. She insisted her mother use it for their lives, that it had been a gift from Blackbird. In the end they decided to split it, half to her account and half for saving to move. To celebrate they had a wonderful dinner that night and watched another movie that her mother fell asleep to. However, Elizabeth couldn't sleep. She felt wide awake the entire night. When she had gotten ready in front of the mirror this morning, the runes etched in the mirror frame were dead; no life shined from them and when she traced her fingers over the engravings, she wished they still glowed.

Elizabeth thought when she woke up today things would be better, be different. But as she made her way towards her first period class it was only getting worse. Groups of different cliques chatted excitedly about nothing important. After her time in Noir, her perspective on life changed. What mattered before was very different from what mattered now. Someone bumped into her shoulder harshly, but Elizabeth just slid back into the blob of locomotion as if it never happened. The one thing she could count on was that she wasn't going to be friends with the mean trio anymore. What could they do to her? After what she went through in Noir, the pain they would try to inflict would be nothing. It was finally time to stand up for herself, and the other people they picked on.

Elizabeth passed her first period class door and headed for the bathroom where the girls always hung out before class. Elizabeth shoved the door open prepared for confrontation.

"Lizabeth!" yelled Raquel as she vainly brushed her long hair. It made Elizabeth want to throw the brush in the trash. Tanya just looked at her, ignoring Elizabeth like she was too cool, and went back to admiring her long fingernails the mirror. Elizabeth wanted all three of them to be here for this. "Where's Nora?" she asked harshly. The change in her tone seemed to go unnoticed by Raquel and Tanya.

"You didn't hear?" Raquel questioned, with the stroke of her brush. "She totally got infected with Pumpkin Pox. She has like some disease or something."

"Yeah, totally," laughed Tanya, as she dangled her long fingers in delight. "She's definitely not in the crew anymore."

"Which is why, we want you to take her spot!" exclaimed Raquel, with a squeal of delight.

"So where's Nora then? I didn't see her," she asked, ignoring the invitation.

"Who knows? Crying off in the corner somewhere with the rest of the losers?" Raquel proclaimed, without a care for Nora's wellbeing.

Elizabeth stormed out without another word. "Hey, wait! Where you going, Lizabeth?" Elizabeth turned as she was halfway out the door. "It's E-Liz-A-Beth. E. The letter E. Do you know your alphabet or does remembering how to count to ten take up all of your brain capacity?" The last thing Elizabeth saw before she walked out was Raquel's jaw nearly on the floor as her gum rolled off her tongue.

Ms. Thorn was in an unusually good mood this morning. Elizabeth hardly paid attention and couldn't remember the name of the story they were reviewing, but it had something to do with someone overcoming a group of people who had wronged her. Elizabeth the betrayer. That's probably what the Cookapeepooh tribe called her. Owah and the elders might be able to forgive her, but what about all those who lost their family and friends in the battle? For nothing? Could Owah really recover the rune? She knew nothing about the extent of Babarosa's power, but it seemed as though Owah was not as powerful as she thought. Both times he had battled another magic user he hadn't fared too well. Would he be able to defeat Babarosa?

"Elizabeth?" Ms. Thorn asked for what must have been the third or fourth time. She was staring at Elizabeth, and the rest of the class had all eyes on her.

"Oh sorry…what was that?"

"Never mind that my dear, it's obvious you were not listening. Are you okay? Why don't you see me after class?" she reprimanded. Snickers broke out in the class and Elizabeth snapped a mean stare at some kids she didn't know. That shut them up quickly, but one met her challenge. Elizabeth looked to where Nora's usual seat was, and it felt weird not seeing her mischievously evil smile. The girl with the pale skin and dark eyes kept staring at her. Maybe she had made a new enemy? If this dark eyed girl wanted trouble, she was barking up the right tree. Elizabeth didn't know why she was so angry. And she wouldn't have any magical powers in this world. She had never gotten into a fight. So why was she acting as if she could defend herself? The girl continued to stare through her soul. It gave Elizabeth the same creeps she felt when she saw the Queen of Mist.

The bell rang at last. Still five more classes to go through. Elizabeth didn't know how she would even get through the day. She walked up to Ms. Thorn's desk to get it over with.

"How's everything at home child?"

"It's fine, better actually."

"Oh? How so? Tell Ms. Thorn," referring to herself in the third person like she normally did. Just like Babarosa always did. But Elizabeth knew she couldn't hold something against Ms. Thorn. She hadn't been the one to manipulate her and use her. Elizabeth wished she could get Babarosa back somehow. And most importantly, get the rune back for the Cookapeepooh tribe.

"My mother got promoted at work." She left out the embarrassing details about how now they could finally eat and hire an exterminator.

"That's good to hear, Ms. Thorn is glad for you and your mother. You deserve it after what you have been through."

"Thank you." Elizabeth didn't know what else to say. She felt awkward; what else could she say to someone she hardly knew? Ms. Thorn stood up from her chair. "Remember if you need anything, just ask me. Ms. Thorn just wants what is best for Elizabeth." Heard that before. It made her trust Ms. Thorn even less. "Be careful out there Elizabeth. It can be an ugly world."

Lunch was the usual. The jocks with jocks, the goths with the goths, and the nerds with the nerds. She slid her tray across the metal poles of the lunch line and received her last dollop of slop. As Elizabeth carried her tray her eyes searched for Raquel and Tanya, but they were nowhere to be found.

Instead she slid down next to a solitary figure eating by himself. "Hey Wally, what's up?" He turned quickly, startled and dropped his spoon on the ground, and looked up at Elizabeth in embarrassment, his glasses drooping over his nose, too loose for his skinny head. "Here. Take mine," Elizabeth said as she handed him her spoon. "Just take it, trust me I'm not going to eat…"

"Uh thanks, aren't you going to sit with your friends?"

"No. They aren't my friends, they never were. I kind of got stuck with the wrong crowd. And I was too scared to speak up. But we're friends, right? Thanks again for all the bug spray. I have the big canister at home to give back to Joe."

"You're welcome," he said sadly, swishing around the goop in his trey.

"What's wrong?"

"Joe… Joe was in an accident over the weekend. I'm surprised you didn't hear; it's been all over social media."

"No, I didn't, I was… out of town… kind of."

"He was taking a group of kids from the church he's a part of to Lakeview Park for a picnic. The bridge collapsed as they were crossing it."

"Oh, my goodness, is he okay? And the kids?" she asked fearfully.

"All saved. All eight of them. He swam them all to shore two at a time. But when he went back for the last two… they aren't sure, but something gave out. He was able to get the kids to shallow enough water for them to get to safety, but he went underwater face first. By the time some adults came over to drag him out, he wasn't breathing. The paramedics came and gave him CPR. He's alive and breathing with a life support machine but he hasn't woken up yet." Wally looked up with tear filled eyes, "I overheard the doctors telling some of the parents there's a good chance he's not going to make it," he sniffled, tears flowing down his face.

Elizabeth was blown away. Joe seemed like such a nice guy. He looked rough on the outside, but he was an angel on the inside, him helping without even knowing her and volunteering at a church proved that.

"Wally…I'm so sorry…" Elizabeth was lost for words.

"Me too… me too," he whispered as he continued sobbing, sloshing his watery lunch around mindlessly. Thankfully Bianca came and sat across from Wally.

"Hey, I heard about Joe. Are you alright?" she asked tenderly while mouthing a silent hello to Elizabeth.

"Yes. I'm fine, thanks for asking," Wally spoke coldly, while wiping his tears and standing up, "I have to go," and took off too quickly and tripped over his own feet but thankfully caught his balance as he ran off through the crowd of cliques in the lunch hall.

"Wally wait!" called Bianca as she stood up, but Wally ditched his tray into the trashcan and took off running. Bianca looked upset as she sat back down and turned to Elizabeth. "Poor Wally, and Joe too... he is such a nice guy and really cares about the kids in our community." Bianca shook her head, "I really hope he pulls through, especially for Wally's sake."

"Yeah, it sounds like they are really close."

"They are... Joe is like family to Wally. Since his dad died... he pretty much looks after Wally since his mother is always working to support them."

"I had no idea. Does Wally belong to the church too?"

"Wally was there when it happened."

Elizabeth's heart dropped.

Bianca continued, "Wally was the one who pulled the last two kids out of the water before Joe went under. Then he screamed for help, but no one came so he went in after Joe. He said he tried and tried but Joe was too heavy, he couldn't pull him up.

"Oh, my goodness," was all Elizabeth could manage.

"Now Wally feels like it's his fault Joe is… Joe is not doing so well," corrected Bianca. Her gaze wandered down to the animal tooth necklace that now hung on top of her grandmother's gold letter "N". Bianca reached under the neck of her dress and pulled out an exact replica. "Where did you get that from?"

Elizabeth froze with the memory of Princess Whitecloud giving it to her. "From a friend, a friend who I may never see again…" she trailed off.

"Well, she must think you're quite special Elizabeth. There are only so many of these in the world. They are passed down from generation to generation. Mine is fifty-seven generations old."

"I had no idea…" Elizabeth replied while running her fingers over the sharp little teeth, "That makes me value it even more. I think I should return it to her if that's the case."

"But I thought you may never see her again?"

"I guess I could if I went back. I just didn't think I ever would."

"Bad memories from a bad place?"

"I mean kind of, not really. Just bad choices that I wish I could take back," Elizabeth confessed. Had her bonds of friendship been that strong to those in Noir? Did she let her one mistake blind her to the good that lay there?

"I understand about bad choices," laughed Bianca, as she seemed to be lost in memories. "Follow your heart Elizabeth. You have a good one. I'm sure your friends will forgive whatever it is you have done." Bianca stood up and slung her backpack over a shoulder. The way she flipped her hair reminded Elizabeth of Princess Whitecloud. "I've gotta go. I promised Thomas that I'd walk him to practice. He's been different since the incident at the lake…he's part of the youth group too and he fell in when the bridge broke. Don't tell anyone, but he can't swim. He feels terrible, feels like if Joe didn't have to drag him out of there, he would be alive. We'll talk soon, see you around!" Elizabeth smiled and said her goodbyes as Bianca walked over to Thomas and took his hand, his muscular stature bursting out of his letterman's jacket with the school mascot on the back: a falcon with a battle axe. Just like Toma.

Elizabeth still hadn't seen Nora all day and assumed she must have stayed home. Maybe the ridicule of Raquel and Tanya was too much for her. She hoped for once Mr. Betto wouldn't bore her to death and make the last hour of the day feel like three, like he usually did. She kept looking at Nora's empty seat. Elizabeth didn't know why she felt bad for her. Nora had been cruel and unkind, and ridiculed people. It was her karma for something tragic to happen to her because of her actions. But what could have caused Nora to get

"Pumpkin Pox" as the girls had said. Something serious must have happened. Maybe she was hurt?

The bell finally rang, and the room emptied. Mr. Betto moved slowly as he bounced a stack of papers on his desk, trying to straighten them out. He finally looked up, "Oh hello Miss Montgomery. How can I help you? I hope you enjoyed today's lecture," he spoke with a warm smile.

"Uh, yes, I did, very much, uh thank you!" she tried to lie, "Mr. Betto, do you know what happened to Nora?"

"Miss Alcina? Oh, I am sorry to be the one to tell you this, she had a terrible accident. I was actually going to visit her today at the hospital."

"Hospital? What happened to her?"

Mr. Betto seemed to not hear her. His eyes were glazed over in a daze and he looked lost in another world. "Unfortunately, my best friend Joe is in the hospital too," he said, in the same monotone he always spoke with.

"Oh…I'm so sorry Mr. Betto. I heard what happened to Joe. I hope that he pulls through," Elizabeth offered, trying to think of a way to make the situation less uncomfortable.

"Thank you, that's kind of you. You're a good friend to care about Ms. Alcina. I heard her best friends haven't even so much as called to check on her. You seem to be able to influence others and make a change in them, Elizabeth.

You're young and don't realize, but you have great power in this world to make a difference. Remember that, because it would be a shame to let it go to waste. Joe is the same way; he was a difference maker in people's lives. Joe sacrificed himself because he knows how precious life is. I can only hope his kindness will be repaid and he makes it." His eyes showed sadness, but his voice stayed the same, a historian's voice of a reporter.

"Ttthank you Mr. Betto," she stammered, unsure how to respond, "Well, I'm going to head over too then. I'll see you there. Is there a trolley that runs to the hospital?"

"Allow me to give you a ride, just let me close shop here."

Chapter 30:

Heart Of Gold

The heart monitor machine beeped in even tones every few seconds, a good sign that Nora was just fine. The walls of the hospital reminded her a lot of their school and the neighborhood, ugly and peeling. A combination of bleach, paint and mildew mixed together made Elizabeth gag when she first got here. The linoleum floor shined with a recent clean, but the years of stains displayed their badges of honor proudly. Nora laid upright in a hospital bed, her usually grinning mouth was flat, face wrapped in gauze and bandages. The television in the corner of her small room had the news rolling. Nora watched but with blank eyes. She had not said a word to Elizabeth since she got there other than thank you. A genuine thank you that Elizabeth felt in her voice.

Mr. Betto explained what had happened on the ride over. Apparently when the school sprayed for insects last week, someone stole one of the containers and replaced the soap in some of the girl's bathrooms with it. For everyone who ended up using it, a few people got sick but nothing serious. But Nora is extremely allergic to pyrethroids which are found in almost any insecticide. Elizabeth knew Nora washed her face during lunch every day and reapplied her make up. And when she went to use some soap to clean her face after using her makeup remover pads, she had a terrible allergic reaction and broke out in hives all over her face. She was going to live just fine, but it could be months before the hives went away and even then, there was a good chance for permanent scarring.

Elizabeth held Nora's hand and waited patiently. If Nora wanted to talk she would; if she didn't, Elizabeth was not going to force her. She looked up at the television screen when Nora grabbed the remote and turned the volume up a few clicks as a woman in a blue dress suit in her late twenties appeared on screen, standing near the entrance to the bridge:

"Thanks Jon! I am standing here where yesterday a heroic yet tragic story at Lakeview Park occurred when the youth group leader from a local church saved eight children, ages five to fourteen after the bridge spanning over the lake, suddenly collapsed. Joseph Benedetto, age forty-three, acted heroically and quickly, swimming nearly four hundred feet in less than a minute. They were estimated to be approximately fifty feet from shore, where he made four round trips total. Tragically on the last trip, Mr. Benedetto went under water before making it back to shore. Luckily for the last two victims, one of the members of the youth group, Walter Patel, pulled the last two to safety," the reporter spoke, as she walked towards the edge of the shore where Wally would have been pulling the kids to safety.

"Walter then reportedly jumped into the lake but was unable to pull Mr. Benedetto onto the shore. Finally, some adults arrived to help, and they were able to get Benedetto to dry land until paramedics arrived. Benedetto is still in critical condition at United Health Medical Complex."

"He must have really cared about those kids," Nora finally spoke, "I wonder what that's like, making someone's life better instead of making it worse."

"I'm sure you do Nora, I'm sure you do," Elizabeth insisted.

"No. I don't. I'm sorry Elizabeth. Sorry for being so mean to everyone. I've been spoiled and had everything I've ever wanted in life. I'm stuck going to Iberville because I've been expelled from every other school in a twenty miles radius of my parents' house. I deserved that. I see that now. Just like I deserved what happened to my face," sobbed Nora, as tears began wetting the bandages on her face.

Elizabeth squeezed her hand with reassurance, "No one deserves to suffer Nora, and if you don't know what it's like to help make someone's life better, well the good news is, you have the rest of your life to do so."

"Why did you come? You hardly know me?"

"Because… because those girls who I thought were your friends aren't. And at a time like this, that's what a person needs the most. They need their family and friends. I'm sure your parents have come right?"

"No…just my grandparents," Nora sobbed, wiping tears through her mummy wrapped face. "My parents are never home. Sometimes I think they don't even care. They're probably going to be upset with me, they cut their vacation in Europe short once they heard what happened and should be flying in sometime tonight."

"They shouldn't be upset with you, it's not your fault."

"Yes, it is. I'm always in trouble."

"It's never too late to change Nora. They might be mad at you, but you can become the person who you really want to be."

"Thank you, Elizabeth. Thank you for being a true friend and not giving up on me. Even though I don't deserve it. You have a huge heart, I wish I could be as half as kind as you one day…"

"Now you're giving me too much credit…I'm no saint. Recently I've done things I never would have considered before."

"I'm sure you had a good reason for them. You seem like a person who follows what is true in her heart. Thank you for showing me the light. When I get out of here… you'll see a new Nora. And I don't mean a new one with a horrendously ugly face, but a nicer person."

"Nora don't say—"

"I just want to cry and be alone for a little bit, thanks for coming," Nora sobbed between tears. Elizabeth felt terrible and wanted to stay. But she knew now what she had to do. Owah was right. She did have power in her world. She could influence people. Was this the key to her magic in Noir? The power of her heart? It seemed every time she had made the Land of Noir a better place, her world, Lumiere, got just a little better. Was it coincidence? There was only one way to find out. She gave Nora a hug and told her she'd be back to check on her before she left the hospital. All Elizabeth got back were heavy sobs.

As Elizabeth was walking to the front desk to find the room for Joe, she saw Mr. Betto. Elizabeth's heart dropped. Mr. Betto, or as the kids at school called him, Robot because he showed zero emotion, sat in a chair in the lobby, eyes red and full of moisture, their usual cheery and youthful look completely drained.

"Mr. Betto," Elizabeth consoled, "Is everything alright with Joe?" He looked up with heavy sorrow in his old eyes; he looked so tired, as if his better days were behind him and shook his head.

"He isn't going to make it. They are waiting for his sister to come and say goodbye before they pull the plug."

Chapter 31:

Back To The Broken Brick Road

The cool cold mist invigorated her nostrils. The thought of the quicksilver's touch filled her veins with pleasure. One last pat down to ensure she had what she needed for the road ahead: Sorcerer's Robe, check. Healing potion, check. Both of her necklaces, check. A long branch from a rosewood tree, check. Babarosa's moonstone ring, check.

Elizabeth would guide Owah right to Babarosa by using her own magic against her to reveal where she hid.

Then it's on to the next two guardians of the runes. I'm coming for you both. Coming for your runes and to fight if you don't surrender peacefully. Then the Queen of Mist. I'm coming for you. You're nothing but a hateful bully. When you look in the mirror, you'll see who you truly are.

The moonlight shined brightly off her magic mirror from the small window in her bathroom. The runes glowed brightly as the gentle forest breeze hit her face. For the first time, Elizabeth stared back at the eye at the top of the mirror.

It was opening wider by the day. She could no longer ignore it. She had initiated The Calling somehow. In the beginning Elizabeth was in denial, but after her adventures in Noir something had changed. Now, her blood burned to seal the portal. Elizabeth's memory recited the engraving she had discovered on the back of the hand colored portrait after searching her father's footlocker again:

Je suis la magie et la magie est en moi. I am the magic and the magic is in me.

Elizabeth took a deep breath, stepped one foot onto the sink, and dove into the mirror.

Her Sorcerer Robe and long gnarled staff became smaller and smaller with each step, until she was nothing but a tiny spec, heading towards a village of firefly lanterns and beating drums.

CPSIA information can be obtained
at www.ICGtesting.com
Printed in the USA
LVHW051221030219
606183LV00004B/5/P